HEAD OVER HEELS...

It happened so fast, it caught them both by surprise. Maddalyn's feet slipped out from under her, her smile vanished, and she landed on the icy ground.

"Are you all right?" Eric dropped down beside her and placed his hands at her back, lifting her so that her head rested against his shoulder. "Where does it hurt? Your ankle? Your back?"

He thought for a moment that she was crying, but soon recognized the sound that was muffled in his shoulder as soft laughter.

"I take it you're not hurt?" he asked gruffly, and Maddalyn pulled her head back.

She slid one arm around his waist. "The fall just knocked the breath out of me, that's all. Goodness." Maddalyn took a deep breath. "I'll be fine, if I can just sit here for a minute or two."

Eric wasn't sure that he could take this for a minute or two. She was practically in his lap, and her face was so close to his he could feel her breath against his neck.

"This ground is awfully cold," Maddalyn said, squirming slightly, and Eric hauled her onto his lap.

"Better?"

"Much, thank you," she said breathlessly. "It will just take me a moment, I'm sure, to gather myself."

Now she was truly in his face, nose to nose, almost mouth to mouth. She should have looked ridiculous wearing Karl's winter cap, her yellow curls framing her face, but instead she looked irresistible.

"I'm not usually so forward," she whispered, wrapping her arms around his neck, "but would you mind terribly kissing me just once?"

LINDA JONES

Someone's Been Sleeping In My Bed

LOVE SPELL ◆ NEW YORK CITY

A LOVE SPELL BOOK®

July 2001

Published by

Dorchester Publishing Co., Inc.
276 Fifth Avenue
New York, NY 10001

ISBN 0-505-52094-X

The name "Love Spell" and its logo are trademarks of Dorchester Publishing Co., Inc.

Printed in the United States of America.

Visit us on the web at www.dorchesterpub.com.

Chapter One

Wyoming Territory, 1884

Her feet hurt, her arms and shoulders ached, and there was a tremendous rip in the hem of her traveling outfit. Maddalyn grasped the edge of the rock and found a toehold, pushing herself higher still. The stone beneath her fingers was surprisingly cold, the air that brushed her face much chillier than she would have liked.

She was surrounded on all sides by extraordinarily tall, very green trees that blocked the sun, stealing the little bit of spring warmth one would normally expect in the middle of the day. The soft light that filtered through the treetops gave the rugged mountain, with its jutting rocks and towering pine trees, an enchanted look. As though none of it could possibly be real. Maddalyn lifted her head. It was time to move ahead, and ahead was up. She managed to climb onto the flat rock, stopped to take a deep breath, and listened.

Nothing. Not a whisper of a breeze, or a twittering bird. No faraway sounds of voices or horses or creaking wheels. How many times in her life had she been surrounded by such complete and deep quiet? This Wyoming Territory mountain was another world, far away from Aunt Ethel's proper Georgia home. There, even at night, she'd not been alone. Cousin Doreen, in the room next door, snored loudly and constantly. Of course, the one time Maddalyn had been impertinent enough to mention it, Aunt Ethel had attempted to lay blame on poor Uncle Henry. Never mind that on several occasions Uncle Henry had been forced to spend the night out of town, and the snoring had continued.

Maddalyn lifted her face to the sloping hill above. It was, she was certain, not quite as steep as the one she'd just mastered. The ground she would have to cover was identical to what she'd seen so far, cold stone, hard ground, and dried pine needles that alternately slipped her up or stabbed her hands. She could always go back down the mountain, but there was no way to be sure that those horrible men wouldn't be waiting for her there.

She closed her eyes and gathered her strength, taking in the cold air as she inhaled deeply. In her twenty-two years, she'd seen a lot. She'd been orphaned, left in the care of a hateful aunt who harangued her every day, attended school and done quite well, watched as her uncle drove away the only man who'd ever been bold enough to express an interest in her . . . but she'd never seen anyone die.

And she'd never expected to see anyone die violently. That poor stagecoach driver, shot not once, but three times. He'd been an odd little man, with very few teeth and horribly dirty clothes. But he'd seemed a nice enough fellow, and smiled frequently even though he was missing so many teeth. The sight of that dusty shirt stained with blood would not leave her mind. And poor Mr. Harrison, the only other passenger on the stage, conked over the head with the wrong end of a gun. He hadn't put up a fight, hadn't even had a weapon. But when he'd had the nerve to stir, the bandits had unceremoniously shot him in the back.

Maddalyn had no doubt that she would have been killed, too. Eventually. The outlaws had seen no threat from her, and had stopped to rifle through the boxes that had been strapped to the roof. She'd taken a couple of steps back and toward the forest, wrung her hands, and begged them not to hurt her.

They'd laughed. Ugly, hateful guffaws.

While they'd been bent over a strongbox that seemed to be of particular interest to them, Maddalyn had turned and run. Into the forest, up that first rise, into the trees. She didn't think they would follow her. One of the outlaws had been almost as fat as Cousin Doreen, and the other had walked with a pronounced limp. They wore masks, dust-covered bandannas that covered most of their faces, but she could tell by the tufts of gray hair that poked out from their dusty hats, and by the wrinkled skin on their necks, that they were not young men.

They wouldn't follow her. They wouldn't. It became a litany she repeated, in her head and aloud, for hours after she'd escaped.

But she was afraid to go back down the mountain.

Time to tackle the next rise. Maddalyn took a single step forward and promptly tripped. She caught herself, but lay there for a moment with her face against the pine needles that covered the ground before she lifted her head. Her hair covered her face, golden curls that were normally well restrained curling wildly and festooned with a number of pine needles. Somewhere along the way, quite a while back, she'd lost the ribbon that had held her curls back.

She brushed the tangled mass away from her face and stood again. It hardly made sense to bemoan the loss of a simple hair ribbon when she'd just lost everything else she owned.

Planting her feet firmly on the ground, giving thanks that she had at least purchased a sturdy pair of boots before leaving Georgia, Maddalyn took yet another deep, calming breath.

"Maddalyn Lorraine Kelly," she said aloud, "you most certainly cannot stop here. There must be something ahead, even if it's clear on the other side of this mountain." The sound of her own voice in the deep quiet of the woods was soothing. Aunt Ethel had dearly hated it when Maddalyn had talked to herself. Said it was a sure sign that she was not quite right.

"Aunt Ethel isn't here, is she?" Maddalyn said as she took a step forward. "And if anyone's not quite right it's that nasty old windbag." Speaking so plainly about her aunt gave Maddalyn a burst of energy and courage. No, she couldn't go back. Not back down the mountain, not back to Georgia.

It was that certainty that propelled her up the mountain. She could move ahead or move back, and going back was not an option Maddalyn was willing to consider. Each steep rise, each cold rock she climbed, became a conquest. A victory. A step toward her new life.

She saw the rising smoke first, and still the sight of the roof took her by surprise. Maddalyn lowered herself to the ground and crept forward until she could see the cabin clearly. Prone, and with her face barely off the ground, she took in the sight. It was quite a large log cabin, solidly built at the top of the mountain. The area around the cabin had been cleared, and that only made the building appear more out of place, a stark contrast to the mountain she had just climbed. Smoke rose gently from the chimney, a welcoming sign that Maddalyn was wary of.

Would it be too bold of her to ask the inhabitants of that cabin for help? Surely they would be shocked to see a woman alone on top of their mountain. Would they greet her with a shotgun? Were they anything like the men who had robbed the stagecoach and killed two men before her eyes?

As she hesitated, the door burst open. Three men filed from the cabin, and at the sight of them Maddalyn held her breath. They were very large, tall and broad, and very hairy, with thick beards and mustaches and long brown hair that hung past their shoulders. What sort of men were these? Not the sort she was accustomed to, certainly. They appeared to be completely uncivilized, unkempt, and as wild as the animals that certainly roamed this mountain. Barbarians, she thought with a chill. Wild mountain men.

And they were arguing, all three of them talking loudly and quickly and at the same time. Even though their voices were loud, she couldn't understand a word they said, since all three of them spoke at once.

It was two against one, she decided as she watched, finally giving in and taking a shallow breath. One of the men turned and faced the others, spreading his arms wide and yelling into their faces. She caught a glimpse of his hairy face as he turned. It was no more than a glance, but her heart beat furiously with a fear as strong as she'd felt

12

when faced by those bandits.

They walked away from the cabin, continuing to argue ceaselessly, and together the three tall men disappeared over a rise on the other side of the dwelling.

Maddalyn remained motionless on the ground for a few moments. What were her chances of finding another cabin on this mountain? Quite small, if not nonexistent. Perhaps there was a woman inside right now, preparing dinner for the three large men.

She crept from the woods, watching the now deserted rise over which the men had disappeared. Desperate as she was for assistance, she wasn't yet so desperate that she'd chance a meeting with those gentlemen.

The door the men had used was slightly ajar, and swung inward slightly as Maddalyn knocked.

"Hello?" she called, her voice a whisper. "Is anyone home?"

The door opened onto a large kitchen, a large empty kitchen. "Hello?" she called, a little louder. Her voice echoed through the silent house.

In the middle of the warm kitchen there was a long table. It was plain, made of rough wood, and there was no tablecloth. But there were three steaming bowls of what appeared to be stew, and a pan of biscuits in the middle of it all, along with containers of salt and pepper.

The aroma was heavenly, and Maddalyn stepped into the kitchen, closing the door behind her. She was starving, and hadn't even realized it until this very moment, as that wonderful smell tantalized her: meat and spices and what was certainly onions. Her stomach growled, and Maddalyn bit one corner of her watering mouth. Surely it was not wrong to take just a little bit of food if one was truly hungry.

She sat in the chair nearest the door, took the spoon that rested by the bowl, and lifted a full spoonful to her lips. Delicious. She closed her eyes and took several bites before the sting of the pepper hit her. There was a tin mug at her right hand, and she grabbed it, chugging down a good half of the mug's contents. Cider, she decided as the warmth hit her belly.

A quick look into the bowl confirmed her suspicions. Someone had dusted the stew liberally with the pepper on the table. It was just too much for her. Without hesitation, still starving, Maddalyn moved to the seat at her left.

She tested this bowl carefully, tasting only a spoonful. This serving had been salted much too liberally, and she took a sip from the mug that rested beside the salty stew before she moved on.

The third bowl of stew was heavenly, and Maddalyn closed her eyes as she devoured it. Aunt Ethel had never served stew, but Maddalyn had come to appreciate a nice bowl as she'd traveled west. This particular stew was wonderful. Tasty, warm, seasoned perfectly, it was just right. She alternated hasty bites with small sips of the cider, until her spoon hit the bottom of the empty bowl.

And she realized that she had just eaten someone's evening meal. A meal prepared for one of those enormous and very cross men.

Maddalyn jumped from the seat and ran to the stove. There was a pot there, and there was a good portion of stew remaining. All she had to do was refill the bowl, clean the spoons, find the cider. . . .

She heard the voices before she had a chance to do any of those things. Angry voices, still, and one of them was very close as she turned away from the table.

Maddalyn hesitated, turned swiftly, and grabbed a biscuit from the pan at the center of the table. Just one, and there were so many, and they looked so good.

She slipped from the kitchen into a large main room. A fire blazed in the fireplace, three chairs were arranged there in a half-circle, and there was another door directly opposite the one she had entered.

Facing the men was impossible. She had entered their home unbidden, and eaten from their table without an invitation. She could not confront them and risk having that barbaric anger turned toward her.

She slipped quietly out of the door off the main room, and found herself on a wide front porch. In spite of her hurry, she stopped for a moment. Straight ahead, the view was unlike anything she'd ever seen. This was just one mountain of many, and the view went on forever. Blue and green and crystal clear, and the most beautiful sight she had ever seen. Such magnificent vastness, such power, such beauty. Maddalyn thought for a moment that she would be content to stand there on the porch at the top of the mountain forever.

But when she heard the kitchen door slam, she lifted her ripped skirt in her hands, ran down the steps, and circled the house to enter the woods.

Eric threw open the kitchen door, allowing it to crash into the wall and swing shut behind him. Four years ago, when he'd asked his two older brothers to join him in his venture, he hadn't expected *this*. He'd assumed that Karl and Conrad would always have the same aspirations for their logging business that he did.

Ranching would change everything. They didn't need more money, and they certainly didn't need to bring cattle and cowboys to the mountain. Eric liked his solitude, needed it the way he needed the cool, clean air and the endless view from the front porch.

It was all Conrad's fault. Eric was certain this was his idea. Conrad, the middle brother, had always been the one to get into mischief. The shortest of the three at barely six feet, he'd always tried to make up for what he lacked in height with his big mouth. Ranching! Karl was quiet, thoughtful, and on occasion too easily swayed. It wouldn't have taken Conrad ten minutes to convince his older brother that ranching was the way to go.

But a deal was a deal. Unless the decision was unanimous, there would be no changes made.

Eric shucked off his heavy coat and hung it on the peg behind the kitchen door. They wouldn't change his mind. He liked his life and his mountain just the way they were.

And to top it all off, his stew was getting cold, and he was famished.

He had taken his seat and lifted his spoon before he noticed that the bowl was empty. A residue of what had been a bowl full of stew just a few minutes ago was all that remained. Eric lifted his tin cup. It had been filled with Conrad's special cider, full to the rim. Now it was empty.

Eric was still staring into the empty cup, a deepening frown on his face, when the kitchen door opened and his brothers entered the cabin.

"Couldn't wait for us?" Conrad called almost cheerfully as he pulled off his coat and hung it next to Eric's. "I guess it's cooled off enough for us to dig in."

Karl was silent as he hung up his coat, then turned to the table with a frown and narrowed eyes.

Eric glanced up at his brothers. They stared first at their own bowls and then at him.

"It's bad enough that you run in here in a fit of temper and wolf down your own supper," Conrad said as he lifted his spoon. A drop of stew ran down the side. "But you had no call to dip into ours as well."

"I didn't. . . ." Eric began.

A glare from Karl stopped him. A glare from Karl could probably stop a speeding train, it was so fierce. His size was intimidating enough, six and a half feet tall and almost as wide in the shoulders, but coupled with that narrow-eyed stare . . . Karl lifted his own tin cup, stared into it briefly, and then returned his stare to Eric.

"Half my cider is gone." His voice was surprisingly soft, not quite a whisper. Men had quaked at the sound of that gruff whisper.

"I didn't—" Eric began.

"Don't deny it, little brother," Conrad said, stepping to the stove to grab the handle of the still warm pot of stew Eric had prepared just that afternoon. He topped off Karl's bowl, and then his own, before turning to Eric and filling his bowl. "What, do you expect us to believe that someone climbed the mountain and crept into the cabin, all for a taste of your stew? It's pretty good, little brother, though it could use a little more salt, but it's not *that* good."

Conrad returned the pot to the stove, sat down, and salted his stew liberally. Again. He'd salted it earlier, when they'd first sat down at the table to three filled bowls of stew that were much too hot to eat. The argument about the expansion Conrad proposed had begun, and they'd taken the discussion—if you could call it that—outside while the stew cooled.

"I know it doesn't make sense." Eric tried to

maintain his calm. Not an easy task when he was already angry. "But someone else was in here. Someone who ate my stew and drank my cider and started on yours before we came back. We probably frightened whoever it was away."

Karl shook his head slowly. Conrad smiled as he ate enthusiastically. Neither one of them believed him.

And he certainly wouldn't waste his time trying to convince his two stubborn older brothers. Eric ate his own stew, and wondered silently about their visitor. An old mountain man who stumbled on the cabin? A trapper? A hunter? No one could have gotten down the road without being seen, and the approach from any other direction was . . . well, difficult, but not impossible.

Whoever the intruder was, he'd been hungry. They hadn't been away from the cabin but a few minutes, and his bowl had been neatly emptied.

"I still say," Conrad began, breaking the silence, "that if we cleared that land at the foot of the mountain, got just a few head to start, hired on a few hands . . ."

"No," Eric said with a frown. "I started this place on my own, and if you don't like the way I live, you can move on and build somewhere else."

"We're partners, little brother," Conrad reminded Eric gently. "I don't want to be a logger forever."

"We make no changes unless we *all* agree," Eric reminded his brother. "Barrett Brothers is and will remain a family business. I want no strangers on my mountain."

"Our mountain," Conrad corrected.

"Our mountain," Eric repeated, grudgingly.

In spite of her fear Maddalyn didn't get very far. It would soon be dark, and there was a deepening chill in the air. A chill that crept through her long sleeves and tattered skirt.

She almost stumbled across the cave. Much of the entrance was covered with fallen limbs and a spreading bush that Maddalyn pushed aside with her hands. The crevice was small, but large enough for her to curl up in, escape the cold wind, take a nap perhaps.

In the shelter of the cave, Maddalyn picked at the still warm biscuit she had taken from the cabin. It was flaky and tender, a real treat after the hard and tasteless bread she'd been served so often on the journey.

She was tired and achy, but no longer hungry. The biscuit, savored after she'd eaten too much of the stew too quickly, had more than filled her, and the cider had warmed her belly and made her sleepy.

Inside the small cave, Maddalyn reached out and pulled the limbs of the bush over to cover the entrance. She could peek out, but no one would see her hiding place unless they looked straight at her.

Of course, no one up here was likely to be looking for her. Unless of course one of those men from the cabin decided to search for the thief who had stolen his stew.

Maddalyn smiled, in spite of the harshness of the day, in spite of her aching bones and sore feet. She pulled her knees to her chest and hugged them tightly, as much in excitement as against the cold. It had been oddly exhilarating to sneak into that cabin and make herself at home. Not that she condoned thievery, of course.

But the very idea of thwarting those three huge men, of slipping into their home behind their backs and making off through the front door as they returned, was somehow thrilling. Surely it was better to take just a little than to starve to death in the wilderness. Surely it wasn't really wrong to steal just enough food to survive.

The uncomfortable fullness in her stomach reminded Maddalyn that she'd taken much more than was necessary for survival. Next time she'd be more discreet, if there was a next time.

As darkness fell, Maddalyn closed her eyes. Without the wind, with her belly full and the cider in her blood, the chill dissipated. Tomorrow morning she would find a way down the mountain. Not back the way she'd come, back to the stagecoach, but some other way.

Surely those three large men occasionally left the mountain. Perhaps there was a road. Perhaps there was even a small town at the foot of the mountain. She would find out tomorrow, Maddalyn thought wearily. By the light of day, after a good night's rest, she would explore the mountain and plan the next leg of her journey. She would have to keep an eye out for those men, though. Those three colossal men . . .

Chapter Two

Maddalyn knelt on the hard ground, peeking between two fully leafed bushes, as the three men left the cabin. After a surprisingly decent night's sleep she'd awakened in the cave, hungry and stiff. She wouldn't have thought it possible, but her tortured muscles were hurting more this morning than they had yesterday.

There was no way she could continue her journey today.

Those large men, all three talking at the same time as they walked away from Maddalyn and the cabin, headed for the rise they'd crossed the day before. She couldn't see it, but surely there was a path of some sort there.

When the time came, she would make her way down the mountain by way of that path. The stagecoach thieves surely wouldn't wait at the bottom of the mountain indefinitely, and besides, the path would take her to a different place. Perhaps a small town.

From there she would catch another stagecoach to Sheridan, move into the small house promised to her as the new schoolteacher, and begin a whole new life. She'd never look back. Georgia had never been home to her. She'd always been the poor relation, had always felt outside the small family that had taken her in. Aunt Ethel, as strict and sour a woman as Maddalyn had ever met. Uncle Henry, sad-eyed, quiet, with nothing more than an occasional wistful smile for his sister's only child. Cousin Doreen, a woman as ugly on the inside as she was on the outside. That was unkind, Maddalyn reminded herself silently, but true.

At one time, Maddalyn had looked forward to marriage as an escape, but that dream died a slow death. For one thing, Aunt Ethel declared that it would be unseemly for Maddalyn to marry before her older cousin, and Doreen's prospects grew dimmer with every passing year.

On Maddalyn's twentieth birthday, a bold and very sweet boy from a nearby farm had dared to ask Uncle Henry for her hand. He had been rudely ousted from the house, and told not to return. Although she'd been initially disappointed, Maddalyn didn't grieve for long. She decided then that she would never marry without love. She'd seen what a loveless marriage had done to Aunt Ethel and

Uncle Henry. They were both miserable, and had produced a truly miserable child in Cousin Doreen.

It would be best to never marry than to bind her life to a man who didn't love her. A man she didn't love. And she didn't buy that hogwash about learning to love as the years passed. Lawrence, that very sweet boy from the farm, had tried to convince her of that impossibility. That love could grow from nothing.

Maddalyn knew that love was an absolute. It was powerful and endless and it was either there or it wasn't. And she had never loved Lawrence, even though she'd been quite fond of him, and she had allowed him to kiss her once. Just once. Of course, Aunt Ethel had caught them, and had spent the next several weeks calling Maddalyn the vilest of names. *Harlot. Strumpet. No decent man will ever have you.*

That final insult had echoed through her head for the longest time. What if it were true? What if no decent man would have her?

The three men had disappeared down the hill several moments earlier, and Maddalyn finally decided that it was safe to proceed. She was starving.

The table was clean, still damp from washing, and Maddalyn sighed loudly as she closed the door behind her. Three men, bachelors most likely, and they didn't leave even a crumb of food on the table!

A quick search of the kitchen yielded two biscuits, still warm, and a half a jar of blueberry preserves. That, along with a small pitcher of water,

25

stilled the rumbling in her stomach. Perhaps now she could think clearly.

She was much too sore to make the trek down the mountain today, of that she was certain. Her legs were practically shaking, they were so weak. This decision not to proceed did not distress her. She rather liked the cabin, and apparently it was left empty throughout the day, while the three gigantic men worked. It was a place where she could think, decide on her next course of action. It was true, she needed to catch a stage for Sheridan, but the stagecoach thieves had taken everything. Her trunk, the small satchel containing her funds—meager as they were—and her mother's pearls. Those pearls were the only item of value she owned, and the only tangible reminder of her mother.

Perhaps the operators of the stagecoach would honor the ticket she no longer possessed, and she could continue on to Sheridan. And even though she dreaded it, she supposed she should make a statement of some sort to the authorities concerning the robbery, the fate of the driver, and that of poor Mr. Harrison.

Maddalyn stepped into the main room, peeking around the corner as if she expected to see someone there, even though she knew perfectly well that she was all alone in the cabin. This room was as neat as the kitchen, with no frills, nothing out of place. There were three chairs arranged in a semicircle around a cold fireplace, and one was flooded with sunlight from a window facing the front of the cabin. There were sparkling panes of glass, but no curtain to block the sun.

Or the view, Maddalyn thought as she sat in that chair. From this spot, warmed by the sun, she could look out over those endless mountains she had admired yesterday. She had never been so high. So close to heaven. She had never even imagined that people lived in places like this. Secluded, but not lonely.

After spending a good portion of the morning gazing out the window, daydreaming about her life once she reached Sheridan, Maddalyn laid her head back and closed her eyes. She could sleep here. Just a short nap. She had rested, of course, but that cave was so cold, and the ground was so hard. The cane seat of this chair was worn, so that her bottom sank down just slightly, and there was a thin padded cushion at her back. It was really quite lovely.

She dozed in the comfortable chair for a while, and dreamed that the three men returned as she slept. In the dream they towered over her, surrounding her so that there was no escape. That one—the man who had yelled and waved his arms so energetically—she'd gotten a brief glimpse of his face yesterday. It was rather nice, in an odd sort of way. It was he who leaned close to her, who accused her silently.

When she woke it was with a start. Good heavens! She couldn't allow those men to find her here!

27

Not much time had passed, she could tell by the direction of the sunlight that streamed through the window, but it would be best if she didn't sleep again.

Laying her head back against the cushioned chair, she spied the photograph that was propped on the mantel. It was a formal portrait of the three men, only they didn't look nearly so intimidating. In the photograph they were clean-shaven, except that the largest one, the man who was seated, had a bushy mustache.

Maddalyn wanted a closer look at that picture. There was no excuse for it, except for her own insatiable curiosity. Unfortunately the mantel was rather high for a woman who stood barely five foot three. She edged the chair she'd dozed in nearer the fireplace, and carefully stood on the cane seat so that she was face-to-face with the photograph of those three men.

Three brothers, she surmised as she studied the photograph. They had the same strong jaw, the same broad shoulders. The seated one, the largest brother, had a gruffer look about him than the other two. His eyes were narrowed, and the edges of his mouth turned down. He looked rather like a moose. The brother standing on the left was the smallest of the three, but still far from normal size, Maddalyn knew from spying the three of them from a distance. He had the brightest smile, a deep cleft in his chin, and a more casual stance than his two brothers.

Maddalyn stared for a long time at the third brother. He had the same broad shoulders and square jaw as the other men, but he didn't scowl, and he didn't grin. He was a man in control, powerful and strong. Tougher, in an odd way, than the larger, scowling brother. And even though it was quite impossible, he seemed, she thought with a shudder, to be staring straight at her. Through her.

He was lovely.

Maddalyn leaned forward just slightly, but it was enough to set the chair off balance. She tumbled to the floor, driving one booted foot through the cane seat and landing in a very unladylike position on her derriere.

The wind was knocked right out of her lungs, and she added a very sore bottom to her long list of complaints. Carefully she pulled her foot from the destroyed seat. Oh, dear. They would know that someone had been here.

She tried, in vain, to arrange the ripped seat so that the damage was not so very noticeable. It was useless. There was a mangled hole right in the center of the cane seat.

Maddalyn passed the remainder of the morning in the kitchen and on the front porch. She rummaged in a full pantry and came up with a quick afternoon meal from the innumerable canned goods there, then cleaned every evidence of her presence from the room. She avoided the main room, and most especially the photograph of those three men. That one brother watched her as she passed, condemning her with his eyes.

The afternoon was mild, and the view from the front porch was heavenly. Maddalyn could look across the mountains and imagine that there was not another person for a thousand miles. It was not frightening, as she might have thought. It was strangely peaceful.

How wonderful it must be, she thought with a sigh, to belong in such a place. To call it home, to wake every morning at the top of the world.

There were flowers growing all around the porch that ran the length of the house, wildflowers in yellow and dark pink and lavender. Unexpected beauty that grew tall against the wood of the cabin and reached for the sun. She picked a handful and placed them in her tangled hair, tucking several blooms behind her ear.

She could almost forget, for a time, that she was certainly in dire straits. Lost, unprotected, penniless. What did that matter in a place like this?

In spite of the feeling that one of those men in the photograph watched her, she made one last trip into the main room. She lingered over the chair she had destroyed, and tried once again to repair the damage. It was useless.

Before she left the cabin for the day she lifted her head one last time to eye the photograph on the mantel. Her eyes lit on the brother who seemed to observe her with such intensity. Would he condemn her for her small transgressions?

"Sorry," she whispered, before she left to make her way back to the cave.

Eric walked well ahead of his brothers. They were ganging up on him, trying to force him to a decision he couldn't live with. A ranch at the foot of the mountain. Cattle, cowhands, a cook, and a foreman. That could mean as many as twenty men, lodging and food for them all, the inevitable families.

At least tonight he didn't have to cook. It was Conrad's turn to prepare the evening meal, and Eric was fully prepared for something tough and salty. Fortunately there would be plenty of cider to wash it down with.

There hadn't been time, as they'd cleared a small section just down the hill, to wonder about the intruder who had eaten his supper the night before, but as Eric opened the kitchen door he searched the room for evidence of a visitor. It didn't take him long to note that the two biscuits he'd purposely left on the shelf by the stove were gone. He listened, motionless in the doorway, for sounds of someone moving through the house, but all was silent.

An unexpected grin split his face, and he was able to forget his problems with Karl and Conrad. Their visitor had been very careful not to disturb anything. The chairs at the table were just as he'd left them—two straight and two askew. Apparently nothing in the kitchen had been moved but the two missing biscuits.

Without making a sound, even though he wore heavy work boots, Eric slipped through the kitchen and to the large open doorway that led to the main room. Something had changed, though he couldn't quite put his finger on it.

To his left was another open doorway. This one led to a wide hallway. There were three large bedrooms off that hallway, a luxury Eric had insisted on. This would be his home for the rest of his days, and he hadn't skimped when building the place.

It only took a moment to walk down that hallway and peek into each room. Every room was furnished with a wide bed, a plain dresser, and an unadorned window. As far as he could see, nothing there had been touched.

Entering the main room, he saw what had teased him before. His chair had been moved. Not much, but it was at an odd angle, turned as if someone had been sitting there and looking out the window. He should know. He'd spent a lot of winter mornings at that window.

He saw the damage, the torn seat, before he reached the chair. If he'd tried to sit on the chair his backside probably would have fallen straight through.

Yes, someone had been here. Someone had come in while he'd been working, and made himself at home. He didn't know whether to be angry or amused. What sort of an addlebrained ass would try to dupe the Barrett brothers? Again he thought of some crazy old mountain man, lost for years in the mountains. If that were the case, he wouldn't be easy to get rid of.

A flash of color caught his eye, and Eric dropped down to his haunches. There, on the smooth wooden floor beneath the damaged chair, was a single wildflower. It had already started to wither, but its color was still a bright spring yellow.

Eric lifted the drooping bloom between fingers that were suddenly too big and clumsy, and an involuntary smile crossed his face. Oh yes, they had definitely had a visitor.

The last of the light died quickly in the cave. Maddalyn huddled, her knees to her chest and her arms wrapped tightly around those knees, trying to hold in the warmth. It was going to be colder tonight than it had been the night before, she decided, promising an unpleasant evening. Perhaps she should have appealed to those three men for assistance. Perhaps she should have appealed to the one who had stared at her from his photograph all afternoon.

She'd never known anyone who looked like that. Uncle Henry was short and round, and Lawrence had hardly been any taller than she was herself. Of course she had seen other men, at church and in town, and on her trip west, but they had been—for the most part—much like Uncle Henry and Lawrence. Ordinary.

Those three brothers—the resemblance was so strong she was certain that they were brothers— were nothing like the men she'd known. They were certainly not ordinary in any sense of the word. Especially the one . . . the very handsome one who stared at her from his photograph . . . and of course she didn't have any idea what to call him, what his name was, nor would she unless she worked up the courage to approach the cabin in the evening hours. It would have to be a very special name.

Ulysses. Atlas. Lancelot. In the dark, Maddalyn smiled at her own foolishness. His name was probably something perfectly ordinary, like Horace or Otis or Elmer. And while she had imagined that he had a pleasing, clear voice, deep and soothing, he probably spoke with an effeminate lisp, or perhaps with a soft stutter, or a nasal twang.

How silly she was to imagine that he was as perfect as his photograph. Perhaps he was tall and broad and handsome to a fault beneath that beard. Perhaps he did seem to have a power as strong as that of his mountain. That didn't mean he was some impossibly perfect specimen of manhood.

Maddalyn relaxed and finally dozed, off and on, trying to find fault with the man in the photograph. He probably had a terrible temper, was one of those demanding sorts who could never be pleased. What if he was like that poor Mr. Harrison, who seemed not to like women at all? Mr. Harrison had actually scowled at her when she'd tried to strike up a conversation during the long stage ride, though of course it was still quite sad that he had died so horribly.

Perhaps the man in the photograph had a laugh like Rev. Eaton, high and grating and horribly loud. Or perhaps he whined horribly, or had poor diction. Would he have a coarse accent like the stagecoach driver and the bandits who had robbed the stage and killed the driver and Mr. Harrison?

Maddalyn prided herself on being practical and down-to-earth. She never would have survived more than twenty years in Aunt Ethel's household otherwise. There was no place for fancy in a place like that.

It was imprudent to give in to such fanciful thoughts, especially where that man was concerned.

But in her dreams his voice was perfectly agreeable.

Chapter Three

Maddalyn rubbed her hands together as she waited for the three brothers to leave the cabin. There was a deep chill in the air, a frigidity that had awakened her hours earlier while it was still quite dark. Perhaps the stove would still be warm this morning, and she could warm herself in that cozy kitchen.

Two of the brothers, the monstrously large man and the fellow who hid a cleft on his chin under a bushy beard, left together, and Maddalyn waited for several minutes, holding her breath. What if the other one was ill? What if he had no intention of leaving the cabin at all? If that were true, what on earth would she do?

She was much too tired and cold to make her way down the mountain, and there was no way she could present herself at their door. They would certainly know that she had been the one to break their chair. She wondered if they'd missed the stew, the biscuits, and the canned peaches she had eaten. Not a single one of them looked to be the forgiving sort.

She didn't have long to wait. The other one, the man with the piercing eyes that had watched her from the photograph, was just a few minutes behind his brothers. Maddalyn was very still, concealed behind a clump of bushes. Yesterday any small sounds she might have made would have been covered by the voices of the bickering men. Today there was just the one. And it had to be *that* one, of course. Just her luck.

He closed the kitchen door behind him, not with a slam but with an easy motion, and set a wide-brimmed hat on his head. Maddalyn sucked in her breath and held it, wondering if he would look her way.

It was the heavy coat that made him appear so broad, she tried to convince herself, the hat that made him appear to be so tall. The beard and long hair that made him look so wild. There was no justification for her unreasonable fear of the man.

He hesitated with his back to the door, pushed that dark brown hat back on his head, and rotated his head slowly, searching the heavy growth that formed a half-circle around the cabin.

He was looking for her.

Maddalyn exhaled the breath she had been holding for too long, and leaned forward just slightly.

He couldn't possibly see her here, and she wouldn't make a sound. . . .

Dried pine needles crackled beneath her hands, making a noise no louder than a whisper, a hushed wind. He looked right at her then, or rather, right at the clump of bushes she hid behind. If he came after her, if he decided to search behind the bushes, there was no way she would escape. His legs were too long, and her own were too sore from the unaccustomed exercise they'd been put through climbing this mountain. Her strength and speed would be no match for his, of that she was certain.

But he didn't come toward her. He did stare just a moment too long, until Maddalyn was almost certain he knew she was there.

Maddalyn licked her suddenly dry lips when he finally turned away from her and headed after his brothers. That had been close. Too close. It wouldn't be safe to stay on top of this mountain for much longer.

A day. Maybe two.

She waited for several minutes, wondering if he would come back and try to catch her, rounding the corner, cresting the hill, shouting *Aha!* as if they were playing a child's game of hide-and-seek. Maddalyn approached the cabin cautiously, but he didn't return. She was much too cold to wait in the woods for very long.

The warmth of the kitchen was heavenly, and she leaned against the closed door and allowed herself to relax. She'd known all along that coming west would be an adventure, but she hadn't expected this. Lost. Destitute. Afraid.

Well, afraid when she was huddled in that cave. In this cabin she felt oddly safe, unafraid even of those gigantic men.

There were biscuits again, and Maddalyn devoured them too quickly. She hadn't come to Wyoming Territory to starve to death on top of some mountain she couldn't name. Nor to be robbed or lost. She had wonderful and specific plans for her future. A few years teaching in Sheridan. The pay wasn't great, but board and a small house were included, so she would be able to save almost everything. She didn't want or need a lot of things. Just the necessities.

And then, in a few years, she would open her own all-girls school. The Maddalyn Lorraine Kelly Academy for Young Ladies. Music, French, literature, even mathematics and science. Maddalyn was of the notion that a lady needed to know everything.

A man could have a specialty, could learn how to do one thing well, and he was set for life. Not so a lady. A lady had to be prepared for whatever life presented her.

Maddalyn readily admitted to herself that nothing could have prepared her for this.

She cleaned the crumbs from the shelf, and from the floor at her feet, squatting down and scooping the bits of tender biscuit into her hand. When she stood, a wave of dizziness swept over her, and she grasped the edge of the stove to keep from falling to the floor.

Maddalyn closed her eyes. She was tired, that was all. It was merely exhaustion that made her head swim. She was not normally a delicate creature who was given to moments of light-headedness. It simply had been much too cold to sleep well in the cave, and dreams of that man in the photograph, that one particularly lovely man, had plagued her well into morning.

When she felt clearheaded she made her way to the main room, and felt sick at her stomach with guilt. There were only two chairs in front of the fireplace today. The chair she had damaged had been taken away. Perhaps one of the brothers had the skill to repair it, so that it would soon be as good as new.

She didn't want to sit on the porch this morning. The wind today was so cold it cut right through her thin traveling suit. Maddalyn looked down in dismay at her dress. It had once been a perfectly lovely shade of blue, but it appeared more gray than blue at the moment.

She had chosen it so carefully, wanting to make the right impression on the people of Sheridan. The neck was high, but not so high that it choked her. It was snug enough to show off her figure, but not so tight as to be ruled indecent. Not at all. Maddalyn lifted her arms and frowned at the sight. There had once been just a touch of lace at the wrists. Dainty. Feminine. Gone.

The yawn caught her completely by surprise. Maddalyn allowed the yawn to take her, and she let her arms fall to her sides. She was truly spent, bone weary, all but insensible. It was still early in the day. She could take a nap and be gone from the cabin long before the occupants returned. No one would ever know.

She had not yet explored the hallway and the bedrooms. It had seemed, yesterday, too much of an intrusion. Not at all polite.

Maddalyn entered the wide hallway and turned right. There were no doors, just doorways, and she stuck her head into the first bedroom cautiously, as if she still expected to find someone there, even though she'd seen the men leaving with her own eyes.

There was a wide, long bed, covered with a tattered quilt fashioned from squares in every shade of yellow. Beyond the bed was a dresser and yet another curtainless window.

Maddalyn lay carefully on top of the quilt and rested her head on a flat pillow. The bed was so long, her feet were a good distance from the foot of the bed. Of course, the tall and broad men who lived here would need such room to sleep comfortably, she imagined, feeling her face grow warm at the very thought.

She rested on her side for a moment, closing her eyes and taking a deep breath. After a minute or two she rolled to her back. She would swear that this bed was every bit as hard as the floor of the cave! There was no yield in the mattress, and when she rolled over it didn't bounce at all. It was, all in all, a poor excuse for a bed.

Maddalyn rolled up and swung her feet to the floor. There was no reason to make herself miserable. There were two other beds in this cabin.

She didn't feel nearly as much guilt when she made her way into the second bedroom, the one in the middle. It was almost identical to the first, except that the quilt was fashioned from many colors. Maddalyn tested the mattress, placing both hands on the side and putting her weight on them. The mattress gave, just enough, and she lowered herself to lie atop the quilt.

For a few moments she was comfortable, and then she rolled onto her back. Had this mattress been stuffed with onions? Not only was it lumpy, the lumps were huge, boulders beneath the ticking.

This would never do. She'd be better off in that hard bed.

There was one more bedroom, and she entered it with just a trace of frustration. Again, this room was like the others, but the quilt was done in shades of blue. Her favorite color. Maddalyn went to the window and lifted the panes just an inch or two. Cold air crept in, over her hands and up her arms, and she closed it again quickly. Could it possibly be getting colder?

The view from that window was almost as spectacular as it was from the porch, and as she stood there her earlier disgust faded away. It was silly of her to fret over hard and lumpy mattresses in her present circumstances.

Turning to the bed, Maddalyn ran her hands over the top of the long dresser. The surface was smooth, polished, and clean. There was only a single item, a small trinket box, sitting on the dresser, and Maddalyn found herself running her fingers over the carved lid.

What would a man keep in such a box? she wondered, picking at the edges. It was wrong, of course, for her to pry, but she was so very curious and she did only want to peek at the contents.

After she'd lifted the lid, she wished she hadn't. Gold coins. Not a lot of them, but . . . well, several. Enough to get her to Sheridan, if she took only one.

Maddalyn snapped the box shut. She must be terribly tired and out of sorts! Not herself at all. Stealing a bit of food to survive was one thing, and occupying an empty cabin for a few hours while the inhabitants were away was harmless enough, but she was not a thief. She did what was necessary to survive, and no more.

Maddalyn rubbed her temples, trying to push back the threatening headache. She was just tired, that was all. It was exhaustion that made her dizzy and crabby.

She eased herself onto the bed. This mattress was heavenly. Soft, but not lumpy. Comfortable, yes, extremely comfortable.

Maddalyn sat up and removed her boots. She

didn't want to get dirt on this quilt, and besides, she'd sleep better with them off. For a moment she rested on top of the quilt, but that seemed silly. She rolled to the side and slipped beneath the quilt, pulling it to her chin.

Muscles relaxed, and Maddalyn melted into the mattress, lost herself in a wonderful cocoon that protected her from the rest of the world.

She was warm. She was comfortable. This was heaven.

"Storm, my ass," Conrad said, dogging Eric's steps. "You really think you're going to catch some old coot in the cabin, don't you?"

"Maybe." Eric smiled. Someone had been in the forest this morning, as he'd left the cabin. Someone who'd been patiently waiting for him to leave. "But you have to agree, there is one hell of a storm coming. Probably the last this season."

"Spring is a long time coming to this mountain," Karl said softly.

A single snowflake, just a hint of what was to come, hit Eric's face. They were returning to the cabin just a couple of hours earlier than usual, and it was true he'd used the approaching storm as an excuse.

He waved his hand to silence his brothers as he opened the kitchen door. There was no one there, but—once again—the biscuits were gone.

"See?" he whispered, pointing to the empty shelf. "I left two biscuits there this morning."

Conrad lifted his eyebrows. "You probably ate them yourself, you pig, and don't want us to—"

Eric placed a finger to his lips, and Conrad rolled his eyes.

He was disappointed to find the main room empty. Conrad had probably scared away whoever had taken the biscuits and broken the chair.

Karl brushed past silently, unbuttoning his shirt and heading for his bedroom. Eric went to the window that looked over the front porch and searched for any sign of the intruder. A smudge on the glass, a rocking chair out of place . . . but there was nothing.

"I'll be damned," Karl muttered, a whisper from his room off the hall.

Eric hurried to his brother's room, half expecting to find the intruder there. But Karl was standing over an empty bed, his dirty shirt in his hands.

"Someone's been here," Karl whispered, and then he shot a narrow gaze in Eric's direction. "Is this your doin's? Did you come in here this morning after we left and do this? Is this some kinda game to make us forget about expanding the business? Did you do this?"

Eric looked down at the perfectly normal bed and then back up at his brother. "Do what?"

"The pillow is in the wrong place, and there's a wrinkle in the middle of my bed." Karl frowned as he leaned forward, bending at the waist, and inhaled loudly. "And I could swear I smell a woman."

Conrad stuck his head into the room and

grinned widely. "Eric, have a look at this." He held one hand high, apparently holding nothing. Eric stepped closer.

"I found it on my pillow."

A single hair, very long, very pale, twisted aimlessly from Conrad's pinched fingers toward the floor.

Eric pushed his way past Conrad and down the hallway, advancing silently to his bedroom.

He stopped in the doorway. At least it was no crazy old mountain man.

Her back was to him, and her hair, gold and curling, covered his pillow. She was snuggled beneath his quilt, hidden from view, the curve of her hip and the line of her legs distinct.

She was a tiny thing, more hair than anything else, from the look of her. What the hell was she doing here?

"Well?" Conrad called from the other end of the hallway. "Is there anything out of the ordinary in your room?"

Eric smiled and leaned against the door frame. "You could say that."

Conrad and Karl started down the hall, and Eric raised his hand to stop them. He wasn't ready to share her just yet, whoever she was.

They did stop, for a moment, and then Conrad barreled forward. "What have you—"

"Quiet," Eric whispered. "You'll wake her."

"Her?" Conrad asked. He continued on, Karl behind him.

Eric smiled. "Someone's sleeping in my bed."

She lifted her head then, and turned a fair face to the door. It was serenely and sleepily beautiful for just a moment, and then fear took over. Her eyes grew wide and she bolted upright with a small, high-pitched squeal, tossing his quilt to the floor.

Eric lifted his hand in what he hoped was a gesture of peace. "It's all right."

Obviously she didn't hear him as she rushed to the window and threw it open, clambering over the windowsill in a panic. Her skirts and her hair flew wildly around her, and then she was out. She was trying to bring her skirt with her, when the material snagged on a nail. Yanking frantically at the material, she glanced at him, and Eric took a step toward the window.

She screamed again, not quite so shrilly this time, and Eric stopped in his tracks.

She was dirty and bedraggled, with smudges on her face and that golden curly hair in a tangle to her waist. She was beautiful, and she was terrified, and she was getting away.

"Come back here," he called, breaking the trance and reaching for the window and the skirt.

She broke away, the snagged skirt ripping free. Most of it trailed after her, but a scrap remained hanging on the head of the nail that had almost stopped her.

Eric leaned out of the window and watched her run. That hair bounced behind her, that torn skirt whipped in the cold wind. The snow was falling fast now, and this was just the beginning of what promised to be a very long, very cold storm.

When she was gone he turned away from the window. His brothers stood in the doorway, Karl stunned and Conrad smiling broadly. It had happened so quickly—they'd found the intruder and she'd escaped. Eric glanced at the rumpled bed, and then his gaze fell to the floor. And there they were.

Two tiny black boots, placed neatly side by side on the floor at the edge of his bed.

"She won't survive a night like this out there," he said, as much to himself as to his brothers.

"Nope," Karl agreed solemnly.

"Got any ideas?" Conrad asked, and Eric could tell by his expression and the humor in his voice that Conrad knew damned well what he was going to do.

She ran, without thinking, toward the cave. Her heart was beating much too hard, and she could hardly breathe, and still she ran.

How incredibly stupid! How could she have slept for so long? Thick gray clouds covered the sun, but she could only assume that it was very late in the afternoon. She'd slept like an innocent baby, and she'd been caught!

She didn't look back. Her last glance at the cabin had afforded her a view of the man with the eyes, that man who had watched her from the photograph, all but leaning out of the window she'd escaped through. Why him? Why not that smaller one with the insolent grin? Why not that very large man who must certainly be slow?

If that haunting man had followed her, if he'd climbed out of the window and given chase, he'd surely have her by now. But Maddalyn didn't slow her pace. She listened for any sound that might indicate she was being followed.

The snow began to fall harder, large, fat flakes that stung her face and clung to her dress. She'd never seen snow before, and would have liked to stop and watch for a while, if circumstances had been different.

But there was no time to enjoy the snow, and as it began to fall faster she only wished that it would stop. Dazzling or not, it was icy cold.

The cold was brutal at her toes, especially as the snow gathered on the ground. In minutes her stockings were soaked, and the cold seemed to travel to the bone. How would she ever make it down the mountain without her boots?

Maddalyn did look over her shoulder as she reached the cave. The snow fell faster and faster, clinging to the green trees and building on the ground, flying thick and cutting her range of vision in half.

The storm would surely keep the men in their cabin, she decided with a breathless sigh of relief. She'd only taken a little bit of food—and that crime certainly wasn't worth a venture into a snowstorm.

Her crimes had been insignificant, petty, almost not crimes at all.

She was confident of her safety for at least this one last night. Would he look for her tomorrow? He hadn't appeared to be the forgiving sort, as he'd rushed to the window and ordered her to stop. Long hair hanging to his shoulders. Short beard hiding what she knew to be a fierce jaw. Hands . . . enormously large hands reaching out for her, to snare her like an animal in a trap.

Maddalyn shivered, and it had nothing to do with the cold wind or the snow that pelted her.

Chapter Four

She'd left a trail a child could follow, broken limbs and tiny footprints in the new snow.

Eric hefted the pack on his back as he plunged forward, angry and worried and curious. He wasn't more than half an hour behind her, having taken the time to pack a blanket, food, a canteen of cider, and her little black boots.

He was angry. She'd made herself at home, eaten their food, broken his favorite chair, slept in his bed. All she'd had to do was ask, for God's sake. Knock on the door and ask for food and shelter. Did she think they would turn her away?

He was worried. Her clothing had been inappropriate, thin and much too light. No coat, no boots, no hat. A little thing like that, she'd be dead by morning if he didn't find her.

And even as he rushed forward, following the path she left, he was curious. Who was she? Where had she come from? It had been months since he'd been to town, but he was certain she hadn't been a resident of Olympia when he'd last been there. He would have remembered her. That face, that golden hair. Those eyes, such a bright blue. Why was she on his mountain? Sneaking into the cabin, hiding? What was she hiding from?

Her footprints were quickly being covered by the falling snow, but not before he followed her trail to a wall of rock. A thick bush grew unnaturally, leaning away from the sun, and Eric reached down to push the greenery aside.

The cave was small, not more than an indentation in the rock, and she was huddled there, her back to the stone, her knees to her chest. She shivered so hard her whole body shook.

"G-g-go . . . go . . . go away," she stammered, her teeth chattering.

Eric dropped down to his haunches, placing his face level with hers, locking his eyes on hers. It was clear that she was scared of him, frightened half to death, when all he wanted to do was save her miserable hide!

"You're turning blue," he said calmly.

"I . . . I don't . . . c-c-care." She lifted her chin stubbornly. "G-go away."

Eric tried a smile, a very small and nonthreatening attempt to show her that he intended her no harm. "I can't do that." He swung the pack off of his back and into the cave, depositing it at her feet, and opened it to remove the wool blanket he had stored on top. At least she had the sense not to argue as he wrapped it around her shoulders.

She hugged the blanket to her, and buried her face in the warm wool. His little invader tried to scoot back when he moved into the cave with her, but she didn't say another word as he shoved the bush aside and built a fire in the entrance.

Her shivering slowed, as she was warmed by the fire and the blanket, and Eric settled himself across from her. There wasn't much room in the cave. Her stocking-encased feet rested between his spread legs, and he lifted one half-frozen foot in his hands.

She jerked her foot away from him, trying to hide it under the edge of the blanket.

"It would be best," he said calmly, "if we dried your stockings and warmed your feet before you put your boots back on."

"You brought my boots?" Her first words to him without chattering teeth.

Eric nodded. "And food. Sorry we were all out of biscuits, but I brought some crackers and a few strips of dried meat."

She blushed, color rising to her cheeks as she bit her lower lip. "I'm not usually a thief," she whispered.

"Not usually?"

She shook her head, and long tangles of yellow curls danced about her face.

Eric reached just under the blanket and gently

grabbed one foot. Through the thin, damp stockings he could feel that her toes were practically frozen, and he kneaded them gently. She tried to pull away once again, but he held fast and continued his massage.

"Your feet need to be warmed," he insisted.

"I'll place them closer to the fire."

Eric didn't let go. "This is best. And we need to get those stockings off and dried." He could feel her foot tense in his grasp. "I'd hate for you to lose these toes. Frostbite can be deadly."

She stopped tugging, and glanced up at him. "Frostbite?"

Eric nodded, massaging her foot gently, rubbing his thumb against the arch. "You're not accustomed to the cold, are you?"

She shook her head, withdrew her foot from his hand, and reached very carefully beneath her skirt. Working beneath the blanket, she didn't show a bit of skin, and he didn't even get a good look at the turn of her ankle. A moment later she withdrew a dark stocking and shook it out by the fire, and Eric took her bare foot in his grasp. The skin was much too cold, still damp, but it responded quickly to his touch, warming nicely.

"You have a Southern accent. Where are you from?"

She hesitated, and for a moment Eric thought she would refuse to tell him anything about herself. "Georgia," she revealed hesitantly. "But I'm not going back there."

She held her stocking close to the fire, and in minutes it was dry. He watched as she cautiously slipped her foot into the stocking and slid it up, never showing even an inch of leg. She worked her hands under the folds of the blanket, up her calf, and out again, and all Eric saw was the stocking-covered toes of one foot peeking from beneath brown wool. She held the other damp stocking in her hand, and waved it near the fire.

Eric placed his hand over her warmed foot and slid it beneath the blanket, and he took the other one, her bare, cold foot, in his hands. She didn't protest this time, but actually relaxed as he began to stroke the chilled extremity. "Where are you headed?"

"Sheridan. I'm going to be the new schoolteacher there."

"Sheridan's a good four days north of here."

"I know. So close, after all this time, and disaster strikes."

"Disaster," he repeated.

She nodded her head. "My foot's quite warm now, thank you, sir."

Eric released her foot, and she drew on a newly dried stocking with as much ease and modesty as she'd removed it, as he reached into the pack for her boots. He didn't even attempt to hand them to her, but instead loosened the laces and slipped one onto her foot himself, hooking the laces and tying them at her ankle.

And a shapely ankle it was. His fingers itched to

climb just a bit higher to her calf, but he restrained himself. She was skittish enough as it was. She allowed him to slip on first one boot and then another, blushing pink the entire time. She didn't like it, but she apparently didn't want to move her hands from beneath the warm blanket she clutched.

"Thank you," she whispered when he was done. "It was very kind of you to bring me these things, and the food, but you can leave now. Go back to your cabin."

She was perfectly serious, lifting her chin stubbornly, settling those blue eyes on him with defiance.

Eric glanced past the fire, into a blackening night aglow with moonlit snow. "Neither of us is going anywhere tonight."

She followed his gaze, and the defiance in her eyes died. "I see."

She obviously didn't like the idea. Not at all. Eric gave her his most charming smile. "Since we're going to be spending the night together, perhaps I should introduce myself. Eric Barrett."

"Eric Barrett," she repeated, with some show of interest. "That's a very nice name."

"Thank you. And yours?"

She looked a little surprised, as if she hadn't expected to have to introduce herself, and then she smiled just slightly. "Oh, how rude of me. Maddalyn Lorraine Kelly, Mr. Barrett."

"Maddalyn Lorraine Kelly of Georgia," he said,

a small part of his curiosity satisfied.

Her smile faded. "Maddalyn Lorraine Kelly of Sheridan," she corrected him, glancing down into her lap and pulling the woolen blanket tighter around her arms and chest.

He was even bigger up close than he had appeared to be from her hiding place behind the bushes, and he filled the too small cave with his shoulders and his long legs. Maddalyn kept her eyes down, but she couldn't ignore Eric Barrett's presence.

She was practically trapped between his legs. If it hadn't been snowing so hard, if he hadn't been kind enough to bring her this wonderfully warm blanket, she would have insisted that he remain outside the cave. These quarters were much too small for her to feel at ease.

"Feeling better?" he asked, and Maddalyn lifted her head. He had such a wonderful voice, deep and clear, strong and distinct. It suited his face.

She nodded her head, not trusting herself to speak.

"Good. Would you like something to eat?"

Maddalyn nodded again, and Eric Barrett smiled. It was that smile that kept her from attempting to flee from the cave. It was as clear and true as his voice, touching his eyes with a spark of real humor.

Well, to be honest, it was more than the smile that kept her in place. The snow was piling up quickly outside the cave, and he had mentioned frostbite, losing her toes! No, she was definitely better off right where she was.

He handed her a strip of dried meat and a hard cracker, passing the meal into the hand she reluctantly slipped from under the blanket. When she had devoured the dry food and returned her hand to its place against her chest, he withdrew a canteen and two tin cups from the pack at his side.

"Drink this," he insisted, handing her a half-full tin cup of liquid. "It'll warm you up."

Maddalyn slipped her hand out, just to the wrist, and took the cup, bringing it to her lips. It was that wonderful cider she had sampled at the cabin, and it did warm her as it went down.

She emptied the cup quickly and handed it to the man who watched her so intently. "Thank you, Mr. Barrett. That really is the most marvelous cider I've ever tasted."

He smiled at her again, his whole face full of good humor. "Thank *you*, Miss Kelly." She was almost certain that he was having fun with her, jesting at her expense. Of course, she had sampled quite a bit of the cider in the past three days, and it was possible that Eric Barrett was quite aware of that fact. "My brother Conrad makes a batch every fall, enough to last the year."

"Your brother Conrad," she repeated. "Is he the very large one or the one with the dimple in his chin?"

"Conrad's the dimple," he said, his smile fading.

"Karl is the very large one."

"I see."

It was getting colder in spite of the fire, in spite of the fact that Eric Barrett was so very close. People didn't normally make Maddalyn nervous, but there was something about Eric Barrett that made her skittish.

"Would you like to tell me, Miss Kelly, what you're doing on my mountain?" There was no humor in that question, and his soothing smile was gone.

"Your mountain?"

He didn't answer. He waited for her to.

"Well, as I told you earlier, I'm going to Sheridan to be a schoolteacher. I believe the present instructor is engaged to be married, and will be moving away from the area quite soon. In any case, I corresponded with a lady there who offered me the position. Her name is Mrs. James Hudson, and she seemed very nice, judging from her letters. Her husband has a ranch very near Sheridan, and they have six children, four boys and two girls, and she is, of course, concerned about their education."

Eric Barrett sighed, just a little, and Maddalyn decided that she'd best get right to the answer.

"The stage was robbed, and the outlaws killed the driver and the other passenger. I suspect they would have killed me, also, but I escaped. I climbed your mountain, found your lovely cabin, and—I must confess—I did enter the cabin while you were not at home, and I helped myself to some food, but

I was quite hungry, so I don't think it was very wrong." Maddalyn looked him in the eye, ready for his condemnation. "Do you, Mr. Barrett?"

"You could have asked."

"I did knock, but no one was home. And then, well, there were just you and your brothers, and I wasn't certain how I would be received."

He lifted his eyebrows just slightly. "Were you afraid of us?"

"No . . . well, yes, just a little. Especially after I broke a chair. I didn't mean to, really. I was looking at that wonderful photograph of you and your brothers, Karl and Conrad, and I lost my balance. Quite clumsy of me, really."

"What do you plan to do now?" he asked softly.

"Now?"

"Do you plan to stay in this cave until the snow melts, sneaking into the kitchen when the three of us are away?"

He was poking fun at her, and she didn't like it at all. "In a day or two I'll make my way down the mountain, find a town or a homestead, and continue on to Sheridan."

Eric Barrett smiled at her, and leaned in until his face was much too close to hers. "No, you won't."

"I most certainly will."

"Being new to Wyoming Territory, I'm sure you don't realize that the past week has been unseasonably warm."

"Warm?"

He nodded. "The snow that's falling might stop tonight. It might not. It might snow for a couple of days. Doesn't really matter. No one's going up or down this mountain until it melts."

"And when will that be?" She didn't mean to sound distressed, but her voice cracked just a little.

"Two weeks . . . four . . . maybe six." Eric Barrett didn't seem at all disconsolate at the prospect of Maddalyn being forced to live in a cave for better than a month!

"I see," Maddalyn said softly.

"I'm afraid you're stuck here." There was entirely too much joviality in his voice, and his smile was quite inappropriate.

"It seems that's true."

"So of course you'll have to come and live with us."

His casual suggestion caught Maddalyn by surprise. "I beg your pardon?"

"Do you cook?" he asked.

"Quite well."

"Good. You can cook, clean, do some mending . . . none of us is very good with a needle . . . in exchange for a room, food, all the cider you can drink."

"Mr. Barrett," Maddalyn said softly. "While I appreciate your suggestion, I must make it clear that I do not intend to seek employment as a cook or a maid."

"Do you intend to live in this cave until the snow melts, Miss Kelly? What I am offering is an arrangement that makes perfect sense."

He sounded so smug, so sure of himself! And, of course, his suggestion *did* make perfect sense.

"All right," she agreed reluctantly. "Until the snow melts."

His smile was victorious, much too smug to be handsome. "Then that's settled. Come over here." He opened his arms and waited for her to move into them!

"Mr. Barrett!" Maddalyn snapped, hugging the blanket tight. "Just because I have agreed to be your housekeeper for the next few weeks . . ."

His laughter filled the small cave, bouncing off the walls and echoing loudly in her ears. It was a very pleasant laugh, full of real and true good humor.

"I don't know what it is you find so amusing," Maddalyn said in her best Aunt Ethel voice.

His laughter died. "I'm sorry, I should have explained. It's cold, and it's going to get colder. If we huddle together we'll stay warmer. It's as simple as that."

Maddalyn didn't have much experience dealing with men, but her instincts told her this one was honest. He looked her in the eye, unflinching, and she could see no artifice there.

"I see. Well, I suppose if we must, we must."

Maddalyn moved forward slowly, inching closer to Eric Barrett, holding the blanket tightly around her shoulders. Frigid air crept in the tiny crevices that opened up as she moved. She'd never known that people lived in places where it was so cold!

Strictly in the name of survival, she placed her body against his. He was so very large—wide chest and long legs, long arms he wrapped around her gently—that he dwarfed her completely. She was lost in his arms, lost in the warmth that enveloped her immediately. It would have made perfect sense for her to feel threatened, even afraid, but that wasn't the case.

She'd never in her life felt safer, more protected, than she did at this moment, wrapped in the arms of a stranger. Not even as a child in her uncle's house. Certainly not as a young woman, growing up under Aunt Ethel's scrutiny. She had never felt threatened, but neither had she ever felt this secure.

It made no sense, she decided as she buried her face against Eric Barrett's chest, no sense at all.

"Mr. Barrett, would you mind terribly if I slept for a while?"

"Not at all, Miss Kelly." His voice was soft, without the thundering ring of his earlier laughter. In fact, she could hear no hint of humor in his clear and beautiful voice.

How did she do that? Fall asleep so fast and so easily? Eric looked down at the bundle trapped in his arms and frowned. All he could see was tangled, curly blond hair and that brown blanket Maddalyn Kelly had wrapped around herself.

But he could feel her warm breath against his

chest, penetrating his clothing, that feathery touch taking him to the edge of madness.

When he'd sensed an intruder, he hadn't expected this. He hadn't expected *her*. She was too delicate for this mountain. How had she managed to climb it?

It hadn't been easy for her. He had seen the dirt and the rips in her dress, the scuffs on her fine boots, the smudges on her face, the scratches on her hand. She was apparently tougher than she appeared to be.

She murmured in her sleep, and rubbed her face against his chest contentedly.

She didn't belong on this mountain, but she sure as hell didn't belong in Sheridan, either. That town was too wild, too dangerous for a lady like Maddalyn Lorraine Kelly.

One thing about a lady. You could put her on a mountain, mess her up a bit, dirty her up a lot, take away her fine clothes and fancy jewelry . . . and you could still tell she was a lady.

And ladies didn't last long out here. The life was too hard, too unpredictable. The best thing little Miss Kelly could do for herself was get back to Georgia as soon as the weather permitted travel.

But she'd been adamant that she wasn't going to return there. Why? A marriage gone wrong? A lovers' quarrel? What had driven Maddalyn Kelly across the country?

Still asleep, she snaked one arm around his waist. A moment later, the other followed. Eric tucked the blanket around her, so that they were wrapped together in its folds, as warm as a body could be on a night like this.

It was too bad that Maddalyn Kelly was so obviously a lady. He wouldn't mind having a *woman* around the cabin for a few weeks. Welcoming arms at the end of the day, a warm and willing body in his bed at night. Someone to hold, like this, when the nights were cold, like this.

But Maddalyn Kelly was a lady who was as out of place on his mountain as he would be in Georgia.

She curled up against him, making her body an even tighter ball of soft, warm, pliable . . . lady.

What a shame.

Chapter Five

Maddalyn woke not with her usual morning lethargy, but with a sudden start, much as she had when she'd awakened to find Eric Barrett watching her from the bedroom doorway. She yanked her head off of his chest, her arms from around his waist, and pulled away.

He was sleeping, his face lit with soft morning light that spilled through the cave entrance, and as she studied him he reached out, eyes still firmly closed, and with those large and surprisingly gentle hands pulled her back into position against his chest.

Maddalyn didn't protest, didn't fight the sleeping man. The air that had rushed between them when she'd moved away had been horribly cold.

The snow had stopped falling, and the sun would

Linda Jones

soon be shining brightly, but the fire he had built between their shelter and the snow had died out. Maddalyn knew that she surely would have died here in the small crevice that had become her haven, if Eric Barrett hadn't come after her.

He murmured in his sleep, something unintelligible, and wrapped his arms around her. He laid his head on top of hers, and she could hear his deep breathing near her ear. Sound and warm and soothing, his breath touched her, and a strand of thick hair brushed her face.

From a distance she had thought it to be a simple brown, but in truth there was every shade of brown and dark blond in those straight strands. She reached up and barely touched the thick hair that fell over his shoulder. It was so soft and thick! Uncle Henry hadn't had much hair at all, and hadn't for as long as Maddalyn could remember. Lawrence's hair had been rather thin, she recalled, though at the moment she couldn't quite picture it. She did remember that it had always been worn short.

Why was she forever comparing Eric Barrett to the limited number of men she knew? He wasn't like any of them. Not at all.

He had undoubtedly saved her life, chasing after her in last night's snowstorm. Why? He could have stayed in the safety of his cabin, warm and well fed, and left her to her own devices. But he hadn't. Eric Barrett had spent the night in a freezing cave, and had eaten the same all but inedible substances

70

he'd fed her. Maddalyn tilted her head back and studied his bearded face.

His beard was trimmed short, but he was definitely better-looking without it. The photograph she'd studied hadn't been all that old, and it was really a shame to hide that wonderfully distinct jaw. He even had a nice nose. She'd never admired anyone's nose before, but Eric Barrett's was quite perfect. Just the right size for his face, straight, not too wide or too narrow.

It was true that Eric Barrett was a very large man, tall and broad in the shoulders. Even his feet and hands were sizable. But he had an unexpected elegance, also, in the way he moved, in the long fingers on those hands.

She had been so afraid, upon spying him from a distance, but she knew now that worry had been foolish. There was no reason to fear a man who would do as this man had done. He hadn't left her to her own devices, but had instead surely rescued her from death. And he'd been quite the gentleman, insisting on their current improper closeness strictly for the sake of warmth and survival.

It was inappropriate, she knew, even shocking, but it was also very nice. Eric Barrett was warm, and she seemed to fit quite nicely here, trapped between his thighs and his long arms.

No one had ever held her so, that she could recall. Her mother, perhaps, but Maddalyn had been orphaned as a child and had no memory of her parents. When Lawrence had kissed her, he had simply placed his hands on her shoulders and leaned in to press his damp lips to hers. There had been nothing warm or quite so nice as this.

Aunt Ethel had never been one for hugging or holding. Maddalyn had never seen her aunt make either of those gestures even to her only child, Doreen. Touching was not approved of in that dreary household. Aunt Ethel and Uncle Henry never even so much as held hands, or planted a kiss on a waiting cheek.

Of course, they must have touched at least once. There was Cousin Doreen to consider. Maddalyn blushed and lowered her gaze. She wouldn't even have known that much, if it hadn't been for Mary Lynette.

Mary Lynette was the best cook in Georgia, or at least that was what she claimed. Maddalyn was never sure why the woman had stayed so long with Aunt Ethel and Uncle Henry, but she was certainly grateful. Mary Lynette had taught Maddalyn to cook, and while they worked in the kitchen, they'd talked. Some days Mary Lynette listened, and some days the cook did all the talking.

Aunt Ethel had never spoken to Maddalyn of men, of marriage or love, but Mary Lynette had. Maddalyn had heard tirades over raisin pie, sweet, soft speeches over hoecake. Mary Lynette shared with Maddalyn everything that happened to her, and the cook led a colorful life.

Maddalyn had never understood the quickening of the heart at the sight of a man, though Mary

Lynette had spoken enthusiastically of it often. The cook had been married three times, and had buried all three of her husbands. *Buried them happy*, she'd said with a sad smile. *Loved them, all three, different as they were.*

"What are you thinking about?" The gravelly question took her by surprise, and Maddalyn drew her head away from Eric Barrett's chest and looked up into narrowly opened gray eyes.

"I can't tell," she said quickly.

He didn't argue with her, but smiled sleepily. "Sorry to intrude, Miss Kelly. I was just wondering what put that smile on your face."

"I wasn't smiling," Maddalyn insisted, reluctantly drawing away from Eric Barrett and the warmth they created in the small, cold cave.

He sighed, reached long arms above his head, and stretched languidly. "I could have sworn you had a smile on your face, Miss Kelly. Must have been a dream."

She wouldn't look at him, and her avoidance of him in such close quarters was so blatant it was almost amusing. Almost.

Maddalyn Kelly stared at the ground as Eric closed and tied the pack. There was little in the lightweight pack this morning. She was wearing the blanket around her shoulders and the boots on her feet, and together they'd eaten what little bit of food he'd packed.

She was embarrassed. Her cheeks were pink—

73

the cold air or a ladylike blush? Poor Miss Kelly, modest and reserved to the point of death. Eric knew he was being too harsh. She had protested only weakly and not for long last night when he'd opened his arms to her. But look at her now. She was properly modest, just this side of indignant, he supposed.

"Hungry?" he asked, his voice gruff with sleep.

Maddalyn Kelly's head snapped up, as if she was surprised. Blue eyes, big as saucers, stared at him. "Well, yes, I suppose I am."

"Karl will have a big pot of oatmeal on the stove when we get back to the cabin. Hot coffee. Pan of biscuits." He grinned, in spite of his aggravation with her. "I know you like Karl's biscuits."

"Will they mind . . . you know . . . my staying there for a while? Until the snow melts?"

Eric stood, stooping slightly in the too small cave. "Not when I tell them you're going to take over the cooking while you're there."

"I hope that's true. I do hate to be a bother."

Eric turned his back to her and stepped into the sun. A bother? He didn't want to review his mental list of her transgressions thus far, but she'd been much more than a bother.

The snow had stopped, but it blanketed the ground, hung in the evergreen trees, caught the sun and reflected its brightness.

"It's so very beautiful."

Eric glanced down at the woman . . . the lady at his side. The top of her head barely reached his shoulder, and as she stepped forward all he could see was a tangle of golden hair to her waist, and the woolen blanket she clutched around her. She should have looked . . . at the very least unappealing. But she turned her face to him, bright, smiling, breathtaking, and Maddalyn Kelly was anything but unappealing.

"Isn't it?" she asked, wanting him to confirm her observation.

"It's cold," he answered.

His lifeless reply did not dampen her enthusiasm. "Of course it's cold. But for goodness' sake, Mr. Barrett, have you ever seen anything more spectacular?"

She saw beauty on his mountain, but she didn't see the danger. He wanted to tell her how quickly she could have frozen to death last night, that it was dangerous, even now, with the sun shining down on them brightly.

But he didn't.

"It is beautiful," he agreed. "Let's go."

He tramped forward, stopping every few minutes to look back. Each time he stopped, Maddalyn Kelly was farther away, struggling to keep up the pace as she waded through calf-high snow. Her battle included an effort to keep her skirt and the trailing blanket from dragging through the snow, a losing battle from the start. Each time, he waited until she was almost to him before he started forward again. After half a dozen stops he cursed under his breath, met her halfway, and lifted her from her feet.

With one arm under her knees and another around her back, he lunged forward again.

She tried to protest, but her breath was already coming too fast. All she could manage was a muttered objection that died quickly on her lips.

"I'm so sorry, Mr. Barrett," she said when she had recovered her breath. "It really isn't right that you should have to carry me."

"I don't mind." She was light as a feather, no impedance at all. "I'm hungry and I'm cold, and we'll reach the cabin faster this way."

"You're cold?"

He just stared at her, at her inquisitive eyes and pink cheeks and pursed lips.

And then Maddalyn Kelly wrapped her arms around his neck and laid her head against his shoulder, wrapping the blanket that covered her around his arms as well.

"Is that better?" she asked, much too softly.

Hell no, it wasn't a damn bit better. "Yes," he lied. "That's just fine."

She curled against him, relaxed and content and apparently no longer embarrassed. When the cabin came into view, Eric gave a silent prayer of thanks. He couldn't take much more of this. Before he'd reached the door, Karl and Conrad were there, bundled in their heavy coats and waiting anxiously to see exactly what he was bringing home.

Eric had a feeling he was the only one who recognized that he was bringing home trouble.

"Is she dead?" Conrad called, his smile fading as Eric neared the door.

"Of course not," Eric snapped.

"What's wrong with her, then?" Karl asked.

Maddalyn Kelly lifted her head from Eric's shoulder, just slightly, but she didn't loosen her hold. Yellow curls brushed his cheek and tickled his nose as she smiled for his brothers. It was a bright smile she flashed at them, with none of her earlier hesitation. "There's nothing wrong with me," she said. "I'm simply keeping Mr. Barrett warm."

He set her on her feet just inside the kitchen door, and Maddalyn found herself surrounded by the Barrett men. Eric, who stayed close, Conrad, with what seemed to be an ever-present smile, and Karl, a rather quiet giant of a man who hadn't taken his eyes off of her.

The cabin was warm. Toasty, in fact, and there was no reason to cling to Eric Barrett any longer.

"Hungry?" Karl Barrett asked, and Maddalyn decided that must be an oft-asked question in this household. "I made plenty."

"We're both starving," Eric said, removing his coat and then taking the blanket from around her shoulders. "This is Miss Maddalyn Kelly. She's . . ." He hesitated for just a moment. ". . . lost."

"What happened?" Conrad took Maddalyn's arm graciously and led her to the table. "How did you come to be lost on the mountain?"

Eric was immediately at her other arm, helping her into a chair. His touch seemed more demanding, urgent, somehow. "After we eat, if you don't mind," he growled.

Conrad and Karl had evidently already eaten, but they sat at the table with Maddalyn and Eric as they ate their breakfast. Eric had been correct. Oatmeal, biscuits, some dried meat that Maddalyn passed on, and a full pot of steaming coffee.

Maddalyn studied the brothers while she ate. Karl should have been frightening, but he was not. Though he stood at least six and a half feet tall, and his upper arms were approximately the size of her waist, there was a gentleness in his eyes that could not be ignored. No, he was not frightening at all . . . but she definitely would want to stay on his good side.

Conrad's constant smile became almost irritating. He had the look of a man who knows a secret he refuses to share, and finds it all terribly amusing. He was the shortest of the three, though she was certain he stood at least six feet tall. His features, including the bearded chin she knew hid a handsome cleft, were sharper than Karl's or Eric's, and his nose was just a tad too long.

All three of them had magnificent gray eyes that were not quite blue, and yet not a completely colorless gray, either.

When she had finished her oatmeal and a biscuit loaded with strawberry jam, she told Eric's brothers what she had told him the night before. She told them about her plans to teach in Sheridan, about the stagecoach robbery, about escaping from the bandits and climbing the mountain.

"It's amazing," Karl said softly.

"So Eric was right all along," Conrad said. "You snuck into the cabin while we were down the hill."

Maddalyn nodded, trying to look contrite. It was difficult. Here she was, the center of attention, three handsome men hanging on her every word. She was warm, she was comfortable . . . she was sinfully content.

"I must say, Mr. Barrett," she said, directing her comment to Conrad, "you make the most delightful cider. I would love to have your recipe."

"Thank you, Miss Kelly, I would be delighted. . . ."

Maddalyn jumped when Eric slammed his mug onto the table. "This is ridiculous," he muttered under his breath. "First of all," he snapped, "you can hardly call all three of us Mr. Barrett. You know our given names. Use them. Secondly, this is not a Georgia drawing room. I'm glad you enjoyed Conrad's cider when you crept in here and *stole* it, but let's not pretend that you're an invited guest. A streak of bad luck brought you here, and we'll deal with it as best we can, but—"

"Yours or mine, Mr. Barrett?" Maddalyn asked, keeping her voice and her facial expression polite.

"Yours or mine what?" Eric Barrett's eyes were angry, and his teeth were clenched.

"Streak of bad luck. Yours or mine?" She was determined to remain calm.

"Does it matter?"

It did, but Maddalyn refused to say so.

"You're tired, Mr. Barrett. I'm afraid you didn't sleep as well as I last night. It's perfectly normal for you to be unnaturally cranky this morning, after the ordeal."

Eric ignored her, turned his gaze away from her and to his brothers. "She's going to stay until the snow thaws, and then one of us will have to take her to Olympia."

"Of course she'll stay," Conrad said with an enthusiastic grin.

"While she's here she's going to cook, clean, and mend. I for one will not miss the nights when it's Conrad's turn to cook."

Karl was shaking his head slowly. "She's a guest. We can't ask her to—"

"It's quite all right, Karl," Maddalyn said before he could finish. "The days will pass much faster if I have something to do, and I really am a good cook. I enjoy cooking, in fact."

Eric banged his cup on the surface of the table again. "She's not a guest, she's a thief!"

Maddalyn forestalled Conrad's protest. "That is correct, I suppose, but I'm not a very good thief. I only took food and Conrad's cider, and even then you knew that I had been here. I don't suppose I'd make a very good bandit."

Conrad and Karl laughed, but it was evident by

the black look on Eric's face that he was not amused. Still, Maddalyn found herself smiling at him. He was quite fascinating, rugged and inflexible, handsome even when he growled at her. He did try to appear to be callous, but she knew better. He'd rescued her from the storm, after all. Had warmed her feet and held her against the cold. Had carried her to the cabin when the task proved too much for her.

There was something else, some sense that she had known him all her life. An inexplicable feeling that he would always be there.

It took a moment, but as Maddalyn watched him the blackly hostile look he cast her way softened. The hardness in his eyes faded, and his thinned lips relaxed. Try as he might, Eric Barrett couldn't stay angry for very long. It was not his nature, even though he apparently wished it could be true.

Tiny goosebumps rose on Maddalyn's arms as Eric continued to stare at her with those marvelous eyes. He didn't blink, didn't move at all, and that stare he cast her way gave her chills. Quite pleasant chills.

Goodness, she'd been right about love all along. It was absolute, undeniable, pure. When it came it was with a flash, a certainty that couldn't be denied, and that quickening of her heart Mary Lynette had spoken of.

Heaven help her, she was hopelessly in love with Eric Barrett.

Chapter Six

"You can have any bedroom you'd like," Conrad said, leading Maddalyn into the main room and nearer the blazing fire that warmed the cabin. "Take mine. It's the room in the middle, so there's never a draft in the night."

"I don't want to be a bother. If I can just have a pallet or a couple of blankets I will be quite comfortable here." She pointed to an uncluttered corner. Besides, Conrad's mattress was lumpy.

"Nonsense," Karl said, his voice soft and coming from directly behind her. "You pick a room, any room, and it's yours for as long as you stay with us."

Maddalyn bit her bottom lip. She didn't want to seem demanding or overly particular. "The bedroom at the end of the hall, where I was . . . napping yesterday was very nice. If it wouldn't be too much bother . . ."

"Not at all." Eric's voice remained gruff, and Maddalyn turned to scrutinize him. He stood in the wide and open doorway between the main room and the kitchen, arms crossed over his chest, his expression black once more. Of course, he had no idea that she loved him, and she most certainly couldn't declare herself outright. Mary Lynette had told her that men who were afraid of nothing else were often terrified of love, because it made them vulnerable. It was often best, the cook had said, not to tell them they were in love until it was too late to fight it.

And of course, the man who glared at her didn't love her. Not yet. And if he didn't fall in love with her—deep, undeniable, forever love that matched her own—before she left this cabin, then her own love was in vain. She'd never marry a man who didn't love her as much as she loved him. She didn't want to end up like Aunt Ethel, a sour, miserable old woman, raising miserable children.

"Please take my room." Eric's forbidding expression faded, as it had before. He was not, Maddalyn was certain, a normally cross person. Something about her presence made him cross, but he couldn't maintain his anger.

"Your room?"

"I'll bunk down in here, or in Conrad's room."

What if I get cold? She couldn't ask that question, of course, but it echoed in her mind.

She pulled her eyes away from Eric to find Conrad and Karl staring at one another with the most comically puzzled expressions on their faces. Karl's bushy eyebrows were pulled together, and his brow was a mass of wrinkles. Conrad had narrowed his eyes, but as Maddalyn watched he broke into a full grin.

Maddalyn turned her back on the three of them, and walked to the window. Even from across the room the view was spectacular. White and green and a marvelous gray-blue—like Eric Barrett's eyes.

But as she neared the window she saw something else. Something horrible. Her own reflection.

Her hair had never been easy to tame, but at the moment it was a mass of tangles that stuck out at all angles, golden curls and knots. There were smudges on her face, and she reached one hand up to touch a dirty cheek. Her dress—she looked down to confirm what she already knew—was nothing more than a rag. Torn and stained, it was ruined. She looked like a street urchin.

"Oh, dear," she murmured, making herself miserable as she continued to study her faint reflection in the glass. "Oh, my." She turned around, away from the awful image, to find the three Barrett brothers staring at her. Waiting. "I don't normally look like this," she said in defense of herself.

"She's not normally a thief, either," Eric said with a half-grin. "Or so she says."

For the first time since this ordeal had begun, Maddalyn got angry. She was rarely cross, but when it happened it came over her quickly, in a flash.

"Thank you for reminding us all of that, Mr. Barrett," she snapped, and her eyes filled with tears. It was a failing, that when she was cross she cried. It made her anger ineffective, childish, but it couldn't be helped.

"Look what you've done, Eric," Conrad said, stepping forward to take Maddalyn's hand. "You've upset our guest, you lout. I swear, you have no manners at all." He turned his face to her. "What do you need, Maddalyn?"

"A bath," she said, sniffling slightly. "Lots of soap. A brush or a comb. Clean clothes." Conrad was holding her hand, patting it consolingly.

"I don't know what we can do about the clothes, but we can handle the rest."

Karl turned abruptly and stalked to the hall that led to the bedrooms. He returned moments later with a bolt of red calico. "You can have this," he offered almost desperately. "Can you make a dress with this?" His face was almost as red as the material he offered her.

Maddalyn did her best to calm herself. Karl and Conrad, at least, were obviously uncomfortable with a crying woman. They had been quite decent to her, considering the circumstances, and she didn't want to cause them any distress. "Not without a pattern, but I can make a skirt, I suppose.

Perhaps if one of you has an old shirt of some sort I can alter . . ."

"Of course," Conrad interrupted.

Maddalyn wiped the last of the tears from her eyes. "You must forgive me. I'm afraid the past few days have been an ordeal, and I'm not entirely myself."

She lifted her face to look at Karl, eye to eye. He was a tremendously tall man, wider in the shoulders even than Eric. But he had a kind face, with regular features and gray eyes like Eric's. "Whatever were you planning to do with this calico?"

"I was going to make curtains for the cabin, but . . ."

"Red?" Maddalyn interrupted. "You can't put red curtains in this lovely house."

"That's what Eric said." Karl placed the bolt of fabric in her hands. "I saw red curtains in a hotel in San Francisco once. I thought it was right pretty." He backed away. "Doesn't matter. None of us can sew."

Maddalyn looked past Conrad and Karl to a silent Eric. "White," she said. "If you must have curtains here, they should be white, with ties so they can be pulled back. It would be a crime to screen even a portion of the view."

"You like the view from this place?" Eric asked.

"Of course I do." Eric was staring at her much too intently, and Maddalyn turned her back on him to gaze out of the window. She looked past the disturbing image—ignored her own reflection. "It's quite magnificent, Mr. Barrett. I never knew that such a land existed. In Georgia, where I've lived all my life, there are hills. Some people call them mountains, but those people have never seen this."

Maddalyn clutched the red calico to her breast, afraid to turn around. Everything here was bigger, better than she could have imagined. The mountains, the cabin . . . Eric Barrett.

Eric and Conrad went down the hill, promising to return with a bathtub to place in the kitchen. Karl stayed behind and opened a trunk that sat in the corner of the main room. It was filled with shirts that needed mending, pants the Barrett brothers had outgrown, needles, thread, a pair of scissors.

"It will take me a couple of days to make a skirt," Maddalyn said, talking to herself. Karl had opened the trunk and stepped away, but he hovered over her, watching her every move as she sat cross-legged in front of the trunk.

Some of the shirts she drew from the chest were beyond hope. Some were simply missing buttons, or had small tears in the fabric. Easily mended. The pants were all much too large, but she set aside a pair that seemed a tad lighter than the rest. They were black serge, a pair of dress trousers that hadn't seen much wear.

She worked there on the floor in front of the trunk, cutting a few buttons from an unsalvageable shirt and sewing them onto one that was in fairly good shape.

"How do you do that so fast without stabbing yourself?" Karl asked. He had a quiet voice, gentle and sweet, even though it was quite deep.

"Practice," she said with a smile, glancing over her shoulder. "I've been doing needlework since I was eight years old. My Aunt Ethel was of a mind that women needed to be able to do two things, and do them well: sewing and cooking. Of course, she couldn't cook at all, herself. That was why we had Mary Lynette. But Mary Lynette taught me to cook."

Karl listened and nodded, and Maddalyn returned her eyes to her work. "It is my personal opinion that women need to know much more. It's all well and good to be able to run a household, but I think a woman should be capable of managing her own finances, of understanding the world we live in. Do you find that terribly shocking, Karl?"

She glanced up again and he shook his head. "My Aunt Ethel found it shocking. She predicted that I would be dead within a month of leaving her home. Scalped by Indians. She was almost right. Not about the Indian part, of course, but about the dead part. It's terribly petty of me, but I think that's what I would have hated the most, if those bandits had killed me. It would have made Aunt Ethel right, and she is always terribly sanctimonious when she's proved correct."

Maddalyn held up the shirt she had been working on, nodded in approval, and set it aside. "But of course, thanks to Mr. Barrett, I'm not dead." She picked up the black trousers and the scissors and began to cut, shortening them dramatically. "I think he's rather peeved with me at the moment," she said softly. "Perhaps because he was forced to sleep outdoors last night, and it was quite cold." Maddalyn let her hands and the black trousers fall into her lap. The night had been cold, but Eric Barrett had been warm. She stared into the trunk full of clothes and sighed, just a little, and then she glanced over her shoulder once again. It was not just Karl who stood behind her, but all three Barrett brothers, Eric included. From her position on the floor, they towered over her.

"Oh, I didn't hear you come in."

"You were talking," Eric said. "The tub's in the kitchen, in front of the stove."

"Thank you, Mr. Barrett."

"And just for your information, Miss Kelly, I am not *peeved* at you." His voice and his expression belied his words.

"I'm glad to hear it. I am very grateful, you know. I don't mean to be a—"

"You're not a bother," he snapped.

In spite of his scowl, Maddalyn smiled at him. "It's very nice of you to say so, even though I don't think you mean what you say. You'll not be sorry, Mr. Barrett." She blushed. She could feel the heat rising in her cheeks, and she could only hope that the smudges there hid her uncontrollable reaction.

"I'm really a very good cook."

"I'm sure you are."

"I can't wait," Conrad said enthusiastically. "All Eric knows how to make is stew, and Karl makes pretty good biscuits, but that's about it."

Maddalyn pulled her eyes away from Eric and stared up at Karl and Conrad. Conrad's words had startled her somewhat. For a moment she had forgotten Eric's brothers were there, and had imagined she and Eric were alone.

"You'll see," she said, returning to her quick mending work. "You won't be sorry."

"I'm already sorry," Eric mumbled as he slammed the kitchen door behind him.

"You don't mean it," Conrad said jovially, and Eric cast a cutting glance in his brother's direction.

"I do."

"Ahhh," Conrad sighed with more meaning than was necessary. "She is a pretty girl. I'll bet she cleans up real nice."

Eric walked down the hill, wishing that Conrad would decide to stay behind. He didn't. A short way down the hill was the barn they'd built to house the horses and mules. Next to the barn was the smokehouse that got them through the long winters.

"It's really too bad," Conrad called from a safe distance, "that the girl's already sweet on you. I should have volunteered to go after her myself, braved the snowstorm and played the gallant."

"Yes, you should have," Eric grumbled.

"But after all, she was *your* intruder. You knew about her first, and she was sleeping in your bed." Conrad closed the gap between them, practically running down the icy, snow-covered hill. "What's your problem, *Mr. Barrett?*"

"My problem is, at this moment, preparing to step into a warm tub of water in my kitchen." He imagined that scene much too clearly. "Hell, it might be weeks before we can make it down the mountain!"

"Is that so bad?"

"Yes!" Eric stopped on the snow-covered path and turned to his brother. Normally Karl was the dense one. "Dammit, Conrad, surely even you can see what she is, in spite of the state she's in. She's already got you and Karl eating out of the palm of her hand, and within a week she'll be bored, and whining about the cold, and—"

"She's not Jane," Conrad interrupted, his smile fading. "I never thought you still . . . that was five years ago, Eric. Jane and Maddalyn are nothing alike."

"They're a lot alike. Pretty, spoiled ladies."

"Jane wouldn't have lasted three hours on this mountain alone, much less three days. She would have stood there and screamed until the outlaws shot her. Hell, I would have shot her myself if I'd had the chance. She spent two days in the cabin five years ago. She brought four servants with her, for God's sake, and all she did was complain about the cold. And it was September! You're the one who told me all that. Have you forgotten?"

Forgotten? Never. Eric saw Karl at the top of the hill, and turned away from his brothers. Conrad's assessment of Jane was correct, and he'd only met her the one time. Eric tried to tell himself that leaving was the best gift she could have given him. He'd been twenty-four, thought himself hopelessly in love with her—the way she laughed, the way she batted her lashes at him. And she hadn't actually acted alone. She'd given him a choice. *Come back to Boston and be my husband, or stay here and live alone.*

It hadn't taken him two minutes to make his choice. He would never survive in the city. This mountain was his home. He'd worked for it, built most of the cabin himself, and by God he'd be buried here.

Jane had been surprised. So had he, in a way. He hadn't loved her so very much after all.

"You'll see," he said softly.

"You're not even giving the girl a chance." Conrad was dogging his steps. "Now if she was a redhead, I'd give you a run for your money, in spite of the fact that she's sweet on you. I can be very charming, you know. Think I could get her to dye her hair? Nah," he answered his own question. "It's not the same."

Eric had rarely regretted asking his brothers to join him in his venture, to leave behind careers none of them were suited for and build something

93

Linda Jones

on this mountain, but at the moment he did. Intensely.

Karl appeared at the top of the hill and lumbered down the road. The oldest of the Barrett brothers had always been shy with women, at times appearing coldly reserved when he was, in fact, scared half to death. He'd taken to Maddalyn right quick, though.

"I told her we'd give her an hour," Karl called as he came near. "At least. So behave yourselves, little brothers." A wide smile split his face. "Hey, Eric," he called. "I think she likes you."

Oh, no. Not again.

Maddalyn stepped into the warm water and sat slowly. She closed her eyes and leaned back, knees raised in the short tub. Not since leaving Aunt Ethel's house had she had the luxury of a tub bath.

Karl had filled the tub quickly, carrying two large buckets at a time in from the pump just outside the kitchen door. Maddalyn had heated a large pot of water herself, but Karl had insisted on emptying the heavy pan into the waiting cold water for her.

He had been very sweet, staying behind to assist her while his brothers all but ran from the cabin.

Maddalyn rubbed a rough bar of soap over her arms. Certainly she'd never been this dirty in all her life. Aunt Ethel never would have allowed it.

As she rubbed that same bar of soap over her feet, she smiled. How well she could remember Eric Barrett's hands warming her freezing feet. Of course, he hadn't meant that touch to be a caress, but rather a necessary act—like holding her against the cold.

She remembered that touch fondly, though, just as she remembered the warmth of his embrace, the strength of his long arms.

Maddalyn leaned back, dipping her head into the water. How on earth could she expect any man to fall in love with her when she looked like a street urchin? She soaped her hair twice, already dreading the necessary attempt to comb out the tangles.

How on earth could she be expected to charm a man with so little at her disposal? She had no enticing gowns, no perfume, not even a ribbon for her hair.

Clean at last, Maddalyn sighed deeply and leaned her back against the tub, relaxing for a moment more before the water became completely cold.

Of course, it was true that Mary Lynette had never possessed any fine gowns, and the cook had usually smelled of cinnamon rather than perfume. Mary Lynette was not, Maddalyn conceded, even very pretty. She had wide hips, and eyes that were set just a bit too far apart, and a pointed chin. Maddalyn had found the cook to be striking, on occasion, usually when she spoke of one of her husbands, but she hadn't attracted even one of them with fetching gowns and sweet perfume.

The way to a man's heart is through his stomach,

Mary Lynette had insisted on more than one occasion.

Maddalyn smiled as she rose from the tub, grabbing the towel that was folded neatly on the floor. She knew how to cook. Pies and cakes, puddings and breads. A roast that would melt in your mouth.

Eric, large as he was, looked to have a healthy appetite.

Chapter Seven

They gave her more than her allotted hour, just to be safe, and when they entered the kitchen a tempting aroma hit them. Eric frowned and wrinkled his nose as the unfamiliar smell hit him. Something sweet. Spicy.

"Gingerbread," Maddalyn said with a smile as she watched the three of them file into the cabin. "I hope you don't mind, but you had all the ingredients there in the pantry, and I do hate to be at loose ends. I was able to start on that calico, as well. The material for a skirt is cut, and there was lots left over. Enough for this sash, perhaps an apron, too."

Karl said nothing. Even Conrad was silent. Eric herded his brothers in and closed the door behind them. He'd known it all along. Dammit, he'd tried

Linda Jones

to warn them, but they'd stubbornly refused to listen.

Maddalyn Kelly stood in front of the stove, holding a pan of fragrant gingerbread in her hands as if it were a peace offering. Conrad had been right. She cleaned up real nice.

He couldn't help but recognize the clothing she had chosen from the trunk full of discarded items. Black pants that hung loosely on her, and a white linen shirt that hadn't had any buttons on it when he'd last seen it. He'd removed the shirt without taking the time to unfasten even a single button. The trousers and shirt Maddalyn wore had been his wedding suit, the clothes he'd worn to Boston that last time, to see Jane. He should've burned those clothes, instead of tossing them into that trunk.

She'd fitted them nicely, adding a sash made from Karl's red calico. Her face was pink, scrubbed clean so that it seemed her blue eyes were brighter than before. And that hair . . . It was soft and shiny, still slightly damp, and it curled around her face and over her shoulders in a mass of fine golden ringlets.

She was much too beautiful.

Her smile died slowly, and the pan dropped from chest to waist level. "You don't like gingerbread?" She had taken their silence as disapproval.

"We love gingerbread," Eric said, hefting the ham he'd carried in from the smokehouse and

98

placing it on the table. "Ham and biscuits for dinner?"

Maddalyn set the pan of gingerbread on the table. "If that's what you'd like."

"If there's any ham left you can use it in a pot of beans for supper tonight."

She looked down at the good-sized ham that sat next to her pan. "If?"

Eric smiled broadly. Conrad and Karl remained silent, and Maddalyn seemed just a little disconcerted. Just a little. It wouldn't take him two days to prove to them all that she didn't fit in here, that a lady from Georgia or anywhere else was lost on this mountain.

"Is that a problem for you?" he asked.

And she was a lady, even dressed in his discarded clothes. She was elegant and poised and fragile. But as he watched her eyes they became a sharper blue, flashing defiance at him. He could add spoiled to his list of ladylike qualities she possessed.

"Mr. Barrett, why don't you and your brothers wait in the other room while I prepare dinner?" Her eyes flickered over his shoulder, and she frowned at the silent Karl and Conrad. "Is there anything wrong?"

"You'll have to excuse my brothers and their terrible manners. We just . . . haven't had any gingerbread for a very long time."

Eric glanced over his shoulder. Karl was now staring at the floor, but Conrad was still watching

Maddalyn intently. It wasn't the gingerbread that had his normally talkative brother entranced.

Karl gave Conrad a shove, and Eric watched his brothers shuffle into the main room. Conrad's hoarse whisper carried to the kitchen, but the words were unintelligible. Eric could only imagine what was being said.

"Do you need any help, Miss Kelly?" Eric offered as she turned to the stove.

"No, thank you, Mr. Barrett." There was a small tremble in her voice, a hesitation that hadn't been there when Karl and Conrad had been behind him. "I'll manage quite well on my own."

It would have made more sense to join Karl and Conrad in front of the fire, but Eric kicked a chair away from the table and sat down, facing Maddalyn's back over the ham and the gingerbread. Her tangle-free hair, a paler gold than he had imagined, fell to her waist, curling softly, twisting this way and that down her back.

She had a nice shape from every angle, he'd already discovered, but in his city trousers she took his breath away. The red calico sash was wrapped snugly around her tiny waist, and her hips swelled nicely downward.

Maybe if he looked long enough, hard enough, he could release himself from the power she had over him. Perhaps if he stared at her, studied her, reminded himself that she was just a woman like any other, a simple glance wouldn't knock him flat the way it had his brothers.

"Are you fond of canned peaches, Mr. Barrett?" Maddalyn asked, her back still to him. "I noticed several cans in the pantry. What about Karl and Conrad?" she continued when he didn't answer immediately.

"Why is it," Eric asked calmly, "that you continue to call me Mr. Barrett? I told you—"

"You told me that I couldn't call all three of you Mr. Barrett, and of course you were correct. That would be very confusing."

Eric leaned back and propped his feet in the chair at the head of the table. "I would prefer that you call me Eric."

Reluctantly, slowly, Maddalyn turned to face him. She bit her full lower lip, then released it. "I suppose—Take your feet off that chair!"

"I beg your pardon?"

"You'll scar the seat with the heels on those boots, and they're such lovely chairs."

Eric smiled. "Thank you. I made them myself." He made no move to lower his feet. "Actually I made most of the furniture in this cabin."

She blushed, her cheeks turning pink so quickly and easily he almost laughed. "Including the chair I destroyed?" she asked. Her voice was soft, not much more than a whisper.

"You didn't exactly destroy it. It needs a new seat, that's all."

"So it can be fixed?"

Eric nodded. "How did you manage to do that, anyway?"

Maddalyn pulled out the chair across the table from him and sat down. "I was looking at the photograph on the mantel. It's much too high, you know. Anyway, I must have . . . slipped, because I fell and my foot went right through the seat. It was such a comfortable chair, too."

She leaned forward, and all that separated them was a large ham and a pan of gingerbread. "I'm so glad it can be repaired."

Maddalyn stared directly at him, her lips parted slightly, her blue eyes wide and clear.

She wasn't just a lady, she was a very naive lady. Didn't she know better than to look at a man like that?

Eric held his breath and clenched his hands under the table. He'd been much too long without gingerbread.

Maddalyn took a deep breath and pushed away from the table, standing tall. Well, as tall as she could, considering that she had to stand a good foot shorter than the man who sat at the table.

She was making an absolute fool of herself, mooning over Eric Barrett. He didn't even seem to like her very much, with his deep frown and narrowed eyes. Why couldn't she have fallen madly in love with Conrad and his easy smile, or that sweet man Karl?

"Scoot," she said, waving her fingers in Eric's direction.

"Scoot?" he repeated, all but mocking her Southern accent.

"Into the other room. I'll call you when dinner's ready. Now get."

That nasty frown disappeared, and he smiled at her, grinning almost wickedly. "Are you ordering me out of my own kitchen?"

Maddalyn placed her hands on her hips, but her pose of defiance only seemed to amuse Eric more. "If I'm to be cook while I'm here, the kitchen is my domain, and I can order you in or out of it at any time." She tried to sound confident, to appear calm.

"I don't like the sound of that," he said softly.

Maddalyn stepped around the table and tried to gently shove Eric's feet off of the chair. "And didn't I tell you to get your big feet out of this chair before you ruin it?" Trying to budge Eric was about as easy as attempting to shove his mountain a couple of feet to the left. An impossible task. She stepped to his knees and nudged them with her own. "You are a stubborn old goat, Mr. Barrett."

He was fast, his arm shooting up without warning. He grabbed her wrist and pulled her toward him so that she landed with a thud on his hard thigh.

"Eric," he said.

"See? You are a stubborn old goat, and a bully as well," Maddalyn said, remaining amazingly calm.

"Add a glutton for punishment to the list," he muttered.

His grip on her wrist was like an iron band, as

immovable as his big feet had been. Maddalyn struggled for just a moment, and then she was still. "Dinner won't get made this way."

"I'm not particularly hungry."

He could look fierce and handsome at the same time. There was anger in his eyes, but it was tempered with kindness. She glanced down at the hand at her wrist, gentle but strong. Eric Barrett was a man of contradictions, and Maddalyn wondered if he ever felt the disharmony. She stared at the hand on her wrist. His fingers looked enormously long next to her small hand.

"I've never known anyone like you before," Maddalyn revealed in a quiet voice, and she lifted her eyes and leaned closer to his face, to his lips. She wanted him to kiss her, to press his lips against hers just briefly. The closer she got to those lips, the harder her heart pounded.

Eric's hand at her wrist was wonderfully warm and gentle, and she felt the warmth at her back as he placed his palm against her spine. "I'm not normally so forward," she whispered.

His hand trailed up and down her back, a feathery touch that made Maddalyn shiver. With what seemed to be reluctance, he moved his lips to the column of her throat and trailed them down, planting little kisses along the way. Hot and gentle, he moved his mouth against her skin.

Her heart was going to explode, her lungs were going to burst, something traumatic and wonderful was going to happen to her. This felt much too marvelous.

Eric pulled away from her with a groan. "You don't have any idea what you're doing," he whispered.

"Does it matter?"

For a moment they were both still. She could feel Eric's warm breath against her neck, and she tingled where he touched her. His hand wrapped around her wrist, the other hand resting at her back.

And then Eric released her hand, set her to her feet, and stood, all in one smooth motion. "Yes, I'm afraid it does."

"Why?"

He was leaving the kitchen, but stopped when she spoke. He had no answer for her, though, and she needed one.

"Eric?" She had known that when she spoke his name it would send shivers down her spine and goosebumps up her arms. And she'd been correct.

He sighed, but didn't turn to face her. "We're going to have to have a long talk, Maddalyn. This afternoon."

"Why not now?"

He hesitated, and for a moment Maddalyn thought he wouldn't answer her at all. But he didn't move away, and she waited.

"After dinner," he finally said in a gruff voice, stalking into the main room and leaving her alone.

Maddalyn touched two fingers to her throat,

there where Eric had kissed her. Mary Lynette had been right. Love was wonderful.

Eric had placed the two undamaged chairs in front of the fireplace, and turned them so that they were facing one another.

It didn't look good. There was a stern expression on his face, and his hands were resting stiffly on his knees. It was a pose Uncle Henry had adopted on occasion, when he had to deliver bad news. *Maddalyn, I'm afraid there's not as much in your fund as we had thought. Expenses . . . Maddalyn, that young man Lawrence Piffler was here this morning. . . . Maddalyn, your aunt tells me . . .*

"Do you mind if I sew while we talk?" she asked, seating herself with the length of red calico in her lap.

Eric's frown deepened, but he shook his head.

"So," Maddalyn began in a cheerful voice, "what is it that we need to discuss so urgently?"

"I just think we need to get a few things straight." His voice was gruff, but Maddalyn ignored that fact as she continued to sew, whipping stitches quickly.

"Did you enjoy your dinner?" she asked abruptly. "You all complimented me so nicely, but I noticed that you didn't eat as well as Conrad and Karl. I do hope you're not getting sick, and on my account. Going out into the cold like you did, carrying me all that way . . ."

"I'm not sick."

"Good." Maddalyn lifted the section she had been working on, checking her stitches, and the calico hung between her and Eric.

She felt the tug, and allowed Eric to pull the calico down. He had leaned forward to grab the bright material, and as it fell away Maddalyn found his face close to hers. He leaned back quickly.

"Maybe you should put that aside for now," he suggested.

Maddalyn took her time, tucking her needle in what would be the waistband, folding the material neatly, setting it on the floor away from the fire.

Eric took a deep breath. "I understand the circumstances that brought you here, but I feel it is my . . . my obligation to advise you to return to Georgia as soon as travel is possible."

He was so calm, so stoic, and Maddalyn wanted to slap his face. "I don't understand. . . ."

"You'll never make it here, Miss Kelly. Life in the West is very hard, unpredictable, and it takes a certain kind of woman—"

"What I was about to say," Maddalyn interrupted, "is that I don't understand why you consider it your obligation to advise me." She was trying very hard to be as calm as he was, but it was difficult. She hadn't expected him to declare that he loved her, or wanted to marry her . . . not yet . . . but neither had she expected this.

"If I hadn't followed you, you would have died out there."

"Should I thank you again?"

"No. You should promise me that you'll go back to Georgia."

Maddalyn stood. As far as she was concerned, this conversation was over. "I'll never return to Georgia. When I can travel, I'll go on to Sheridan."

"Sheridan is a wild town, Maddalyn. Gunslingers, gamblers, cowboys . . ."

"Sounds exciting," she snapped.

"Sit down," he ordered.

"No." Maddalyn crossed her arms over her chest. Eric glared up at her, and she promptly sat down.

"I would like for you to promise me—" he began.

"I'll promise you this," Maddalyn said, leaning forward just slightly. "I promise you I won't ever return to Georgia. You think I don't belong here, but the truth is I belong there even less. You don't think I'm strong enough to survive out here. I should introduce you to my Aunt Ethel, and the two of you could compile a list of all the horrible ways I can die in the West."

"Maddalyn—"

She held up her hand to silence him. "I'm not finished. I also promise that if you ever dare to lay a hand on me again, to . . . to pull me onto your lap and . . . and kiss me, and place your hands . . . well." Maddalyn felt the heat in her face, and knew she was blushing horribly. And she certainly hadn't intended to stammer like that. She took a deep breath to calm herself. "If you do any of that again, I'll slap you silly. I swear it."

"I'd appreciate that," Eric mumbled.

Someone's Been Sleeping in My Bed

If she'd thought it would do any good, she would have stood and slapped him silly right then and there. But it wouldn't have done any good, she knew. He was like a rock, hard, immovable. She couldn't hurt him, even if he did deserve it.

And besides, it would have meant touching him again, and she couldn't face that challenge at the moment.

Mary Lynette had been right. Love was horrid.

Chapter Eight

Eric left by way of the front door, just to avoid passing through the kitchen. He would have thought it impossible, but it seemed he'd just made matters worse.

What was he supposed to do? Sit there and look her in the eyes and be honest with her? *I want you, but you don't belong here, and no matter what happens between us, you can't stay.*

He'd thought his solution was a good one. Concern for her welfare, which was real, instead of the ugly truth.

He hadn't intended to hurt her, but she was so damned sensitive. Was it really so terrible to suggest that she go home? Apparently it was, at least to Maddalyn. Who was Aunt Ethel? He'd noticed the spark in her eyes when he'd spoken her name.

Fear? Hate? It certainly hadn't been love or affection of any kind.

Karl and Conrad weren't even working. They were blatantly waiting for him at the bottom of the first small hill. Damnation, they'd already recovered their senses.

"Trailing a bit behind this afternoon, aren't you, little brother?" Conrad's grin was much too wide. "Our Maddalyn is something, isn't she? What a beauty!" He slapped a hand over his heart. "Redhead or no, I wouldn't mind having a go at her myself."

Eric didn't speed his pace, but when he reached his grinning brother he swung his fist into Conrad's jaw. It was automatic, an uncontrollable response.

Conrad's head snapped to the side, and then he dropped down, hands on thighs as he shook his head slowly.

"Damn!" Conrad came up holding his chin. "What was that for? Karl, did you see—"

"I woulda popped you myself, if I hadn't seen that Eric was going to take care of it."

Conrad rolled his eyes. "I was just joshing."

Karl nodded once. "Glad to hear it. Maddalyn's a sweet little thing. We can't have you talking about her like she was one of Bucktooth Annie's calico girls."

Eric remained silent, listening. They were only human, after all, all three of them, and it had been a long winter. It was a good two-day trip to Olympia, if the roads were clear and the weather was fine, and they were all overdue for a visit to Annie's.

"I told her she should go back to Georgia," Eric said, turning away from his brothers and toward the barn. "That's why I stayed behind."

"How'd she take it?" Karl asked.

"Not too well," Eric muttered.

"Why not, I wonder?" Conrad stepped quickly so that he walked beside Eric. There was no anger in his voice, just his normal curiosity. It usually led to nothing but trouble. "I mean, after all that's happened to her, you'd think she'd be anxious to go home."

Eric frowned. Why was she so adamant about not returning to Georgia? "I'm not sure, but I think it has something to do with an aunt or something."

"Aunt Ethel," Karl said, joining Eric at his other side.

"How'd you know?" Eric stopped abruptly, and Karl and Conrad stopped with him.

"She told me, while you two were fetching the tub. Aunt Ethel told her she'd be dead within a month, scalped by Indians. Doesn't sound like a nice lady to me."

"Maybe she can stay here," Conrad suggested brightly. "It'll be nice to have someone around the place besides you two, and besides that, she's a great cook. Ahhh, that wonderful gingerbread . . ." He sighed loudly. "I can still taste it."

"She'll stay here until the snow melts," Eric began.

"No, that's not what I mean." Conrad worked his

Linda Jones

jaw, reminding Eric of his impulsive action. "I mean she should stay. Indefinitely. For as long as she wants."

"Won't work," Eric said sharply. "A lady like Maddalyn living under the same roof with the three of us?"

There was a moment of complete silence. Eric decided that both of his brothers had gone daft over the sight of a pretty woman.

And then Karl proved him right.

"One of us could marry her," the oldest of the Barrett brothers suggested. "She could stay, and if she was married to one of us it would be right proper."

Unbelievable.

"Which of us do you suggest she marry, Karl?" Eric snapped. "You?"

"Oh, no," Karl said quickly, shaking his head slowly. "She's just a tiny thing. I'd always be afraid I was gonna break her, or smash her."

Eric turned to Conrad. "What about you?" he asked dryly. "What do you think of Karl's brilliant idea? Ready to volunteer?"

But Conrad shook his head. "Nope. For one thing, she's not a redhead. And I'm a man who not only recognizes his obsession, but embraces it. Besides"—he rubbed his jaw for emphasis—"I don't think I could take it."

Karl leaned down, placing his mouth close to Eric's ear, as if Maddalyn could hear from the top of the hill. "You're the one she's sweet on."

Eric couldn't believe what he was hearing. The lady, the subject of their bizarre conversation, had been their guest for a few hours, and Karl all but had him hitched to her.

"Are you suggesting that I marry Maddalyn Kelly, a complete stranger who crept into our cabin and made herself at home, who slept in my bed, who ran out into the snow without even her boots . . . that I marry her so you two won't have to cook?"

If Maddalyn was listening, she'd surely hear him. His voice had risen steadily, until he was shouting up into Karl's face.

Karl remained calm. "Not just because I don't want to cook. Think of that poor little thing all alone in Sheridan, Eric. She needs us. You're a *little* sweet on her, aren't you? Just a little bit?"

"If I was it wouldn't matter," Eric snapped, trying to step away from his brothers. They followed closely. Too closely. "She just told me that if I touched her again she'd slap me silly."

He realized his mistake as soon as the sentence was out of his mouth.

"Again?" Conrad asked, enjoying himself much too much. "Did you say *again?*"

"What happened to you?" Maddalyn asked, watching Conrad bite into his corn bread carefully and with a crooked set to his mouth.

"He fell," Karl said, before Conrad could swallow his corn bread and answer for himself.

115

"That's terrible," she said, toying with the beans on her plate. As much as she would have preferred to ignore Eric, it wouldn't be right. "And you?" she asked, staring at Eric's blackening eye.

"He fell, too," Karl answered in a soft voice. "It's the ice. And besides, they're both clumsy."

"I see." Maddalyn wasn't hungry, but she ate several bites of the beans and ham anyway. "I guess that's a hazard you're accustomed to, with all the snow and ice you get here."

Eric grunted, Conrad tried to laugh and couldn't, and Karl just nodded his head.

It was to be her first night in the cabin, and this was not at all how she wanted it to be. If only Eric hadn't insisted on ruining everything with his little speech. Back to Georgia, indeed!

At least he'd made it clear that whatever she was feeling was one-sided, so she could refrain from making a fool of herself. She just had to look at her time here as a job, no different from teaching in Sheridan. She was a cook, a housekeeper, no more, and there would be no more sitting on Eric's lap, and if she was cold there was always the fireplace.

"Eric tells me that Sheridan is quite a wild town." Maddalyn looked across the table at Conrad, and then to her left, at Karl. "Have either of you ever been there?"

"I haven't been there," Karl said, "but Conrad spent some time in Sheridan a few years back."

"Really?" She turned her attention to Conrad,

and he smiled at her crookedly. "You must tell me all about it."

Conrad cradled his jaw for a moment, and then he began. "All I really remember is a couple of saloons and the hotel."

"Didn't you propose to some little redheaded dancer in Sheridan?" Eric asked, rather nastily.

"Probably." Conrad didn't even look at his younger brother as he agreed. "I'm sure it's changed a lot since I was there. That was five or six years ago, when I was still with Pinkerton's. I was looking for Frank James. . . ."

"You were a Pinkerton's detective?" Her question was whispered with awe. She'd read such stories!

Conrad nodded, oddly silent.

"He was a Pinkerton's detective until he got shot at a few times," Karl said softly.

"You were shot?"

"Shot *at*," Eric added caustically. "Conrad worked railroad security until the bullets started flying too close."

"What about you?" Conrad shot, turning to Eric. "You didn't last three years."

"Yeah, but I quit because I didn't like the people I was working with, not because I was jumpy about getting shot at."

"Well, you hear those bullets whizzing by your head a couple of times and see if it don't make you think twice about sticking it out there again."

Maddalyn raised her hand to quiet the two of them. "Do you mean to tell me that both of you were Pinkerton's detectives?"

"Karl, too," Conrad added. "But he was usually assigned to personal security."

Maddalyn looked at each of them in turn. "I just assumed . . . somehow I imagined the three of you growing up here, or near here. You're a part of this place. I can't imagine this mountain without the three of you here."

"We grew up on a farm in Kansas," Eric said, for the first time that evening really looking at her, seeing her. "Flat, not a decent tree in sight. Pa wasn't a very good farmer, but he made enough for the family to get by. No more than that. When he died, not one of us wanted to stay there."

"Your mother?"

"She'd died years earlier, when I was seven. Got a bad cough one winter that never went away."

"I'm sorry. I shouldn't have asked."

"It was a long time ago."

Maddalyn searched Eric's face for a sign that he was angry with her for asking, but his eyes were calm. "Do you remember her?"

"Yes."

"I wish I could remember my mother. She died when I was two, and that was when I went to live with Uncle Henry and Aunt Ethel."

"What about your father?"

"He died in the Northern Invasion, just two months before I was born."

"The what?" all three of the brothers asked at the same time.

118

"The Northern Invasion," Maddalyn repeated. "General Sherman? Eighteen sixty-four?"

"She's talking about the War Between the States," Conrad said with a crooked smile.

"Call it what you will," Maddalyn said, lifting her chin defiantly.

"Is that what Aunt Ethel called it?" Karl asked. "The Northern Invasion?"

"No." Maddalyn nodded toward the oldest and largest Barrett brother. "Aunt Ethel always referred to that time as The Late Unpleasantness."

Only Conrad had the temerity to laugh aloud, but Karl and Eric smiled much too widely.

And when they left the kitchen for the comfort of the main room, leaving her with a terrible mess, Maddalyn was almost certain that she heard one of those men utter the phrase "the *Southern* Invasion." She should have been insulted, but she ended up clearing the table with a soft smile on her face.

Eric faced the fire, lying on his side. The side of his face ached, just a little, where Karl had hit him. The punch had been as calm and unexpected as the one he'd delivered to Conrad himself.

The pallet beneath him was hard, but the wool blanket that covered his legs was warm enough. And, like it or not, the plain brown blanket reminded him of Maddalyn Kelly. *Are you cold, Mr. Barrett?*, the question delivered as she wrapped the ends of the wool around his arms and shoulders.

119

He tried to dislike her, even tried to convince himself that he hated her for invading his mountain, for intruding into his well-ordered life, for making him want her . . . but he couldn't. There was something about Maddalyn . . . something he couldn't define. It went beyond her beauty, and it was much more than her charm, the charm of a well-bred lady.

She touched him somewhere deep inside. He felt it when she smiled, when she'd cried. Hitting Conrad had been an instinctive action, one he couldn't have stopped even if he'd wanted to. Some instinct made him want to follow her to Sheridan, protect her from the scum she was bound to encounter there, keep her safe.

But that was impossible. She was so naive . . . so damnably innocent . . . he could almost give Karl's addlebrained suggestion serious thought. Almost.

Marry her? Keep her here? Impossible. She wasn't the kind of woman to live her life in an isolated cabin. Maddalyn was much too sociable for this life. She'd probably teach for a few months, marry some rich rancher, throw parties for the people of Sheridan every spring and every Christmas. He could see her, dressed in silks, that golden hair piled on top of her head, smiling at every guest that came to the door. She had such a bright smile. The rancher would probably be older, old enough to be her father. They would have children, lots of children. . . .

"Are you awake?" she whispered, and Eric bolted upright.

The woman he'd been thinking of stood there wrapped in his quilt. It was gathered around her shoulders, and she clutched it to her chest so that all he saw was her face and her hair. He hadn't heard her coming, not a step or a breath.

"I couldn't sleep either." She took a step forward, and he saw bare toes peeking out as she came toward him. "My feet are cold, and I thought that maybe if you were awake I could warm them by the fire. Do you mind?"

Eric shook his head and swung his legs to the side, making a place for her to sit beside him. She lowered herself to the pallet and extended her legs toward the fire so that just her bare feet were exposed. He already knew that she had tiny feet, but he stared at them for a long moment, as she wiggled her toes and then flexed her feet.

"Does your eye hurt?" She spoke softly, thinking no doubt of Conrad and the faintly snoring Karl, and Eric pulled his gaze away from her feet and to her face. Her expression was merely curious, and he was certain she would have asked Conrad the same question if he'd been sitting in Eric's place.

"Not really."

"You look so displeased at the moment. I guess that's on my account, rather than because of your fall this afternoon."

He didn't deny it.

She turned away from him to stare into the fire.

"I forgive you, you know."

"For what?"

"For suggesting that I return to Georgia. I realize now that you couldn't possibly have known why that suggestion was so repugnant to me." She let the quilt fall open just a little, and he saw what she was wearing. A blue shirt that was in much worse shape than the one she'd worn with his trousers. He remembered ripping the sleeve from the cuff to the shoulder, and tossing it into the box of clothing that needed to be mended and probably never would be.

"Would you like to tell me why?" he asked.

She glanced at him, just briefly, and then returned her gaze to the fire. "I suppose I could. After my mother died, I went to live with her brother, Uncle Henry, his wife, Aunt Ethel, and their daughter, Doreen. I really don't remember living in any house but theirs, and I have no other family. Still, I always felt . . . like an outsider. I was an obligation, a burden, Aunt Ethel's cross to bear. For most of my life I thought I'd done something wrong. I thought they'd love me if I were prettier, if I had dark hair like they all did, if I were smarter." She was quiet for a long moment, and she took a long strand of golden hair and wrapped it around her finger. "It was really Lawrence who made me think that maybe it wasn't me. Maybe it was them."

"Lawrence?"

She smiled brightly, still staring into the fire, and Eric felt a moment's pain. Jealousy? Impossible.

"Lawrence Piffler. He asked me to marry him, but Uncle Henry forbade it."

"And you . . . wanted to marry him?"

She hesitated, pursing her lips thoughtfully and gathering the quilt tighter, as if she were embracing it.

"No. I thought about marrying him anyway, just to escape. But I didn't love him, and I knew I never would, so it didn't seem fair."

"You headed for Sheridan instead."

"Not right away. I answered an ad in an Atlanta paper, discreetly, of course. 'Schoolmarms needed for civilized West.' Several towns participated in the ad, I believe, and I soon heard from Mrs. Hudson of Sheridan."

"What did your uncle have to say about that?"

She looked at him again, unflinching, eye to eye. "Nothing. I didn't tell him, but I did tell Aunt Ethel. She laughed at me, and told me I'd be dead within a month if I did anything so foolish."

"She tried to stop you?"

"No." Maddalyn hesitated, but only for a moment. "I went to the bank and withdrew some funds. My mother left me a little money, but most of it was already gone, used to clothe and feed me over the years. It wasn't much, but it was enough to travel to Sheridan. I mailed Uncle Henry a letter from St. Louis." She told the story almost emotionlessly, but Eric could see the flash in her eyes. It wasn't the firelight; it was anger or fear or determination.

He wanted to reach out, to take her in his arms and hold her, but he didn't. He didn't want to comfort Maddalyn; he wanted to possess her, to crush her beneath his body and rid himself of this obsession for her. But Maddalyn wasn't the kind of woman to be satisfied with being a man's mistress for a short time . . . and he wasn't the kind of man to offer anything more than that.

"So you see, you don't have to worry about me overstaying my welcome. As soon as I can travel, I will." She turned away from him and stared into the fire. "I won't stay again where I'm not wanted."

It would have been so easy to tell her that she was wanted, to show her just how much he wanted her. But Eric was no fool. She wasn't that kind of woman, and he didn't have anything else to give.

"My feet are quite warm now. Thank you for allowing me to share the fire for a while. I hope I didn't bend your ear too terribly."

"You didn't."

Maddalyn stood, gathering the quilt close around her. "You're very lucky to have Karl and Conrad. I envy you."

The response that came to his lips and died there was caustic, and he was glad he didn't speak it aloud. Envy?

"Good night, Eric."

He watched Maddalyn walk away, the quilt trailing the floor behind her. She faded into the darkness, and he didn't hear so much as a whisper as she disappeared.

Eric fell back onto the pallet with his hands over his eyes. He hadn't been prepared to face her, the way she'd sneaked up on him. And now . . . now he surely wouldn't sleep. He hurt, and it wasn't just his eye any longer.

"Eric?"

This time he nearly exploded, jumping into a sitting position. "What the—"

"Never mind," she whispered hoarsely, backing away into the darkness. "I didn't mean . . . sorry," he heard as she faded away from him.

Eric sat there for a long minute. He should leave it alone. He didn't need or want to see her again tonight.

But he stood anyway, raking the hair away from his face and stepping silently on bare feet to the hallway, finding his way easily in the dark. He could just apologize and tell Maddalyn that she'd startled him. There would be no need to enter the room. He wouldn't have to see her lying in his bed in the dark, huddled beneath his quilt, and he wouldn't have to get close enough to touch her.

He was as silent as Maddalyn had been, slipping down the hall to the open entrance to his room.

The bed was empty, and Maddalyn stood at the window, looking out on the snow-covered landscape lit by the moon. No wonder she'd been cold. She stood there without the quilt, his shirt hanging to her knees, her legs and feet bare. With the moon-lit window behind her she was a perfect silhouette, soft curves and flowing hair, and as he watched she

125

lifted a hand slowly to the window, laying her palm on the cold panes of glass.

It would be so easy to cross the room, to lay his hand over hers, to wrap his arm around her waist and pull her away from the cold window and into that empty bed. He could almost feel her tiny hand beneath his own, her supple skin beneath the shirt she wore yielding to his touch.

Eric knew that he couldn't speak to her now. He could deny it all night, and probably would, but at the moment he had to admit that it was painful just to look at her. And in spite of his determination to see her gone from this place, in spite of the fact that he called her a thief and a lady, at that moment he wanted her more than he'd ever wanted anything . . . including his mountain.

And that just wouldn't do.

He backed away as silently as he'd crept down the hall. Let her think he didn't want her, didn't even like her. Let her think he was rough and rude. Let her think he couldn't wait to get her off his mountain.

It was easier than the truth.

Chapter Nine

Maddalyn frowned at the perfectly browning pancakes on the griddle. They bubbled in the middle and she flipped them easily, but her frown never faded. It was barely light outside, and Eric was already gone.

When she'd tiptoed into the main room, before the sun had fully risen, she'd expected to see him sleeping on the floor near the fireplace, curled up like a content child, his hair a mess. She'd expected, and wanted, to catch him in an uncontrolled moment, but the pallet he'd used had been rolled up and placed in the corner, and Eric was out of the house.

She hadn't slept all that wonderfully herself, until quite late. Probably early morning. She hadn't been particularly sleepy until then, and had spent much of the night at the window, looking out over the incredible view that stretched before her. With the moonlight on the snow and ice, the shadows the tall trees cast, it was easy to imagine that it was an enchanted land she surveyed, there on the other side of that cold window.

Rest might have come earlier if Eric hadn't snapped at her, and for no good reason. She'd only wanted to offer him his own bed, so that he could sleep well. He'd looked so uncomfortable, his long body stretched before the fire. The pallet would suit her just fine, and she'd felt guilty for taking over Eric's bed.

No more. She'd stay in that room until one of the Barrett brothers took her to Olympia.

The pile of pancakes grew. She could eat two, if she was incredibly hungry. How many would Karl eat?

Conrad was the first of the brothers to enter the kitchen, a wide and unnaturally crooked smile on his face, a reminder of his *fall*. "Flapjacks!" he exclaimed. "You're an angel, Maddalyn."

"Of course," she agreed, setting a full plate before him. Syrup was already on the table, and she placed a cup of coffee beside the plate.

Karl came in next, sniffing the air, blinking his eyes repeatedly as he came fully awake. He was as thrilled as Conrad to find breakfast waiting, and sat down to a leaning stack of pancakes.

They were almost finished when Eric came through the kitchen door. He looked as if he hadn't

128

slept at all, and he was covered with wood shavings, his boots and his coat and his trousers powdered with sawdust and the occasional wood chip. His eye was truly black this morning, and he growled at his brothers as he disappeared into the pantry.

"What's Eric been up to?" Conrad directed his question to Maddalyn, as if she would have any idea what the ornery man had been doing. She shrugged her shoulders and continued to eat.

Eric ignored them all as he puttered about the kitchen, filling a pan with water, adding a handful of salt, and dropping something into the salty water that clanged loudly against the tin.

"What's that?" Karl asked through a mouthful of pancakes.

"Hinges," Eric answered, not even bothering to turn and face the table.

"Hinges," Conrad repeated. "For what?"

Eric turned, and what could have been a smile passed over his face. "I've made Maddalyn a door."

"How sweet," she said insincerely. "No one's ever made me a door before."

"I intended to hang doors on those rooms years ago, but I never got around to it. I know a lady enjoys her privacy." Eric shucked off his heavy coat and hung it on the peg by the door.

"Why on earth are you soaking the hinges in salt water?" Karl asked. "They'll rust overnight. That door'll squeal like the dickens."

This time Maddalyn was positive it was a smile

that passed over Eric's face. "I know," he said, and then he helped himself to a heaping plate of pancakes.

It was late afternoon before Eric finally got around to hanging Maddalyn's door. By God, she wouldn't sneak up on him again, wouldn't catch him off guard and make his heart race the way it had last night.

She watched him sporadically, poking her head around the corner and into the hallway. She never said a word, and never watched for very long, but her curiosity got the best of her on a regular and frequent basis.

Eric didn't glance her way, even though he was very well aware of her. He knew when she was watching him, heard her quiet movements and her steady breathing. When she had gone back to her sewing, he listened to the empty silence.

When the door was hung, he opened and closed it several times. It squeaked, but not nearly loud enough. A day, maybe two, before the rust really set in. For good measure, he tapped the hammer against the top hinge, warping the mechanism.

"Are you finally finished?" Maddalyn asked, her Southern accent pronounced. He'd already learned that when she was out of sorts her speech changed slightly. She didn't drawl, exactly, but she came much closer to it when she was put out.

And that wasn't his only clue to her disposition. She lifted her chin, as if she wished to be taller, and pursed her lips as if she were waiting for a quick kiss. She presented that pose to him now, adding to it hands on hips. Maddalyn made quite a tempting picture in his discarded wedding suit.

"I hope the noise didn't distract you," he said, doing his best to be pleasant. He swung the door open, and it all but screamed. The tap had done the trick.

"It seems you did a poor job of it," she said smugly, and the corners of her pouting mouth turned up into a satisfied smile. "It's quite noisy."

"Yes, it is," Eric agreed in a pleasant voice as he swung the door closed and then open again.

It was so simple to tell what Maddalyn Kelly was thinking. In that way she was different from Jane—and the other ladies he had known. Her pouting lips relaxed, her hands fell to her sides, and her eyes softened. Eric watched as the knowledge of his reasoning came to her, and he felt almost guilty. She looked like a little girl who'd had her fragile feelings hurt. "So that's supposed to be some sort of alarm?" she asked in a voice that was much too soft. "A warning noise, so that I can't sneak up on you in the night and intrude upon your peace?"

It was too true, too right. She did disturb his peace, in more ways than one. "No," Eric said, but there was no conviction in his voice. "It's just a door. I thought it would give you a little much-needed privacy."

"Oh, yes," she said, reclaiming some control over

Linda Jones

her easily read face. "You did mention that earlier, that a lady needs her privacy. You don't care for *ladies* much, do you, Eric?"

"They have their place."

"Oh, really, and where would that be?"

"Boston, New York, Atlanta."

"Not here," she said, catching on quickly.

"Not here," he agreed.

She took several small steps down the hallway, coming toward him like a mountain lion stalking her prey. Silently pondering him through narrowed eyes. "I see," she said thoughtfully. "Don't you ever get lonely up here, just you and your brothers?"

"Not that lonely," Eric muttered, more to himself than to Maddalyn.

To his dismay, she smiled. She still resembled a mountain lion, one who had just finished off her dinner. He didn't care for the blatant satisfaction that crept over her face. "I've never warranted my own distress signal before." Obviously the thought didn't disturb her as it had originally. "Would you like to tell me exactly what it is you have against ladies?"

"No."

"We're not all so bad, you know." Thankfully, she stopped a couple of feet away. "I won't tell you that I'm not a lady, because I am. My aunt, crone that she was, saw to that. It's the one endowment she gave me, unwittingly, of course."

She was a little thing, a good foot shorter than

he was, but Eric still felt as if Maddalyn were blocking the hallway, and he was trapped.

"I suppose I should thank you for the door." Maddalyn tilted her head back to look him straight in the eye. "It would, of course, be the ladylike thing to do. Your motives are suspect, but I'll forgive you once again. I do have a forgiving nature."

"Lucky for me that you do," Eric said dryly.

"Yes, indeed," Maddalyn agreed with a smile that was much too wide. She reached out her hand, and with tiny, pale fingers brushed a speck of sawdust from his shirt. "You've made quite a mess of things, Mr. Barrett."

He agreed with her in a voice that he wasn't certain would carry.

Her other hand came slowly to his shoulder, and she brushed away a wood chip that fell to his feet. She caught her lower lip in her teeth and took a short step forward, until she was so close he could feel the heat that came off her body and touched his own.

Eric plucked a short piece of red thread from her arm, his fingers brushing against his wedding shirt and the skin beneath it. He dropped the wayward length of thread to the floor. "Have you finished your skirt yet?"

"Almost." She tapped a fingernail against a button at his chest. "This button is loose, you know. You should let me secure it." He wouldn't have believed that such a light, innocent pressure against his chest would drive him to distraction, but it surely did. Maddalyn's attention seemed to be riveted on that one damn button she touched with her fingernail.

"Sure." He spotted it then, a faint dusting of flour on the red calico sash that circled her waist. Just a light sprinkling that had probably been there since breakfast. He dropped his hand slowly and brushed his fingers over the bright red sash, over Maddalyn's side.

She lifted her face and stared into his eyes, boldly and silently questioning him. Her fingernail stopped rapping against his chest, but her hand remained. Eric stopped brushing against her waist, and settled his fingers against the curve of her hip.

Maddalyn continued to look him in the eye without a hint of indecision. She was so close, not pressed against him, but almost close enough. He slid his hand from her hip to the small of her back, and with a gentle pressure pulled her to him.

The kitchen door slammed, and Maddalyn jumped back, breaking the spell that had made Eric forget, for a moment, that he didn't want her. He turned to the newly hung door, attempting to give it all of his attention, as heavy footsteps echoed through the cabin.

"Eric built me a door," Maddalyn said in a voice that was much too fast, her words almost clipped.

"I know," Karl growled.

Eric only glanced at his oldest brother.

"Do you like venison pie, Karl?" Maddalyn asked, moving away quickly. "There's going to be venison pie for dinner, and fresh-baked bread."

It was a blatant and initially successful attempt to capture Karl's interest. Maddalyn darted past Karl, making quick and small movements as she moved into the main room.

But Karl cast one last glance at Eric, narrow-eyed and suspicious, and Eric's head throbbed a warning, there where he'd been pounded.

He'd allow that Maddalyn was different, that she was nothing like Jane. He'd even concede that she was for the most part imminently agreeable. She was a good cook, had a nice smile, and when she puckered those lips she appeared to be totally kiss-able.

So why was he still so anxious to get her off his mountain?

It didn't take half a second to come up with the answer. You didn't have your pleasure with a lady and then send her on her way. They wanted—they *expected*—more. They expected everything. The worst part was, he could almost see it happening, in his mind.

It would be wonderful, for a while. God, she was beautiful, and soft and rounded in all the right places. He could hear her, her soft Southern voice whispering to him. He could feel her, under him, around him, and it was almost enough to make him forget the rest and throw caution to the wind.

But he knew what would come next. She would, of course, expect him to marry her. So would Karl and Conrad, if they didn't kill him first. No. They wouldn't kill him. They'd beat him senseless, and then they'd fetch the preacher themselves.

No more cooking. Even better, no more of Conrad's cooking. It was best that he think of Maddalyn Kelly as a piece of fresh meat in a deadly trap, one that was especially appealing after a long, lean winter.

Eric had no intention of considering marriage again. Ever. His one experience with the institution had been enough to cure him of any such longings. To teach him even the prettiest face could hide nasty secrets.

"Would you stop that?" Karl thundered, and Eric turned his narrowed eyes down the hall.

"Stop what?"

"Opening and closing that damn door." Karl seethed. Then he glanced over his shoulder and into the main room. "Sorry about the language, Maddalyn."

Eric looked down at the knob in his hand, and with an unexpected burst of energy slammed Maddalyn's new door shut.

Maddalyn hummed as she rolled out the crust, smiling brightly even though she was all alone. So, Eric wasn't completely hostile toward her after all. The way he'd looked at her that afternoon, standing there in the hallway with the doorknob grasped in his hand, the way he'd pulled her against him, stared at her as if he wanted to kiss her throat again but was somehow afraid.

Afraid. What a ridiculous notion. Eric Barrett was likely afraid of nothing at all.

Except maybe of falling in love.

If Karl hadn't come in, Eric likely would have kissed her. Not on the throat this time, but on the mouth where she could almost taste him already. It was a wanton thought that surprised her, for she certainly was not a hussy who was given to such thoughts.

But, of course, love made all the difference. It made thoughts that would have been scandalous otherwise quite acceptable, in her mind.

As Mary Lynette had said on more than one occasion, all's fair in love and war.

So much for making her way to Eric's heart through his stomach. He ate decently, but it was Karl and Conrad who complimented her with spirited enthusiasm as they devoured their supper.

Conrad regularly added rolled eyes and a hand clapped over his heart, while Karl simply ate enough for three hungry men, all by himself.

Eric ate silently, staring at his plate throughout the meal. Maddalyn kept expecting him to lift his head, to look at her and smile. But he didn't.

When he had cleaned his plate Eric stood, scraping the legs of his chair noisily across the floor. He finally complimented her on the meal, but he muttered almost unintelligibly.

With his back to the table, Eric slipped on his coat.

"Where are you going?" Conrad asked. Maddalyn could tell, by the bewildered tone of Conrad's voice, that it was not normal for Eric to leave the cabin in the evening after supper.

"I didn't like the way my horse was limping this morning. Thought I'd have a look at her foreleg," he all but growled, and looked toward the table reluctantly.

"Limping? I didn't notice any—" Conrad began.

"Limping," Eric repeated, and then he opened the door, allowing a cold wind to momentarily rush through the kitchen. He slammed the door behind him, and even though she'd been expecting just that, Maddalyn jumped in her seat.

She knew exactly what Eric was doing. He was, for some reason, uncomfortable in her presence. That was why he had refused to look at her throughout the meal, why he felt compelled to leave the cabin with a poor excuse.

His reasons were, she was certain, the same he'd had for hanging a door that screamed when it was opened or closed.

He didn't want to fall in love. Didn't want to be caught alone again, when he might have to speak to her, or touch her, or kiss her.

Maddalyn started to rise, but thought better of it halfway and lowered herself to her seat slowly. She couldn't very well chase blatantly after the man, following him whenever he left the cabin.

Of course, it wouldn't hurt perhaps to tell him that he had no reason to be frightened of her.

Maddalyn stopped herself again, half-standing, half-sitting. And exactly how would she accomplish that? Tell him straight out?

Her eyes were on the door as she lowered her bottom into the chair. No, no, no. That would never do. She could only show him, when the opportunity arose, that he had no reason to be afraid. She wouldn't push, wouldn't press herself too closely to him. If it was to be, if he was going to fall in love with her, he would. If not—well, that was a possibility she'd face when the time came.

Maybe it wouldn't hurt to talk to him just one more time, alone.

"Maddalyn?"

She looked down at Conrad, and realized that she'd risen to her feet again, her mind on what she would say to Eric.

"Are you all right?" he asked.

Maddalyn smiled wanly. He had put aside his eating utensils and gave her all his attention. A quick glance to her right proved that Karl had done the same. How long had they been watching her?

"I'm fine, I was just . . . I made a cake for dessert, and I was going to bring it to the table. Maybe I should fetch Eric?"

A look passed between them that Maddalyn didn't quite understand. It was almost as if they communicated silently, excluding her completely.

"That's not necessary," Karl said. "We'll save Eric's dessert."

"Oh." Maddalyn sat down. Conrad and Karl continued to stare at her until she realized that she'd told them she was going to fetch the cake she'd made. She shot to her feet and busied herself. It was just a small sweetcake without any icing, but Karl grinned widely when she placed it in the center of the table.

She'd found the way to Karl's and Conrad's affections. Good food, and lots of it, and they seemed to be supremely happy. Karl smiled, and Conrad called her *angel* and *sweetheart*, without any romantic implication, of course.

What was the path to Eric's heart? It seemed no matter what she did, how hard she tried, she only made him cantankerous.

Maybe it was her imagination. Perhaps Eric was always out of sorts.

But Maddalyn didn't think so. He'd held her too tenderly, watched her with expressive eyes that made her heart flutter. He'd touched her too well.

Eric had a tender heart. All she had to do was find it.

Chapter Ten

It was her favorite part of the day, the evening hours after supper. Eric had repaired the chair she'd destroyed, and had brought in a rocker from the front porch.

The rocking chair was hers, and had been from that first evening, and she always had something in her lap to mend or sew by the light of the fire.

It was a special time of day because everyone gathered before the fireplace. Karl and Conrad told her what they'd done that day, and sometimes Eric joined them. Most evenings he was quiet, though, and Maddalyn left him alone. She didn't ignore him, but she didn't lavish any attention on him, either. He seemed to be more comfortable when she neglected him, and since the afternoon he'd hung her door, he'd done his best to pretend she didn't exist. It was difficult to decide how to proceed when he scorned her so blatantly. If only Mary Lynette were here to advise her.

Almost two weeks had passed since Eric had found her in that little cave, and the snow and ice on the ground showed no indication of thawing. The days were cold, even when the sun shone brightly, and Maddalyn had already reluctantly admitted to herself that she was not anxious for the warm weather that would make it possible for her to leave this place.

Karl looked out for her, making certain that she didn't lift anything too heavy, or stay too long in the kitchen. He had been concerned about her constant mending, until she'd explained to him that she found it impossible to sit still.

Conrad made her laugh. There hadn't been much in the way of amusement in Aunt Ethel's house, and she found laughter to be stimulating and restorative. He told such stories, mostly about his own exploits, occasionally about his brothers'.

And Eric. What could she say about Eric? Of course she still loved him. Love didn't come and go like the wind. Some evenings she was content just to watch him furtively, casting quick glances in his direction. Some evenings she found the same activity quite frustrating. How could she capture his attention again?

They were quarreling halfheartedly tonight, rehashing an argument she'd heard a hundred times since she'd come to this mountain.

Finally, weary of hearing the same tiresome bickering, Maddalyn placed her mending in her lap, took a deep breath, and cleared her throat. The room was suddenly silent.

"Why?" she asked softly, directing her simple question to Karl and Conrad.

"Why what, Maddalyn?" Karl asked.

"I would like to hear your reasons for wanting to add ranching to your logging business." She folded her hands in her lap and gave the two older brothers her full attention.

"We could make a lot of money here," Conrad said with his customary smile.

"And why would you want to do that?"

Conrad laughed, but Karl and Eric could see that she was perfectly serious. They didn't laugh at her. In fact, Eric looked as if he were impressed by her question.

"Everybody wants money," Conrad insisted.

"You have everything you could possibly want here. A lovely cabin, a full pantry, several fine horses, if Karl is to be believed. What would three confirmed bachelors do with any more than you already have?"

"We're not all three confirmed bachelors," Conrad informed her. "Why, I've proposed to several women. . . ."

"All redheads," Eric interjected. "Saloon girls, actresses, dancers, women who were already married . . ."

"I had no way of knowing that Lucille had a hus-

Linda Jones

band in Texas. . . ." Conrad began.

"What about you, Karl?" Maddalyn asked lightly.

"I wouldn't mind being married," he said softly. "But it takes a special kind of woman to live up here. This is springtime, Maddalyn. We go for months without seeing the ground, sometimes. And the cold . . . this isn't the half of it. It's deadly."

"Eric was almost married once," Conrad supplied with a hearty slap to his brother's back.

"I find that hard to believe," Maddalyn said with a perfectly straight face. "He seems so disagreeable."

"Remember, I said *almost*," Conrad added.

"And what kind of woman was she?" The question was delivered casually, and with what Maddalyn hoped was a mildly curious expression. She'd bet her last dollar—if she had one—that a *lady* was involved.

"Jane was a prissy little thing, always fussing about something or another. I only met her the one time, but it was enough for me. She lived in Boston, and her pa had all kinds of money—"

Maddalyn had already heard enough of Conrad's description, so she didn't think it would be too rude to interrupt. "Well, there's your answer," she said calmly. "My goodness, you've been looking for a rose on a honeysuckle vine."

"A rose on a what?" Karl asked.

"A honeysuckle vine," Maddalyn repeated. "It has the sweetest, most fragrant bell-shaped flowers." She closed her eyes, and she could almost

144

smell the powerful perfume. "I used to sneak into Mr. Ellington's yard in the summertime, when the scent was just too much to bear. If you pick the small blooms carefully," she said, leaning forward slightly in her rocking chair, "you can taste the honey. You have to remove the stem carefully." She performed a simple pantomime, holding an invisible bloom in her fingers. "And lick the drop of honey from the tip." She brought her fingers to her lips. "And then, you hold the end of the flower to your lips, and very carefully suck the rest of the syrupy essence onto your tongue. There's not a lot there, just a small drop, but it's so very sweet. . . ."

She was lost for a moment, remembering clearly the warmth of a Georgia summer. When she focused her attention on the Barrett brothers again, they were staring at her with the strangest expressions on their faces. Not stunned, exactly, but . . . distracted.

"But of course that has nothing to do with what I was saying," she continued. "You're looking in all the wrong places for the kind of woman you want to marry. Really, Conrad, saloon girls and entertainers."

"Only one actress."

"Did you really expect any one of them to say yes?"

"No."

"Karl, have you ever actually proposed?"

The big man shook his head.

"Surely you've met women who could survive the

winters on this mountain."

"Well," he growled. "Maybe somebody like Daisy Colter."

Maddalyn smiled. Six and a half feet tall, broad as a barn door, and the man was blushing at the mention of a woman's name. "Who is Daisy Colter?"

"Her father runs the general store in Olympia, and Karl's been sweet on her for the past four years," Conrad divulged. "I swear, Maddalyn, you should see this woman. She can look me straight in the eye. She's got to be six feet tall, and she's got shoulders. . . ."

"I think she's pretty," Karl said defensively.

"Well, she is; there's just an awful lot of her."

"All right." Maddalyn raised her hand to silence the bickering. "Karl, do you think she's sweet on you, as well?"

He just shrugged his shoulders and stared into the fire. "No. She's never said a word to me."

"Even when you've spoken to her first?"

Conrad started to laugh, but a biting glare from Maddalyn stopped him.

"Karl's never worked up the nerve to actually speak to her," Eric explained, and Maddalyn was forced to look at him. His face was impassive, cold even.

"Not in four years?"

Eric shook his head.

"Well, we can certainly take care of that," Maddalyn said with assurance.

Someone's Been Sleeping in My Bed

"I still think one of us should marry Maddalyn," Karl grumbled.

"What?" She leaned forward slightly. "Have you actually discussed this possibility?"

"Just once," Karl divulged. "We like having a woman around, and you're agreeable. A good cook, too."

"Hardly reason for marriage," she said lightly. "As if I'd have any one of you."

She leaned back and rocked slowly for several quiet minutes. Most all the mending was done, and cooking only took up so many hours of the day. She needed something to occupy her time, to make the days pass quickly.

"You really should marry, each and every one of you," she said, her earlier anger gone. "If only you'd look in the proper places, learn to . . . talk to the women you're sweet on. I could help, you know."

"How?" Eric's voice was biting, disbelieving.

"For starters, you could all use a bit of cleaning up. The beards should go, and at least some of the hair. A few pointers on charming a lady, a little advice as to the proper sort of woman you need here." She smiled, and her head was filled with all sorts of ideas. "We'll start with you, Karl, since you're the oldest. I'll have to meet this Daisy Colter, of course.

"You'll be second, Conrad. It's only proper that we proceed in order of age. Must she be a red-head?"

"Yes," all three of the brothers answered at once.

"I hate limitations, but I'll see what I can do. Eric, as the youngest, you'll go last."

"Leave me out of this."

"I couldn't do that. It wouldn't be at all fair."

"I don't want—"

"Nonsense," Maddalyn said as she picked up the shirt she was mending and returned to her stitching. When he saw how happy Karl and Conrad were, when he saw that there were women out there who would happily settle on this mountain . . . when he saw that a lady could also be a woman . . . he was bound to come around.

"How do you do, Daisy?" Maddalyn asked in a clear voice as she stared up into Karl's face. "My, what a lovely hat you're wearing."

He was supposed to repeat what she said, but Karl remained silent.

"How do you do, Daisy?" she said more slowly.

Karl ran beefy hands through his long hair. That would have to be next, she supposed. It was bound to be more of a success than this lesson. Who would have thought that a man like Karl would be struck dumb at the very thought of approaching a woman?

"All right," she said patiently. "Perhaps that's too personal for starters. How about this: 'What a lovely day we're having.'"

She was answered with silence.

"This is not such a good idea, Maddalyn," Karl said when he finally spoke.

"Well, how do you expect Daisy Colter to know you're interested if you never say a word to her? For goodness' sake, women are not adept at reading the male mind, even when they do speak plainly. You've never had a bit of trouble speaking to me."

"That's different," Karl mumbled.

"I should be insulted," Maddalyn said in mock indignation, and Karl actually smiled.

"Is it my turn yet?" Conrad asked, sneaking into the kitchen.

"Of course not," Maddalyn said, giving up on Karl for the moment. "Your lessons will have a totally different purpose. If only we can teach you to be silent for a few moments." She tried to put a heavy dose of despair into her voice, and Conrad laughed at her.

"What if I find the perfect woman for you, and she's not a redhead?" Maddalyn poured three cups of coffee and placed them on the table.

"Then she's not the perfect woman for me," he said seriously.

"You do realize"—Maddalyn seated herself at the table and the brothers joined her—"don't you, that's a completely irrational response."

"I know, but it doesn't make a bit of difference. I see a length of red hair, and it drives me mad." He shook his fist playfully in the air, and Maddalyn could only smile.

"And do you wish to be mad for the rest of your life?"

"Desperately."

They were all laughing when Eric came storming through the kitchen door.

"I'll do my best to find you a redheaded woman who'll make a suitable wife. I consider it a challenge."

After a quick, scowling glance at the table, Eric shook his head and sighed loudly. "Maddalyn," he said, the sound of her name on his lips labored. "I'd like a word with you, if you can drag yourself away from the kitchen for a few minutes."

"Of course, Eric." She smiled, in spite of his obvious annoyance. He'd never agreed to her matchmaking proposal.

"I would love a short walk outside, if you'll give me a moment to collect my coat."

"Didn't know you had a coat."

"Actually," she called as she made her way through the main room and down the hall to her . . . to Eric's room, "I found it in the bottom of the trunk. It's a trifle small for any of you, so I assumed that it was outgrown and cast aside. I've been anxious to try it out."

When she returned to the kitchen, wrapped snugly in the warm coat, Eric was waiting impatiently by the door. Goodness, they hadn't been alone in ages. Maddalyn smiled brightly at Eric, despite the fact that she assumed this talk would not be a pleasant one. At least, it wouldn't begin that way.

* * *

"Can we walk over here?" Maddalyn asked, heading toward the trees without waiting for an answer.

Eric followed, wondering just exactly how he was going to word his objections.

She didn't seem to mind the cold. Of course, his old coat was warm enough, and her hands were lost in Conrad's gloves, gloves Karl had insisted she wear even as he set his own hat on her head.

The red skirt whipped around her legs as she walked briskly toward the cover of trees. He'd been so anxious for her to finish making that damned skirt, certain that she would not be as appealing in it as she was in his wedding suit, but he'd been wrong.

"Don't go too far," he called as she entered the shade of the forest. He was right behind her, and the temperature dropped several degrees when they left the sunshine.

She stopped in a glade, surrounded on all sides by tall ponderosa pines. A few feet farther past the pines and the descent down the mountain began. Maddalyn turned around slowly, her face upturned as she made a complete circle. "Isn't it magnificent?" Her voice was almost a whisper as she turned to him.

Eric said nothing. He was too busy silently reciting to himself all the reasons he had for keeping his distance from her.

"I suppose you've called me here to tell me that I'll make a terrible matchmaker, and that I'm ruining everything, and that I should leave you and your brothers alone. I suppose you'd like me to believe that the three of you are perfectly happy here, and will be happier still when you're rid of me."

She smiled, not at all distressed at the idea that all her suppositions might be true.

"What do you think you're doing?" Eric asked, taking a single step toward her. "Teaching Karl and Conrad how to court the perfect wife? Choosing the perfect woman . . ."

"It seems that Karl has already chosen his perfect woman. He just needs a little help and encouragement. You're just dismayed to find that your brothers don't hold the same low opinions of women that you do."

"I don't have a low opinion of all women. . . ."

"Excuse me," Maddalyn said brightly. "Ladies."

"I like things the way they are."

"Do you really?"

Her smile told him that she didn't believe his insistence that he wanted nothing to change. "Life is constant change, Eric. Ups and downs, like climbing your mountain and falling down and getting up to climb it again. Don't you think Karl will make a wonderful father?" She didn't wait for a response. "Conrad, too. Every child needs a father who will protect her, and even make her laugh. And what about you, Eric? How old are you? Are you thirty yet?"

"Almost."

"That's rather young to get set in your ways, don't you think?"

"No."

Maddalyn took a step toward him, her smile constant. "I thought you brought me out here to have a discussion of some sort, but you've hardly said a dozen words. Why did you really ask me to walk with you, Eric?"

Eric wondered if she knew what she was asking, if she had any idea what he wanted.

It happened so fast it caught them both by surprise. Maddalyn's feet slipped out from under her, her smile vanished, and she landed on the icy ground.

"Are you all right?" Eric dropped down beside her and placed his hands at her back, lifting her so that her head rested against his shoulder. "Where does it hurt? Your ankle? Your back?"

He thought for a moment that she was crying, but soon recognized the sound that was muffled in his shoulder as soft laughter.

"I take it you're not hurt?" he asked gruffly, and Maddalyn pulled her head back.

She slid one arm around his waist. "The fall just knocked the breath out of me, that's all. Goodness." Maddalyn took a deep breath. "I'll be fine if I can just sit here for a minute or two."

Eric wasn't sure that he could take this for a minute or two. She was practically in his lap, and her face was so close to his he could feel her breath against his neck.

"This ground is awfully cold," Maddalyn said,

squirming slightly, and Eric hauled her onto his lap.

"Better?"

"Much, thank you," she said breathlessly. "It will just take me a moment, I'm sure, to gather myself."

Now she truly was in his face, nose to nose, almost mouth to mouth. She should have looked ridiculous, wearing Karl's winter cap, her yellow curls framing her face, but instead she looked irresistible.

"I'm not usually so forward," she whispered, wrapping her arms around his neck, "but would you mind terribly kissing me just once?"

Eric placed his mouth against hers, barely touching her waiting lips. She pursed her lips, closed her eyes, and held her breath.

"Pretend," he whispered onto those pouting lips, "that I'm a honeysuckle."

Maddalyn touched her tongue to his lower lip, and when Eric pressed his mouth to hers, she sucked against his lightly. He teased her with his tongue, and she twitched just a little, surprised at the intrusion. She didn't pull away, but pressed her body to his and mimicked him, slipping her tongue past his lips.

Eric heard the trap he'd been trying to avoid close, not with a clang but with a whisper. And he didn't care.

He pulled his lips away from hers because he had to. It wasn't enough. He wanted more, he wanted all of her.

"I certainly can't stand now," she said breathlessly, returning her head to his shoulder.

"Neither can I," Eric growled.

Maddalyn laughed lightly, and Eric wondered if she had any idea what she'd done to him.

"But I guess we should get back," she said half-heartedly.

"Give me a minute," he mumbled, and then he tried to think of everything but the woman on his lap. Logging, the snow, the cold lake at the foot of the mountain—what Karl would do if he found them as they were.

"All right," he said, and Maddalyn rose shakily from his lap.

"Will you hold my hand?" she asked, offering it hesitantly, lifting her arm and presenting to him a hand that was lost in Conrad's glove. "So I won't fall again?"

He took her hand, closing it in his own. Beneath the large glove, there was a small warm hand, tiny and trembling.

Maddalyn was unusually silent as they retraced their steps back to the cabin. Her smile had vanished, though she didn't appear to be unhappy. Her mouth was red and slightly swollen, lips that had obviously been kissed.

He was caught, well and true.

Karl was waiting outside the kitchen door, bareheaded, feet planted solidly apart, arms crossed. Eric considered dropping Maddalyn's hand, but they'd already been seen, and he had no intention of running from his big brother.

Karl's eyes were fastened on their joined hands as they approached the cabin.

"Don't look like such a bear, Karl," Maddalyn called sweetly. "I asked Eric to hold my hand after I fell. I was afraid I'd lose my footing again."

"You fell?" Karl asked, his eyes leaving their clasped hands and fastening onto Maddalyn's face. "Are you hurt?"

"Not at all," Maddalyn said lightly. "I just had the wind knocked out of me." Eric didn't release her hand until they were at the kitchen door. "Do promise me that you won't black Eric's eye again," she said easily.

How had she known?

"Don't look at me," Karl said defensively when Eric glared at him. "I didn't say a word."

Maddalyn smiled then, wide and clear. "Did you really think I'd fall for that ridiculous story about you and Conrad stumbling in the snow? Honestly, you must think I'm incredibly naive."

Naive? Perhaps, but the smile on her face was that of a woman, not a proper lady, and the light in her eyes danced with the memory of their kiss. When she pulled Karl's hat off of her head, golden curls rose and fell, giving her a tousled look, as if she'd just risen from bed. And he could see it much too clearly in his mind.

Her cheeks pink, but not from the cold.

Her golden curls across his pillow.

The warm flesh beneath that too large coat revealed, while Maddalyn gazed at him with clear eyes and gifted him with that same not-quite-naive smile she wore at the moment.

That smile didn't fade as she returned Karl's hat, slipped into the kitchen, and closed the door in their faces.

Chapter Eleven

Sleep would not come, no matter how hard she willed it. Her mind was filled, as it had been all afternoon and evening, with the memory of that wonderful kiss. Warm and thrilling, the intensity had surprised her.

Something in Eric had changed with that kiss. He'd watched her more closely that evening, had even smiled on occasion. Maybe he could love her, with the proper encouragement.

Maddalyn slipped from the bed, bringing the quilt with her. The door was partially open to allow the heat from the fireplace to circulate in her room, but she had to push it several inches in order to slither through the opening.

The hinges screamed, and Maddalyn stopped and waited. Nothing moved. Karl continued to snore. No one whispered or called out or even turned in their bed.

But Eric was turned toward the hallway, lying on his side with the firelight behind him. His head was propped up in one hand, and he was waiting for her.

"I couldn't sleep," she whispered as she sat down beside him.

"Neither could I." Eric smiled, and when he did Maddalyn was certain that her heart stopped. He had such a lovely smile.

Would it be too bold to tell him that their kiss was the reason she couldn't sleep? That, illogically, she thought that if he'd only kiss her again she'd be able to sleep soundly?

She didn't say a word, but she expected that he knew. Perhaps the memory had been keeping him awake as well.

Eric reached up and pushed one side of the quilt off of her shoulder, so that the shirt she slept in every night was exposed. He touched the collar with one finger, then ran that finger over her shoulder and down her arm.

"Another of my old shirts," he whispered, smiling easily. "Do you realize that almost every shirt you've mended and taken for yourself is one of mine?"

"I'm sorry—" He silenced her with a finger at her lips.

"Don't be. I like it, the thought of you sleeping in my bed in something that I once wore."

"How very wicked," Maddalyn whispered, and Eric's smile widened.

He sat up and faced her, and Maddalyn had to lift her eyes to see his. More than anything she wanted to fall into his arms and let him hold her the way he had in the cave. If he held her like that, and kissed her again, she would be sinfully content.

The quilt fell to her waist, and Eric laid his hands on her shoulders. Hands so large and strong they could shield her from anything. Hands so warm they could keep the chill from her on the coldest night.

He pulled her against his chest with those hands, guiding her gently so that she knelt between his legs. He kissed her, and she didn't even have to ask.

It was truly wonderful, warming her from the center of her soul, making her bones quiver. She was bewildered, her mind curiously muddled by the touch of his lips. His mouth claimed hers as he parted her lips with his tongue, but she felt his touch all over her body, like a drug that rushed through her blood, like a wave that crashed over her.

She knew she should move away, that this was more than she could handle, but it was impossible to move her lips from Eric's. It was much too wonderful, and she felt as if she were falling into a deep, dark hole where she'd be happily lost forever.

Eric was lost, too. She could feel it in the hand that tangled in her hair, in the heartbeat that pounded against hers, in the lips that devoured her.

Perhaps this was the way to Eric's heart.

Maddalyn slipped her arms around his waist, held on to Eric for support. Her bones were liquid, and it would be so simple to slip to the floor.

She'd never known her mouth could be so sensitive, that anything could feel so good it bordered on an ache. Eric's lips and tongue against hers were heavenly. Surely a pleasure this deep was sinful.

It was the clearing of throats behind her that broke the spell, and Maddalyn fell backward in her attempt to move away from Eric.

Karl and Conrad stood, forbidding sentinels on either side of the entrance to the hall. Both were dressed in long red underwear, but only Karl had had the decency to wrap his quilt around his waist. Conrad stood there with his arms crossed over his chest, an uncustomary frown on his face.

Karl was furious. She would have quaked had that anger been directed at her, but the older Barrett brothers were staring at their little brother.

"I couldn't sleep," she said, rising as elegantly as she could manage to her feet. Late at night, trying to sleep in her bed in Aunt Ethel's house while Cousin Doreen snored in the next room, Maddalyn had wondered what it would be like to have a real family. Brothers, perhaps. She couldn't stop the smile that spread across her face. This was what it was like.

"Don't be cross," she said. "I was just about to go to bed."

"So I see," Conrad said darkly.

"Get back to bed, both of you," she ordered. Neither of them moved. Maddalyn spun around to face the fire and Eric. He still sat on his pallet, and his expression was as dark as his brothers'. "Good night, Eric," she said sweetly.

She spun back around to find that Karl and Conrad hadn't moved. "For goodness' sake," she hissed. "It was just a kiss."

They escorted her to her door, and Conrad watched as she crawled into the bed. He closed the door, leaving just enough of an opening for the air to circulate. Then he opened the door wide, smiling at the grinding squeak, and returned it to its proper position.

The opening was too narrow for her to pass through.

"It looks like soaking these hinges in salt water wasn't such a bad idea after all," Conrad whispered. "Good night, Maddalyn."

The bed was cozy, and she had the memory of yet another kiss to warm her.

"Good night, Conrad. Do tell Karl to leave Eric alone, will you?"

She couldn't understand Conrad's mumble, but it sounded suspiciously like "fat chance."

Eric expected that something would come of last night's somewhat innocent kiss, but he hadn't expected to be confronted over the breakfast table.

Maddalyn's back was to him as she fried a pan of ham to replace the slices Karl had wolfed down. Once she'd glanced over her shoulder to smile quickly at him. The brightness of her smile stunned him so, hit him so hard, that he didn't even smile back.

Karl cleared his throat loud and long, a sure sign that he was ready to speak and wanted everyone's attention.

"A good thaw's coming soon," Karl said, "and when it does we'll be taking you and Maddalyn down to Olympia to be married. That's all I have to say." He returned with appropriate seriousness to his eggs and biscuits.

"You're kidding, right?" Eric asked, pushing his own plate aside. "I kissed her twice. If Conrad had to marry every girl he kissed he'd have a harem by now."

Karl banged a meaty fist on the kitchen table. "Don't be comparing Maddalyn to those hurdy-girls Conrad has a liking for. Anyways, it looked like a marrying kiss to me."

"Excuse me." Maddalyn's voice was soft, but it carried through the room and caught Eric's attention. Karl's and Conrad's, too, from the look of them. There was an oddly serene expression on her face, and her bright smile was gone. "Is there not even one of you who thinks I should be consulted?"

"Well—" Karl began, but he didn't get far.

"I'll not marry Eric. What you saw has a simple

explanation. I asked Eric to kiss me, being fairly ignorant of such things. If I'm to catch a suitable husband in Sheridan I should at the very least be able to kiss properly. It's no different from the lessons I'm giving you, if you can call them that." The calmness that had come over Maddalyn struck Eric for a moment as being a kind of disguise. A soft but inpenetrable defense.

"We thought—" Conrad began, but Maddalyn interrupted him as well.

"Surely you don't think that I intend to stay on this mountain in the middle of nowhere. I can only imagine that it is a cold, lonely place in the wintertime." Her voice was perfectly reasonable, soft and serene, but she didn't lay her eyes on any one of them. Her attention remained on her cooking. "It's certainly not the sort of place I plan to continue my life in."

"You said there were women who would love to live here," Karl argued.

"I did," Maddalyn said, sliding several slices of ham onto a platter in the middle of the table. "But I never said that I was one of them."

Eric managed a wry smile. He had known all along who she was, what she wanted. She lifted her eyes to him, then, clear blue and bright. A little too bright, or was it just his imagination?

"In any case," Maddalyn continued, "when I do marry I'll expect my prospective husband to approach the altar with some emotion besides fear. With at least a crumb of enthusiasm."

"I don't like it," Karl grumbled.

"You don't have to like it," Maddalyn said as she took her place at the table. "Goodness, Karl, you'd condemn me to a marriage to Eric, all for a simple kiss or two? We all know good and well that Eric dislikes proper ladies. When I'm finished with you and Conrad, think what a time I'll have finding a bride for Eric."

"I don't intend—" Eric began, but he got no further in his attempts to join the conversation than his brothers had.

"If she can't have ladylike qualities, I suppose I'll have to resort to Conrad's . . . what did you call them? Hurdy-girls?" She picked at a biscuit, tearing off crumbs and depositing them on her plate. "Either that, or some rough-and-tumble true Western woman who can shoot a gun and ride a horse and chase a cow, or whatever it is such women do."

"Maddalyn, don't—" Eric began.

"Well, I've had quite enough," she said, pushing away from the table and leaving her breakfast uneaten. "If you don't mind, I have some cleaning to do in my . . . in Eric's room this morning. I'll take care of the breakfast mess after y'all leave the cabin. It's much easier that way."

She talked as she left the kitchen, giving none of them a chance to speak.

Karl and Conrad were stunned, but Eric was not at all surprised. Maddalyn was, after all, a lady. It didn't matter much that she was pretty, that she felt good in his hands, that she kissed with every fiber of her being . . . like she did everything else. He'd never expected her to stay. He'd never really wanted her to stay.

Still, he felt like Karl had just knocked him senseless, a possibility that was still a very real one. You'd think Karl and Conrad had adopted the girl.

"Happy now?" Conrad snapped as the bedroom door screamed shut. "Look what you've done."

"What I've done? What about Karl?" Eric turned to his oldest brother. "He's the one who upset her, telling her she was going to have to marry me and stay on the mountain. That's a fate worse than death for a lady like Maddalyn."

"I really thought she was sweet on you," Karl said apologetically. "And that you were sweet on her, too."

"Yeah, well." Eric pushed away from the table, losing his appetite suddenly. "It's time you learned, Karl, that you don't marry a woman just because your pecker stands up when she enters the room. It's best you remember that when Maddalyn tries to get you hitched to Daisy Colter. As for Maddalyn, when she gets to Sheridan I'm sure she'll get sweet on somebody else."

He must be getting as bad as his brothers, because the thought of Maddalyn kissing another man the way she'd kissed him last night made him feel sick.

"I have a feeling," Eric said, leaning in close to Karl, purposely goading him, "that Maddalyn is not real particular about who she gets sweet on.

Play your cards right, and maybe she'll ask you to kiss her. Play your cards flawlessly and maybe she'll ask you to—"

He'd been expecting the blow. Karl was predictable, if nothing else. But usually it was a clip on the jaw, or a right cross that caught him across the cheek.

So he wasn't prepared for the fist that pounded into his gut. It knocked the air right out of him, and he fell to his knees.

"Don't be talking like that about Maddalyn," Karl warned needlessly as he put on his heavy coat. Eric couldn't speak at all. He rolled onto his back and tried to breathe, but that was an impossibility. Conrad stepped over him, grimacing down.

"You asked for that one, little brother," he said sympathetically.

"I know," Eric answered hoarsely.

"Maddalyn asked me not to black his eye," Karl explained to Conrad. "But I had to do something."

Conrad agreed, as if Eric weren't lying on the floor trying to find his wind.

Hell, that hadn't helped a bit.

Maddalyn listened to them leave, listened to the kitchen door open and close three times, and still she remained in the bedroom.

She shouldn't have been surprised by Karl's suggestion or by Eric's reaction—but she was.

Of course he had said that he didn't care to marry, but she hadn't really thought it was true.

She'd thought it a halfhearted protest. Everyone wanted to be loved, didn't they? Everyone wanted a companion, someone to grow old with, a family.

It was what Maddalyn wanted more than anything. And she was selfish. She wanted it all. Love. Family. Home. She refused to be second-best for another moment of her life. The man she married would love her, or she would never marry.

And she certainly wouldn't marry a man who looked at taking her as a wife as something he was forced to do. Aunt Ethel and Uncle Henry had been forced to take her in, and they'd never let her forget it.

Eric certainly didn't love her, and he never would. He'd had time. She'd cooked for him, mended his clothes, sat with him at the end of the day. They'd kissed. Twice. And each time had been breathtakingly wonderful, at least for her. Hadn't he felt it? Hadn't he felt that powerful glow?

Eric Barrett had had every opportunity to fall in love with her, and he hadn't even come close.

Perhaps he was incapable of love. Perhaps he still loved the lady who had rejected him. Perhaps Jane had broken his heart and it had never healed.

She would never tell Eric that she loved him. Never. When the snow thawed she'd go to Olympia, take care of getting Karl and Conrad married, and then she'd move on to Sheridan. There was no reason for her plans to change.

Maddalyn sat on the edge of the comfortable bed. Should she try to find a suitable wife for Eric as well? It was only fair, but it would certainly be difficult. For goodness' sake, if Eric married he and his wife would sleep in this very bed!

Since Eric was so determined to remain a bachelor, Maddalyn decided with a frown, perhaps she shouldn't interfere with his plans.

Eric set up outside the barn, grateful for the frigid air and the much-needed quiet.

Karl and Conrad were even farther down the hill, intent on felling a few more of the pines that stood where they already pictured their ranch. Maddalyn was warmly and safely ensconced in the cabin, a domain she had quickly and surely claimed as her own.

He whittled at the chair leg, giving it form beneath his hands, making it curve in and out again like a woman's shapely leg.

When the leg had a shape he was satisfied with, Eric placed it carefully next to the other completed pieces and picked up the final leg.

They didn't really need another chair. The one Maddalyn had broken had already been repaired, and there were four perfectly good chairs in the kitchen and a couple of sturdy rockers on the porch.

But this was the only activity that could take his mind off of Maddalyn, and even then . . . he found his mind wandering. Picturing her face as she'd told Karl that she had no intention of living on a desolate mountain, that she'd been practicing in order to learn how to kiss properly.

It was the most ridiculous notion he had ever heard, and he didn't believe for a minute that she'd been doing nothing more than research when she'd kissed him.

He had no trouble believing that she wouldn't live on his mountain. Hell, he'd known that all along. That didn't bother him, because he didn't want her to stay.

As if something inside him recognized the lie, his hand slipped and the knife he wielded sliced the tip of a finger. He cursed and wiped away the welling blood impatiently. It could have been worse.

It was so cold that he didn't really feel any pain. The blood ran slowly down his index finger to his palm, and Eric clenched his fist.

There were some things that couldn't be denied. He'd admit readily that Maddalyn had surprised him, continued to surprise him daily. If he could've gotten away with spending every moment of her stay here watching her, he would do it.

He also had to admit to himself that watching Maddalyn for too long would be disastrous. Hell, all he had to do was look at her and he was ready to take her in his arms again, to show her that the pleasure didn't stop with a single kiss. He wanted to touch her, to bury himself in her, to claim her for his own, the way she'd claimed his cabin and his sanity.

He couldn't, he wouldn't do it. He knew her,

knew that deep down she wanted more than he could ever give her.

And so he wouldn't watch Maddalyn at every opportunity. If she sneaked into the room where he slept at night again, he'd pretend to be asleep, even if she stood over him with a smile that could tempt the devil.

He looked at the gray sky and prayed for a brighter sun to melt the last of the snow. It couldn't come soon enough.

Eric opened his fist slowly, spread the fingers wide. The bleeding had already stopped.

He picked up the last piece of the new chair, proceeding more carefully, with his mind on his work instead of the woman who had stolen into his home and his soul to tempt him with unspoken promises she wouldn't keep.

Chapter Twelve

"Don't tell me. Conrad cut it with a dull ax." Maddalyn lifted a length of Karl's hair. It was nearer blond than Conrad's or Eric's, thick and hanging well over his shoulders. But it seemed to be of every length, ragged at the ends, longer on one side than on the other.

Without further comment, she took the scissors to Karl's hair. She wouldn't call herself a barber, but most anything would be an improvement.

They sat in front of the fire at the end of another long day, three days after Karl's outrageous suggestion—order—that she and Eric marry. Eric hadn't spoken to her since. He was at this very moment sitting at the kitchen table, cradling yet another cup of coffee that he didn't need.

Today had been noticeably warmer than the past

two weeks or so. No one mentioned it, but even Maddalyn had felt the difference in the air.

Spring was coming to the mountain, and she would have to leave.

She cut carefully at Karl's hair, leaving it a little long, but even and not so wild-looking. Conrad was next. Like Eric's hair, there was every shade of brown under the sun represented. Conrad's hair, though, was dominated by the darker browns, with the lighter shades widely interspersed. Like Karl's, it was thick and wild and uneven.

"Come on, Eric," Karl insisted, and Maddalyn looked up from the back of Conrad's head to see that Karl was all but dragging Eric into the room.

"If he doesn't want his hair cut—" she began.

"If I needed a haircut, Eric needs a haircut," Karl insisted.

She couldn't argue too much. It would be suspicious. They might correctly suspect that she had feelings for Eric that she hid from them all.

"Well, have a seat," she instructed sharply as Conrad left the chair. Eric sat down almost reluctantly. Was he nervous? She was at his back, and there was a sharp pair of scissors in her hands. "Relax," she instructed more softly. "I'll try not to take an ear or a piece of your scalp."

"I feel much better now," he mumbled.

Maddalyn trimmed his hair as she had Karl's and Conrad's. Eric's hair was not so fair as Karl's, or so dark as Conrad's, but it was just as thick, just as unruly. She cut away the uneven ends, leaving it a bit longer than was truly fashionable.

The longer hair suited the Barrett brothers, all three of them. They were untamable, wild, free as the wind. Maddalyn didn't know whether she should envy Daisy Colter and Conrad's redhead, or pity them.

"There you are," she said lightly. "All done. Tomorrow morning the beards go."

"The beards, too?" Conrad moaned dramatically.

"Karl," Maddalyn said in her best schoolteacher voice, "would you hand me the photograph on the mantel?"

He reached up without even having to stretch and grabbed the photograph, handing it to her carefully.

"What handsome men we have here," she said succinctly. "The girls of Olympia wouldn't have a chance against three such men intent on marriage."

"Two," Eric mumbled.

Maddalyn ignored him. "When was this taken?"

Naturally it was Conrad who answered. "Right before Eric bought this place. Karl and I were still with Pinkerton's at the time. What was that . . . five years ago or so?"

Karl nodded.

"You all look much nicer without the beards. Trust me, that's a woman's opinion."

"I'll have to grow it back next winter," Karl said, rubbing a hand through his beard, missing it already, by the look of him.

"Certainly," Maddalyn agreed. "By next winter you'll be married and I'll be in Sheridan, and you can grow as much facial hair as you please."

Karl nodded, accepting Maddalyn's suggestion. It even seemed that Conrad would comply. As for Eric . . . she had no idea what he would do. But she would love to see him just once without his beard, just once as he was in the photograph she'd studied so intently when she'd sneaked into the cabin.

He had watched her closely even then. He had made her heart flutter even then.

"Tomorrow morning," she repeated. "I do hope I won't have to shave each and every one of you myself. Good heavens, there's no telling what sort of awful accidents I might have with a razor in my hand."

Conrad made a playful noise of dismay, Karl grimaced, but only Eric promised to shave first thing in the morning.

Eric ran a hand over his newly shaven jaw. He felt naked without the beard he'd worn for the past four years, and foolish for actually shaving it off because a woman told him to. If he needed reminding why he had sworn never to marry again, this was a good one. He dressed as he pleased, cursed when he felt like it, and led his life—beard and all—without instruction from anyone.

Until now.

Maddalyn Kelly had the three of them wrapped around her little finger, and had managed that feat with little effort. Karl and Conrad were seriously considering marriage, as Maddalyn had suggested. Everything in the cabin looked a little brighter, cleaner, neater, now that she was here, and they even, by God, ate when and what she decided. He'd been ousted from his own bed, in his own cabin, and he was damned tired of sleeping on the floor.

He pushed open the kitchen door, not even lifting his head to see her. He knew she was there, humming as she stirred some new concoction in a large bowl. Eric hung his coat on the rack behind the door, and turned toward the main room. Conrad and Karl would be home soon, but evidently supper was not yet ready.

Not that either of his brothers was likely to complain. If she served them dried beans and burnt bread they'd eat it and compliment her as if it were a fine meal.

He didn't get very far before he ran into the table, catching his shin on the sturdy leg.

"Damnation," he shouted through clenched teeth. "You moved the table."

He had no choice but to lift his head and look at her. She'd deposited her bowl on the shelf by the stove and wiped her hands on an apron she'd made from Karl's red calico.

"Yes, I did, and it's quite heavy."

It seemed almost a complaint.

"What do you think? It gives me a little more room to maneuver, and I think it balances that side of the room nicely."

She was evidently going to ignore the fact that he had damn near broken his leg since the table was now directly in the path from the back door to the main room.

"I think you should have left the damn table where it belongs," he growled.

She shook her head slightly. "It doesn't hurt to change a few things."

It was the wrong thing to say, at the wrong time. "Dammit!" Eric pushed the table back where it had been when he'd left the cabin after dinner. "I don't like change." The legs of the table screamed across the floor. "Can't you just leave everything the hell alone?"

"Nothing stays the same forever," Maddalyn said softly. Still, he could hear a hint of anger in her voice. "There's nothing wrong with trying to make your life better."

"Better?" he snapped. Why the hell did she think placing the table in his path was better?

She didn't care for his response. Her face paled, and she gripped the apron skirt in her hands. "You'll be glad to be rid of me, won't you Eric?" Her voice was soft, and he felt it, deep and painful. He didn't have an answer for her, didn't have an answer for himself. Yes, he would be glad when she left. No, he wouldn't. He would be miserable. Hell, he didn't know.

"Fine," she said, as if she had her answer. Maddalyn turned her back to him and began to vigorously mix whatever was in that large bowl.

Eric started to ask her what she was making, just to change the subject, but the words stuck in his throat. So he turned away and left the kitchen, and left Maddalyn to her preparations.

Why had he lost his temper like that? Over something so insignificant. His shin still throbbed, but if he hadn't been so intent on avoiding Maddalyn he would have been watching his step.

She'd be gone soon, and whether he liked it or not, he knew that was for the best.

He stood at the window and looked out at the mountains that stretched before him. As it always did, the sight filled him with a peace he needed, a reminder that he was a very small part of this world, and that his inner struggles were insignificant.

Eric knew he should apologize to Maddalyn, but he delayed returning to the kitchen to do just that. He took a few minutes to cool down, to remind himself that a knot on his shin or a misplaced table were unimportant.

But he knew that wasn't the reason he'd lost his temper. It was this frustration that was driving him mad, facing Maddalyn day in and day out and pretending that he didn't feel anything for her. It was lust, it was possessiveness, it was even, now, affection.

He owed her, at the very least, an apology. An answer to her question wouldn't be out of order, but he wasn't sure he could handle that. Anxious for her to go? Yes. No. Hell, he didn't know what he wanted anymore.

"Maddalyn," he called, turning away from the window and crossing the room in long strides. "Listen . . ." He stepped into the kitchen, and found that he was talking to himself. Her red apron was laid neatly across the back of a chair, and the bowl she'd been using was still sitting on the shelf. Eric crossed the room and looked down at the mess inside the bowl. Batter, of some sort, with a spicy scent.

He picked up the spoon and ran it through the batter, watching the swirls his movements created.

Where was she? Outside cooling off? In the outhouse? Down the hill crying to Karl and Conrad about the cruel treatment she'd received?

He dropped the spoon into the batter and stuffed his hands into his pockets, and as the minutes passed an uneasy feeling grew.

She wouldn't have complained to Karl and Conrad. There hadn't been a word of complaint from her since he'd found her. Outside cooling off? He'd been the one who'd gotten so hot. In the outhouse? All this time? While her batter sat on the shelf and spoiled?

His uneasiness grew when he turned toward the door. His coat, the coat he'd hung behind the door when he'd come home, was gone.

A low limb brushed her face, but Maddalyn didn't slow her pace. There had been no time to plan, no time to consider her options, so she was leaving the mountain by the same route she'd climbed it.

Anger had carried her this far, anger and a deep frustration. Eric wanted her off his mountain. He didn't want any changes in his life, and that included her.

She slipped on an unexpected icy patch, and stumbled down a short incline, cushioning the impact with her hands as she tumbled over and landed on her backside. Going down the mountain was not much easier than climbing up it. She took a moment to rest, to calm her frazzled nerves. It was unlike her to lose her temper, even in the face of supreme stupidity such as Eric's. For goodness' sake, it would soon be dark. There was no way she could make it down the mountain before dark, and she certainly couldn't travel at night.

Had she been thinking, she would have returned to the cave that had provided shelter for her in the past, but of course that was the first place Eric would look. If he bothered to look for her at all.

Maddalyn huddled in the too large coat. She shouldn't have taken it, but it was still quite cold, and going to Eric's room for her own coat would have alerted him as to her plan. If she could call this a plan.

The sound of her name reached her, a faint cry from the top of the mountain.

It was that sound that gave her the strength to stand and face the slope before her. It looked sharper going down than it had coming up, and she hesitated.

Running had been impulsive, and perhaps foolish. If she had an ounce of sense she'd turn around, climb back up the hill she'd just stumbled down, and make some excuse for her short trek.

She heard Eric calling her name again, closer this time, angrier. Maddalyn took a deep breath, looked down, and continued, sitting on the edge and all but crawling downward.

As she slid down the hill she made a tremendous amount of noise, crackling and crushing noises of earth and stone, dried leaves and pine needles. At this elevation the patches of ice and snow were sparser than at the top of the mountain, even though she hadn't traveled all that far. There were just a few stubborn spots that didn't see the sun.

On a rare level spot, Maddalyn stopped and assessed her situation. She stood on smooth stone that ended abruptly, and she peeked over the side. There was a substantial drop, and there didn't seem to be any good way to descend.

"Drat," she whispered. "I must have taken a wrong turn somewhere."

She faced the slope she'd just plunged down with a sigh of exasperation. There was nothing for it but to climb back up again and try another course.

It would soon be dark, and she had no idea where she was. She would have cried if she'd thought tears would do any good at all.

Tiredly, she raked her eyes up the hill, over rocks

of all sizes, dirt and leaves and those nasty pine needles. More rocks, a patch or two of ice, and then those two enormous boots at the top of the slope.

Maddalyn looked back down the cliff, wondering if she'd missed a possible pathway, before she turned her eyes back to Eric.

He was furious, and this time his fury was not tempered with indecision or softening eyes. His arms were crossed over his chest, and of course he was wearing no coat.

"What are you doing here?" she asked haughtily, in lieu of a better defense.

"What am *I* doing here?" he repeated. "Where the hell do you think you're going?"

"You asked me to leave. . . ." she began.

"I did not!" he bellowed, and Maddalyn took a single step away from Eric and his potent anger.

Her right foot hit a small patch of ice, and she plunged downward. There was a moment of true breathlessness as she fell, a moment of time where everything stopped: her heart, all sound, any ability to move. When her elbow brushed against the side of the rock, Maddalyn reached out with both hands to grasp the edge of the cliff.

Her arms were not strong enough to support her for long, but she found a toehold for her left foot and held on as best she could. She could hear her own heartbeat, could hear the rush of her own blood in her veins. Her elbow throbbed, but there was no way to take a look at that injury and see how bad it was.

Eric was there, his face thrust over the edge, his hands gripping her wrist.

"Are you all right?" he asked briskly.

Maddalyn stared at his face, a strangely pale face that no longer displayed his anger. In fact he looked frightened, as if he'd been the one to tumble over the cliff.

"Answer me, dammit!" he demanded, even though he could certainly see that she was unhurt.

"Given the circumstances I'm fine," she said calmly.

His grip at her wrist was too tight, but she wouldn't for the world have asked him to loosen it.

He didn't release her, but did slide one hand under the coat's wide sleeve, almost to her elbow.

"Let go of the rock and grab my wrist," he instructed, nodding to her left hand.

It took a moment to work up the courage to release her hold, but Eric was patient, merely nodding his head when she flexed her fingers hesitantly.

"It's all right," he said, his voice bland and peaceful. "I won't let you fall."

She knew that. She'd never doubted Eric's ability to hoist her from her current predicament.

Quickly she released the rock and grabbed Eric's wrist, wrapping her fingers tightly around the hard bone and muscle there. He nodded to her other hand, and she easily released her hold and clutched his forearm.

He pulled her effortlessly up, seeming to take

care not to bash her too horribly against the side of the cliff. He didn't say a word until she was on her feet, and he had moved her away from the ledge.

When he did speak his words were even and emotionless, but he gripped her wrists tightly. "Don't you ever do that again."

"Do what?"

He looked at her as if she were daffy, and the color came back into his face, but he did not release her. He looked, a time or two, as if he were about to answer, but he finally released her without answering her question.

"Are you hurt?" he asked gruffly, and Maddalyn rubbed her elbow. Eric took her arm, as if she were incapacitated, and slid it easily from the arm of his coat. The heavy coat hung from one arm as he pushed the sleeve of her shirt up and examined her elbow.

It was red, and Eric moved her arm this way and that before he declared that she would be bruised, but that her injury was not serious. Oddly enough, that realization seemed to make him angry again.

"What were you thinking?" he shouted. Maddalyn started to back away, but he reached out and grabbed her arm, forcing her to stay in place. Of course, that move had gotten her into this mess.

"You asked me to leave, so I was leaving," she said calmly, as if it meant nothing.

"I did not. . . ." he began angrily, and then he calmed himself with a seemingly great effort. "I did not ask you to leave," he said quietly, placing her arm back into the sleeve of his coat.

You didn't ask me to stay, either, she accused silently.

"Come on," he said, taking her arm and assisting her up the slope. "Karl and Conrad will be starving."

At the top of the slope he released her, and Maddalyn turned away from him and searched for another way down the mountain. Eric had taken several steps before he realized that she was not behind him.

"Maddalyn," he said, his voice deep and threatening. "What are you doing?"

"Going down the mountain," she said plainly.

"No, you're not," he insisted.

It was an argument that was likely to go nowhere. There was very little light left, and Maddalyn was beginning to doubt her ability to make her way without another disaster.

"It's time," she began.

"Tomorrow," he said, interrupting her with the single gruff word.

"What?"

"Tomorrow," he said more softly. "We'll leave tomorrow."

He turned his back on her, perhaps confident that she would follow this time. She did, keeping a distance, watching Eric's broad back, ignoring him when he turned to check on her progress.

Tomorrow.

Someone's Been Sleeping in My Bed

* * *

In her weeks on the mountain, Maddalyn had stayed close to the cabin most of the time. Her brief walk in the woods and her attempted escape had been the only deviation. But today the three brothers walked with her to the bottom of the hill.

On a leveled-out section of ground at the foot of the slope they had built a smokehouse and a stable for their horses. Both buildings appeared to be sturdy, and like the cabin they were unpainted. The area was framed by towering evergreen trees.

Sporadic spots of snow remained on the ground, primarily in the shade directly beneath the trees, but the path was clear, and the air was pleasant. It was time for her journey to Sheridan to continue, but without the anger that had spurred her last night, Maddalyn didn't want to go.

Just look at the three of them! Bathed and shaved, in decent clothing—much of which she'd mended herself—they made quite a picture. She didn't really expect that Karl would compliment Daisy Colter on her accessories, or that Conrad would be anything other than his gregarious self—but they were lovely.

She would miss the cabin. She would miss most of all the evenings around the fire—all four of them exhausted from the work of the day—and the mealtimes—when Conrad laughed and Karl complimented her cooking and ate like a horse.

And she would miss Eric. He had angered her to distraction, had hurt her feelings terribly, had ignored her whenever possible . . . but he had also saved her life, kept her warm, and kissed her silly, and Maddalyn never doubted for a moment that she would love him until her dying day.

The observation was overly dramatic, she knew, but true.

They were excited about going to town after the long winter, and Maddalyn stepped back to watch them finish their preparations. The horses were saddled, one mule was loaded down with bedrolls and packs of clothing and food, and another mule was saddled, she presumed for her.

They laughed at one of Conrad's jokes, even Eric, and then all three of them came to assist her onto the saddle.

She didn't know which was more overwhelming, the prospect of actually climbing into the saddle, or the three men who towered over her to assist.

Conrad held the reins and talked to the mule, while Eric took her hand and she stepped into the stirrup. Karl positioned himself on the other side of the mule, apparently in case she slid all the way around and to the ground. A distinct possibility.

"I've never done this before, you know," she said, unable to disguise her reluctance. "What if I fall?"

"Winchester won't let you fall," Conrad crooned, still talking to the mule.

"I assume this animal is Winchester?" Maddalyn asked. The mule moved, not forward or back or to the side, but in some strange undulation that made Maddalyn grasp the horn of her saddle.

In due time they left her alone with Winchester, and very gracefully mounted their own horses. Their mounts were much taller, dwarfing her and Winchester, and they were so at home in the saddle Maddalyn was somewhat jealous. The Barrett brothers were tall and elegant and powerful, while she struggled to keep her seat. Graceful? Never. Not on Winchester's back.

But they did make their way down the mountain, down a path shaded by tall pine trees. Here all was quiet, and even Conrad seemed to respect that. It was as if the forest were enchanted, or a holy plot of ground.

Karl led the way down the gentle path, and Conrad followed him. Maddalyn was next, and Eric led the pack mule behind her. She wanted, several times, to glance over her shoulder at him, but she didn't.

The path became steeper for a time, almost as precipitous as the side Maddalyn had climbed. Maddalyn held on to Winchester for dear life, trusting her safety to the mule who seemed very adept at maneuvering down the slope.

With every step the mule took, Maddalyn knew she was closer to her original goal. A teaching position in Sheridan, a bank account to begin saving for the Maddalyn Lorraine Kelly Academy for Young Ladies. A new life, far from Georgia and the family who'd never wanted her.

She should be happy, elated even, to be so close

189

to her goal. But her heart was sinking as she descended the mountain.

At the end of the steepest part of the path were several large felled trees, even more gigantic on their sides than in their natural position. Two wagons were sitting to one side, one of average size and one that was tremendously wide and long.

"Do you pull those wagons on occasion?" she asked Winchester softly. "I suppose if you can haul those you can handle me."

From there the path widened and curved, making a more leisurely course down the mountain. The trees thinned, the sun warmed the ground, and they left the mountain.

There was a lump in Maddalyn's throat the size of the saddle horn she grasped. Would she ever be back?

She knew she shouldn't, but she glanced over her shoulder and up to the mountain she had begun to think of as home. The cabin couldn't be seen from here, for the thick trees that covered the mountain, but she knew it was there at the peak.

She lowered her eyes to find Eric staring at her openly. No smile, no frown, just studying her as she had studied the mountain. He was so handsome, clean-shaven and dressed in a pale blue cotton shirt that made his gray eyes almost blue.

Reluctantly Maddalyn turned her eyes to the front. It wouldn't do to stare at Eric all the way to Olympia, especially since she had to crane her neck to do so.

They traveled at a leisurely pace, but Maddalyn soon grew weary of sitting on Winchester's back. She didn't complain, of course, but traveled in silence as they left the mountain behind.

Her rear end was numb before Karl called a stop to the day's travel. There was no way she could dismount on her own, so she waited. She didn't have to wait long. Eric was there, a hand at her waist as he helped her to the ground. When her feet touched the ground he released her, and her knees buckled. Her legs were as numb as her rear, and apparently totally useless at the moment.

Eric caught her, of course. She'd never doubted that he would. He dragged her up and across his body, until her feet were on the ground once again.

If only he would kiss her just once more. After all, he was right there, and she was right here, and it would make perfect sense. . . .

"What's wrong with Maddalyn?" Karl called, and she was reminded that Eric's brothers watched from no more than a few feet away.

"She's not used to riding, Karl," Eric snapped. "I guess her legs went out on her."

"They're getting better," Maddalyn informed him. "Just a moment more, and I should be able to stand on my own."

He shifted to her side, placing one arm over her shoulder. Maddalyn slipped her arm around his back as he forced her to take a few steps. The feeling came back into her legs and her aching rear all at once.

"Are you all right now?" Eric asked, and when Maddalyn nodded he released her.

"Sorry." She glanced up and to the side. "I'm not usually so feeble."

Eric laughed, even though Maddalyn saw nothing whatsoever amusing about her apology.

She turned her back on him, callous man that he was, and left him to care for Winchester. How could he laugh at her? How could he send her away with thoughtless laughter? Her rear end ached horribly, and he found amusement in her pain. Why should she expect him to behave otherwise, when he'd been heartless all along?

Maddalyn soon dismissed her irritation with Eric when she saw the lake that waited just over a small bluff.

It was wide and flat and clear, and as blue as the sky. The bank was lined with bushes and smooth rocks—large and small—and just a few low-hanging willow trees. The afternoon sun sparkled on the surface of the water.

"How magnificent," Maddalyn breathed.

"Pretty, isn't it?"

She looked up to see Conrad gazing out over the water as she had.

"More than pretty," she said. "You don't suppose I could take a brief swim, do you?"

Conrad shook his head slightly. "I don't know, Maddalyn. The water is . . ." He stopped suddenly and narrowed his eyes. "Pretty deep when you get about ten feet out."

"I'm a wonderful swimmer."

"Are you?" Conrad looked down at her and smiled. "Do you really swim, or do you just splash around in the water and squeal?"

"There is a beautiful lake about a half-hour hike from my uncle's house. I'll have you know this past summer I swam from one bank to the other more than once. Splash and squeal, indeed."

"Do you know what I love to do?" Conrad whispered his question. "See that rock over there?" He pointed just past a thick stand of bushes. A flat rock jutted over the water. "For the first swim of the year, I like to jump off of that rock right into the water."

"It sounds like such fun."

"It is," Conrad confided, looking over her shoulder. She could hear Eric and Karl as they set up camp. "Let's not tell them. You know how Karl is. He'll likely come up with some excuse why you shouldn't go for a swim. I'll get you a towel, and perhaps a blanket to sit on when you finish your plunge into the lake."

"I don't know. . . ." Maddalyn glanced back toward the camp.

"And I'll make certain Karl and Eric stay away from the water for a while. You'll have complete and total privacy."

Maddalyn bit her lower lip. "It does look heavenly."

"It does, doesn't it?" Conrad assured her.

"Wait right here," he whispered, "while I fetch a towel and a blanket."

Maddalyn returned his wide smile, and when he left her she turned her attention back to the lake. She'd never seen water so clear, so beautiful. It was as enchanted as Eric's mountain, as magical and as breathtaking.

Conrad was by her side moments later with the promised towel and a woolen blanket, and then, with a broad grin, he returned to his brothers with a promise to keep them occupied for a while.

Maddalyn felt as decadent as she had when she'd sneaked into the cabin and taken Eric's food. Atop the rock she slipped out of her clothes. She would have preferred to swim in her underwear, but there would be no time for them to dry before the sun set, so she removed her chemise and bloomers and placed them neatly beside her red skirt and white blouse.

From atop the rock, she could see clear to the bottom of the lake. It looked wonderfully inviting, and she took a deep breath, held her nose, and jumped.

Chapter Thirteen

Eric sat with his back to the lake, watching the coffeepot and the flickering flames beneath it with more interest than was necessary. On the other side of the camp Conrad was whispering intently and using his hands to punctuate certain statements, apparently arguing with Karl over something or another. At least it was finally an argument in which Eric was not involved.

Conrad had told Eric moments earlier that Maddalyn was walking along the lakeshore, trying to work out some of the kinks in her legs, and that she had promised not to go too far.

His instinct was to join her, to watch over her and make damn certain that she didn't wander too far from camp. But it wouldn't be a good idea. It would be best if he managed never to be alone with

Maddalyn Kelly again. That was when he got into trouble, when he began to have impossible thoughts.

He'd never forget the moment he'd seen her fall over the edge of the cliff, seen her disappear from view while he stood helpless too damn far away. He'd likely have nightmares about it for the rest of his life.

But the image that was burned into his brain reminded him that Maddalyn had been willing to risk her life to escape from the mountain, from him.

He didn't want her to go to Sheridan, but he also understood why she refused to return to Georgia. Her life there had been hard, and she deserved better than that. Surely there was an alternative, some compromise between Georgia and Sheridan.

Of course, he knew very well that she wouldn't stay on the mountain, and as he had no intention of ever marrying, that was fine with him.

Wasn't it?

The splash was just a whisper, but Eric's head snapped up. The scream that followed was a blood-curdling one, and he shot to his feet and ran toward the lake.

She'd fallen in, just as she'd fallen over that damn cliff yesterday. Could she swim? Would her skirts drag her to the bottom? Most of the water along the bank was shallow, but if she'd ventured out onto a rock and slipped the water could very well be over her head.

Karl and Conrad would be right behind him, he was certain, but when he glanced over his shoulder Eric realized that he was all alone.

The first thing he saw as he reached the lake was her head, above the surface, thank God, and her blond curls floating on the water. As his heart rate returned to something near normal he saw the neatly folded stack of clothes on the rock, the towel and blanket waiting beside them.

"Are you all right?" he called, and she lifted her head.

Her chin touched the surface of the water, but Maddalyn had apparently forgotten how clear the water was. She was totally bare, and he had an unobstructed view of her breasts, her shoulders, her waist and hips. She had a perfect shape, flawless skin, and it would be so easy to walk into the water and join her.

"It's l-like ice!" she called, her teeth chattering.

"Yes," Eric agreed, "it is." The water danced around her as she moved, distorting his view. "What are you doing?"

"S-s-s-swimming," she called, hugging her arms to her chest and covering her breasts.

"This water's too cold to swim in this time of year." Eric walked out onto the rock and picked up Maddalyn's clothing, the towel and blanket.

"I know that now," she snapped. "What are you doing with my things?"

Eric returned to the bank. "Nothing. You can walk out here easier than you can climb the rock."

He placed her neatly folded clothing on the ground, and held the towel and blanket. Waiting.

"Well, you're going to have to leave," she insisted. Her lips were turning blue.

"I know," he conceded, but he didn't move.

"Eric! I'm going to freeze to death!"

He felt almost sorry for her. Her lips were trembling; her whole body was shaking. "How about if I turn my back?"

"Eric!" she screamed.

"Maddalyn," he answered calmly, "I think it's a little late for modesty. Look down."

She did, and a groan of dismay escaped her trembling lips as she looked down at her own shaking hand through the clear water.

Eric turned his back then, holding the towel over one shoulder and the blanket over the other. He listened as Maddalyn left the lake, splashing the water with every step until she was on solid ground. He didn't have to turn around. He could see her clearly in his mind, stepping through the shallow water near the bank, emerging from the lake with her arms across her chest and her hair hanging over her shoulders and down her back.

The towel was yanked out of his hand; the blanket followed fairly quickly.

"You're not a gentleman," she accused hotly.

He listened with punishing intensity as she rubbed the towel over her skin. "Never claimed to be one."

He turned around. Maddalyn was holding the

blanket around her and trying to dry her hair with the towel. She was shaking violently, her lips were still blue, and she didn't protest when he took the towel from her and began to dry her hair for her, rubbing the damp cloth briskly over the wet tresses. It curled, wild yellow spirals in his hands and down her back.

"Whatever possessed you to go swimming?" he asked.

"The lake looked so beautiful, and Conrad said—"

"Conrad," Eric interrupted. "I can only guess that's why I was the only one who jumped out of my skin when you screamed. One of Conrad's stupid jokes."

"It wasn't funny," Maddalyn insisted. "Not at all."

Eric ran the towel down the length of Maddalyn's hair, and then he dropped it to the ground. He had a feeling this was one joke Conrad hadn't intended to be funny.

He pulled Maddalyn's back against his chest and wrapped his arms around her. She was still trembling, still cold to the bone.

"What are you doing?" she asked quietly.

"Trying to get you warm."

"Oh." It was a whisper, an exhaled breath.

He could feel her body beneath the thin blanket, the curve of her backside, the trembling that wouldn't subside. This wasn't a joke; this was torture. Conrad knew he wouldn't leave her alone, cold and shivering. Did he know that it was harder every day to resist her?

Eric turned Maddalyn so that her face was against his chest, and she circled easily, without protest. She rested a cheek against his chest, curled into him, and he did his best to surround her completely.

His erection was pressed against her belly, and Eric wondered if Maddalyn had any idea what she'd done, what she did to him whenever she looked at him or touched him.

It was Maddalyn who lifted her lips to him, and Eric bent to take her mouth. At first touch her lips were cold, but they warmed quickly under his. She needed no encouragement to part her lips and tease him with her tongue, tasting him as he tasted her.

A hand snaked from beneath the blanket, and she laid her palm against his neck. Fingers brushed his jaw, light, feathery touches against his newly shaven skin.

It was so easy to lose himself completely in her warm mouth and cool skin. He closed his eyes and allowed himself to forget that she was a lady, that she wanted more than he could ever give her. He was tired of fighting, tired of pretending that he didn't want her.

She returned his kisses ardently, almost feverishly, and Eric threaded his fingers through her wet hair, buried his hands in the thick golden tresses while she drove him wild with her unrestrained responses.

Eric slipped his hand inside the blanket and cupped a silky breast, caressing the silky-soft skin beneath his fingers. Maddalyn gasped when he brushed his thumb against a taut nipple, but she didn't pull away. Her breathing changed, became more rapid and insistent, and she deepened their kiss, driving her tongue into his mouth.

He wanted her. He could take her now, here on the ground. Bury himself inside her and be done with this obsession once and for all.

He let his hand slide down her side, over satin skin. Across the curve of her hip, to the small of her back, and down to caress two intriguing dimples. He moved slowly, waiting for her to pull away, to protest his actions and proclaim her innocence.

But she didn't. She opened her mouth to him, pressed her body against his, moaned deep in her throat.

Eric held her tightly and allowed his hands to roam over Maddalyn's flesh that was no longer cold. She responded to his every touch, pressing herself harder and harder against him. Her lips, her chest, her hips. She had to be able to feel his throbbing erection pressed against her. She had to know they had gone too far to stop.

"Time's up!"

Maddalyn drew her lips away from his. "What was that?"

"Conrad, I think." Eric continued to hold her tight, refusing to release her.

"What does that mean, 'time's up'?" Her eyes were dazed, her lips were red and swollen, her breath was coming as fast as his was.

"It means I wish right now that I was an only child. It means if I don't get back to camp in a hurry, they're coming after me."

"Oh," she whispered, her mouth puckering so prettily he felt compelled to kiss her again before he released her. She kissed him back with a desperation he felt to his very core. He didn't want to leave her there, quivering and clutching the blanket, but he had no choice.

Eric stalked back into camp, only to find Karl and Conrad sitting calmly by the fire, coffee cups cradled in their hands. Conrad was smiling wickedly, and Karl . . . Karl's face was strangely impassive. Eric presented himself to his oldest brother, arms out, feet planted far apart.

"Go ahead," Eric said in a low voice. "Let's get this over with."

Karl didn't stand. He raked his eyes over Eric from his boots to the top of his head. "Not this time."

"What do you mean, 'not this time'?" Eric asked, refusing to move. "If ever I deserved it . . ."

"Don't press your luck," Conrad called. Eric ignored him.

"It was more than a simple little kiss this time," Eric said through clenched teeth. "I thought you were Maddalyn Kelly's staunch protector."

"It couldn't have been much more than a simple kiss," Conrad muttered. "I was very careful about the timing. . . ." He might as well have been talking to himself.

"Conrad explained to me that a solid punch or two might take your mind off of your . . . obvious discomfort," Karl said seriously. "I think you've suffered enough." He grinned briefly. "I think you're suffering plenty right now."

Eric turned his attention to Conrad. "You're the one who should be pounded, telling Maddalyn it was safe to swim here. Letting her jump into that icy water."

"I knew you'd be there to rescue her, little brother. Besides, if Maddalyn can play matchmaker, why can't I?"

"Because you're terrible at it," Maddalyn said, stalking into camp. She headed directly for Conrad and pulled back her hand, as if to slap him.

But she didn't. She lowered her hand slowly.

"My, but you dressed quickly," Conrad said with an innocent smile.

"My cold bones were great incentive."

"Forgive me?" Conrad begged insincerely.

"Never," Maddalyn said, and then she sat down beside Conrad, paying the dirt no heed. "I should give you a lesson in matchmaking if you're determined to try your hand at the craft. First of all, your subjects must not be completely averse to the idea of marriage. A confirmed bachelor, such as your little brother Eric, makes a poor candidate. Trying to truss him to a woman who's on her way to a new life elsewhere only adds another element of stupidity to your scheme."

For the first time since entering the camp she looked at Eric, and she tried to smile. She did a poor job of it. She'd lost that happily dazed look she'd had when he'd been forced to pull away from her. There she was, chin up and spine straight, ready to take on the world if she had to.

"All your efforts, Conrad, gone to waste," she said, but her eyes were glued to Eric.

She was a wanton, no better than one of Conrad's hurdy-girls.

Maddalyn faced the dying fire, her hands beneath her cheek. It had felt so terribly wonderful, standing there and kissing Eric, the touch of his hands on her body. She hadn't wanted to stop. She *wouldn't* have stopped if Conrad hadn't called out.

She was a lustful woman, a hussy, just as Aunt Ethel had claimed when she'd caught Maddalyn kissing Lawrence.

Of course, this was much more serious. Lawrence's kiss had been . . . not even all that pleasant. Cold and wet and quick.

She could still feel the heat, the insistent need that had come over her when Eric had touched her, and it was warm and wonderful and frustrating all at once.

She wanted it again. The kissing and the touching. The loss of control that was so exhilarating. The resounding beat that coursed through her body. And she wanted more. Needed it. She wanted Eric. Perhaps she wasn't truly wanton if her desire was for only one man.

If she rolled over she would see him just a few feet away, sleeping on his own bedroll. Karl and Eric were there as well, the three of them lined up less than five feet from her bedroll.

Had any woman ever been more protected? They'd placed her bedroll nearest the fire, and then positioned themselves so that she was surrounded.

No, she wouldn't turn. It would only torment her to watch Eric sleeping so near.

What on earth had come over her? She couldn't allow what she wanted so desperately. If she fell any deeper in love with Eric it would surely ruin her life.

Oh, but it had been pure heaven.

Maddalyn forced her eyes closed. She would think of him as she fell asleep, remember clearly the stroke of his hand against her body, the feel of his mouth on hers.

Perhaps in her dreams, Conrad wouldn't call.

Olympia was a nice-size township, larger than Maddalyn had imagined. She had been expecting a village at the foot of the mountains, a single street with the necessary shops.

There was a main street where it seemed most

of the businesses were located, but there were several cross streets, lovely houses bordered with white fences and flowers, and people . . . people everywhere. On the raised boardwalk and in the street, looking through windows and riding on horseback.

Karl led the way to the hotel, a three-story building that seemed to have a fresh coat of paint. He sent Conrad in to secure rooms, and Eric assisted Maddalyn from her mule.

She'd tried to ignore him, thinking it best for everyone's sake, but it wasn't easy. The attraction had only been intensified. She could now add to that attraction frustration, pure and simple.

Eric held on to her for longer than was necessary.

"I don't want you to fall," he explained.

"Thank you." Maddalyn stared at his chest. It seemed a perfectly safe portion of his body to peruse. "I think I can stand on my own now."

He released her slowly and she turned to the hotel. "It looks quite nice," she said innocently.

"It is."

"You've stayed here before?"

"Many times," he whispered.

Maddalyn lifted her eyes to the windows on the third floor. "I can't wait to settle in."

"Neither can I," Eric said as he began to unload the pack mule. His voice was so low, Maddalyn was quite sure no one else could hear him. "It's where we'll finish what we started."

He passed her, carrying two bags in his hands, glancing at her briefly but so hard she trembled. There was a new and almost passive expression on his face, but she wasn't indifferent to the burning fire in his eyes.

That fire frightened her. She understood it too well, understood that Eric shared her frustration.

She wondered if he'd dreamed of her last night, as she had dreamed of him just a few feet away. Her dreams had been wonderful, reckless, surprisingly desperate.

But they had been only dreams. As difficult as it might be, Maddalyn knew that she could never give herself to a man who didn't love her. It was all she demanded of life, real and true love. A man who cared for her deeply, a husband she could count on to be there when she needed him. To love her in good times and bad.

Eric refused to give that much of himself away. As tempting as it was, Maddalyn knew she couldn't take comfort in the arms of a man who cared nothing for her, and she could never convince herself that the love she needed didn't matter.

Her love for Eric had never wavered, and in moments of weakness she began to believe that she could love enough for both of them, that her love alone would be enough.

But it wasn't.

How could she tell him that they could never finish what they'd started on the bank of the lake?

Chapter Fourteen

Eric watched Maddalyn enter the hotel, Karl at her side. She didn't look back, not once, and that was not a good sign. Not at all.

The trap had closed completely. Surely she knew that.

She had become his obsession, a fixation as strong and illogical as Conrad's fancy for redheads.

A sobering thought occurred to him as the hotel doors closed on Maddalyn and Karl. What if, now that he wanted her to distraction, she was finished with him? Had that been her game all along?

No. He couldn't believe that. She would have taken him without hesitation on the lakeside.

"Eric!"

He turned toward the hearty welcome, and came face-to-face with James Colter, Daisy's father and the owner of the general store.

Eric offered his hand, and Colter grasped it heartily.

"I was hoping you boys would be here soon. I have a business proposal for you." His wide grin told Eric it was something big.

Eric always handled the logging business. Karl was too quiet, too easily swayed. Conrad was too quick to make a deal over a couple of drinks, a girl on each knee and a half-empty bottle of whiskey on the table.

"Railway ties," Colter said without further delay. "The Burlington Railroad's headed this way, Eric, and I've spoken to a couple of their officials. They're looking for ties, as many as you can provide, and they'll need lumber for a number of depots, as well. We're talking top dollar here, Eric."

Eric could only assume that Colter was looking to be the middle man, to make a little profit for himself. It was only fair. Eric would be happy to pay if it meant he didn't have to deal with the railroad employees.

Karl and Conrad could have their money in the bank. Maybe then they'd forget about this ranching business and leave his mountain just as it was.

Eric followed Colter to the general store, with a promise of a cool glass of Daisy's lemonade.

"Who was the, ummm, lady I saw going into the hotel with Karl?" Colter asked casually. Eric didn't like the way he hemmed and hawed before the word *lady*.

Someone's Been Sleeping in My Bed

"Maddalyn Kelly," Eric said, stepping onto the boardwalk and into the shade. "A schoolteacher headed for Sheridan. Her stage was robbed, and she ended up staying at the cabin for a few weeks."

"I see," Colter said, the tone of his voice implying that he certainly did *not* see.

Eric had no intention of explaining how Maddalyn had climbed the mountain. How he had followed her and found her huddled in a cold cave.

While the Colters' general store wasn't ever dirty, Eric had never stepped in the place that it hadn't been filled to capacity with goods. Every inch of space was well used, even the counter that was just inside the door, giving the place a cluttered look. There was a pile of cookbooks, candy, tobacco, all there on the counter.

Eric stepped behind the counter, out of the way of the flow of any traffic that might pass through the door.

Daisy Colter brought him a glass of lemonade while her father ran home to collect the notes he had prepared on their prospective deal with the railroad. She didn't even look at him, not really. Her eyes were cast down, and Eric leaned against the wall and took a good, hard look as Daisy walked away.

She was a good-looking woman, with dark hair and high cheekbones, dark brown eyes, a nice figure. The only problem was she was taller than most of the men in Olympia. Not gangly at all, just tall.

Eric suppressed a smile. She wouldn't stand a

211

chance against Maddalyn.

He thought for a moment he had conjured up her voice. A bright hello in that Southern accent. She hadn't wasted a moment. Eric dropped down so that he was concealed behind the counter, hidden from Maddalyn's view. He took a sip of cool lemonade, sat down with his back to the wall, and prepared himself to be entertained.

"I'm not normally so brazen," she began, and Eric almost choked on his lemonade. "You must be Daisy Colter," Maddalyn said. "Let me introduce myself. Maddalyn Lorraine Kelly. I know I should have waited to be properly introduced, but I may only be in town for a few days."

"You rode in with the Barretts, didn't you?" Daisy asked, her voice soft.

"Yes, I did. Lovely men, aren't they?" Maddalyn confided in a low voice.

"Ummm, well . . ." Daisy stammered, being well aware of his presence.

"Not perfect, of course," Maddalyn continued, "but they're really quite nice, when you get to know them. Oh, I must ask you, Miss Colter . . ."

"Daisy."

There was a brief pause, and Eric could only imagine the bright smile that would cross Maddalyn's face.

"Daisy," Maddalyn repeated. "Are you presently being courted? Are you engaged? Are you spoken for in any way?"

"No, but . . ." Daisy still didn't have a chance to

warn Maddalyn that Eric was sitting behind the counter, listening to every word.

"I have a proposition for you, Daisy," Maddalyn said. "Is there someplace we can talk more privately?"

Eric cursed silently as Daisy led Maddalyn to the back of the store. He could hear her voice, hushed, conspiratorial, excited.

Karl was as good as married.

"There's to be a dance social on Friday," Maddalyn said brightly as she cut into her steak. The Olympia Hotel dining room left much to be desired, in her opinion, but the men seemed to enjoy the platters of meat and potatoes that had been set before them.

The table was a little small, especially for Karl, and they continually brushed elbows. Nothing was spilled, however, and no one seemed put out by the inconvenience.

"A dance!" Conrad replied with evident excitement.

"Yes. In the saloon, of all places," Maddalyn revealed. "Daisy assures me that when the place is cleaned up and decorated it will suit just fine."

Karl didn't say a word. He stared down at his plate and ate without comment.

"It will be a wonderful opportunity for Karl to socialize with Daisy. Dancing, refreshments . . ."

"I've changed my mind," Karl mumbled.

"What?"

"This was a mistake," he said more clearly. "Maybe next time I come to town I can talk to her pa, walk with her, maybe."

Maddalyn sighed dramatically. "You can't do this to me, Karl." It wouldn't do to tell him that she'd already spoken to Daisy about the possibility of marriage, that Daisy was more than interested. You couldn't push a man like Karl too hard. He might push back. "Can't we just give this a few days and see how things progress?"

"Why don't I just ask her tonight?" Karl suggested. "Run on up to her house and tell her I'd been thinking of getting hitched and thought she'd do just fine."

"No," Maddalyn said sternly. "A woman is courted by her prospective husband for such a short time, it should be special. Memorable. Something to recall when you come in late after a hard day and forget to tell her how beautiful she is. When you forget her birthday, or track mud onto a clean kitchen floor."

She'd been neatly ignoring Eric, for the most part, even though he was seated at her right side. Evidently he was tired of being ignored. He placed his hand on her knee, beneath the table and the tablecloth that hung clear to her lap, and Maddalyn used all her calm reserve not to jump out of her chair.

"I can't—" Karl began.

"Of course you can," Maddalyn said with a smile directed only at Karl. She lifted the linen napkin from her lap, dabbed it at the corners of her mouth, and when she returned it to her lap she quickly brushed Eric's hand off of her knee.

Not that it did any good. The hand returned, but this time it was placed higher on her leg, on her thigh. He moved his fingers just a little, brushing them against the calico, barely pressing into her skin. Maddalyn knew her face was red. She could feel the heat in her cheeks.

"You don't understand—" Karl began.

"I understand perfectly well," Maddalyn said brightly. "You're nervous, and rightly so. This is a big step, but it's the right one, Karl."

Impossibly, Eric's hand climbed her thigh, inching upward slowly. She finally gave in and looked at him, only to find a half-smile plastered to his face, a wicked gleam in his eyes. He was tormenting her. He knew she wouldn't make a scene in a public place. When she locked her eyes on his, those fingers inched higher. Good heavens, any higher and he'd be . . .

"Something wrong with your steak, Eric?" Conrad asked casually. "You've hardly touched it."

"I'm enjoying the potatoes," Eric growled, but the smile never left his face.

Conrad placed his own knife and fork on his plate, and leaned forward. "Enjoy the steak."

Those fingers trailed down her leg slowly, as Eric removed his hand from her lap. Maddalyn recovered from her shock and kicked him soundly in the shin.

Oddly, throughout the scene Karl didn't even lift his eyes from his plate.

"Really, Karl," Maddalyn said, doing her best to reassure the big man. "There's nothing for you to worry about."

He lifted his eyes to her then, and Maddalyn could see that he was truly worried. Not terrified, exactly, but not all that far from terror, either.

"I can't dance," he said softly. "I'll make a fool of myself if I go to that social."

"Oh, Karl," Maddalyn whispered. "We have two days. I can teach you to dance."

He shook his head, but Maddalyn was determined.

Eric had behaved himself for a few moments, wolfing down a large portion of his steak to appease Conrad. But now he returned his left hand to his lap, and a moment later it was perched on her knee once again. It inched upward.

It wasn't that the feel of his hand on her leg was unpleasant. It certainly was not. His hands were large and strong, his fingers long and callused—but he knew how to be gentle.

But to take such liberties in a public place, carrying out his assault beneath the tablecloth, and with his brothers present—it was shocking. Very improper, in fact, even if it did feel quite nice. Even if it did make her heart beat fast and her temperature rise in a most pleasant manner.

"All three of you in my room," Maddalyn said sweetly. "Half an hour." She stood abruptly, and

Eric's hand fell from her leg. Maddalyn backed away from the table, bumping her elbow against the tall glass of water near the corner of the table. It fell, almost as if she'd intended it, directly into Eric's lap.

"Oh, dear," she said, snatching up her napkin and trying to mop up some of the water that dampened his trousers, patting the linen against his thighs. "How very clumsy of me."

"Indeed," he growled.

"Indeed," she answered with a broad smile.

"I'll do it," Eric said, snatching the napkin from her hand.

"Of course," Maddalyn said, standing tall. She lowered her voice. "I'm so sorry.

"Thirty minutes," she said, raising her voice and speaking to all three of the brothers as brightly as she could manage.

"Like this," Maddalyn instructed primly, looking up into Karl's solemn face. "One, two, three . . ." It was like trying to dance with a boulder. "You *do* have to move."

Her room was very nice, and she had not seen a single insect, thankfully. The bed that had been pushed against one wall was wide, though it was not as large as Eric's bed, and the dresser and single chair were polished and solidly built. There was even a pale yellow curtain in the window that faced the street.

Conrad and Eric watched, neither of them daring to say a word. The clearing in the middle of her room was not spacious by any means, but it would do for Karl's lesson. If only he would cooperate.

"It's very simple. We'll start with a slow waltz, and then pick up the pace a bit."

Still he refused to move. "I can't," he said somberly. "You're too small. If I trip and fall I'll crush you, or break something. . . ."

Maddalyn smiled, but she didn't laugh. Karl's fears, about dancing and Daisy and crushing a too small dance partner, were very real. She released Karl's hand and turned to his brothers.

Eric and Conrad sat on the edge of the bed, not daring to show that they were being entertained. Conrad grinned as always, and Eric watched with an air of detachment. He had changed into a clean and dry pair of trousers, and he hadn't said a single word about her clumsiness.

"Conrad," Maddalyn said with a bright smile, "you'll be Daisy."

"I beg your pardon?" His grin faded.

"You did say that you were about the same height." It seemed a reasonable request to her.

"Yes, but . . ."

"And I know you would do anything for your big brother," she cajoled.

Moments later, Conrad and Karl stood face-to-face, the very picture of motionless dancers. Conrad scowled, but Karl was taking the lesson seriously.

"Do you dance, Conrad?"

"Not like this," he grumbled. "Might as well tie a kerchief to my arm and let the soldiers line up for a jig."

Maddalyn ignored him. "Can you sing? Never mind. Music would probably only confuse us at the moment."

She guided them, step by step, with her hands resting lightly on their arms. Conrad was a fair dancer, but he kept wanting to take the lead. Karl stumbled and almost fell, and Maddalyn was thankful not to be in Conrad's place, after all.

She had patience, and wouldn't dare let her despair show, but it looked to be a hopeless cause. All Karl did was stumble.

"All right," she said, repositioning Karl's hands. "Let's try again."

"It's no use—" he began.

"Like this," Eric said. Before Maddalyn knew what was happening, he had her in his arms. Eric stood beside Karl, and Maddalyn was next to Conrad. "Do what I do," Eric said to Karl.

His steps were slow, calculating, and Karl mimicked Eric perfectly.

"If anyone ever finds out about this . . ." Conrad mumbled.

Eric picked up the pace slightly, and Maddalyn took her eyes off of Karl's big booted feet.

They were dancing. There was no music, and what she wore was far from a fancy gown, but Eric held her in his arms and they danced.

She lifted her eyes to him, and he smiled. Not an

insolent grin like the one he'd worn earlier. There
was a touch of real happiness in this smile.

He was so handsome without his beard. If they'd
been alone she would've reached up and traced the
line of his jaw with her fingers. It was strong and
angular, with just a touch of a pale beard at the
end of the day.

It would be rough beneath her fingertips, compared to the smoothness of his full lips. His mouth
had such a lovely shape, such an attractive hue.

He held her too close. Surely when they'd begun
she hadn't been pressed against him like this. He
was moving too fast, spinning her around on the
too small dance floor, taking her breath away.

She held his hand tightly, and she didn't want to
let go. Ever.

What if they never danced like this again? She
savored the moment, finally endeavoring to return
Eric's smile. For a few moments the man she loved
held her fast and they danced.

It was the applause that broke the spell, and
Maddalyn whipped her head around to find that
Karl and Conrad were standing against the wall.
Watching.

Eric stopped, and Karl began to shake his head.
"I can't do that."

"Of course you can," Eric assured him. "Practice
with Conrad."

Conrad objected, but soon they were dancing,
side by side, the lesson under way once again.

Eric held her at a proper distance, and their

movements were slow so that Karl could follow.

"Will you dance with me on Friday?" Eric asked quietly. His moves were effortless, easy, and Maddalyn felt at home in his arms.

"Of course," she said, and her heartbeat quickened. "You need only to ask."

"I want you to save me every dance," he insisted hoarsely.

"That would be highly improper."

"Propriety be damned," he growled, never missing a beat of their musicless dance.

Chapter Fifteen

The hotel room he shared with his brothers was too small, but Eric admitted to himself that it would have felt that way even if it had been the size of the dining room downstairs.

It wasn't just the room, it was the town. Buildings on all sides, people everywhere, and the noise . . . even now, the laughter and shouts from the saloon reached his ears. Muffled sounds of merriment broken by an occasional moment of silence.

The window was open, but the air remained stuffy. No lamp burned, but the room was lit well enough by a full moon. Karl was snoring lightly, spread across the bed that was much too small for his frame. And Conrad, well, Conrad was raising the noise level in Olympia a notch or two, adding to the sounds of merriment coming from the saloon.

And Maddalyn slept right next door.

She hadn't known that Karl had specifically requested these rooms. Hers was at the end of the hall, so that anyone going to Maddalyn's room would have to pass by this one first. They would hear any noise, a soft knock on her door, a cry in the night.

Not that Karl expected any sort of trouble in Olympia. It was a quiet place, for the most part. There was a well-known canyon hideout that was not too far from Olympia, but the hideaway was closer to Buffalo, and that was where the outlaws did their drinking and hell-raising. Still, his oldest brother had become protective of Maddalyn quickly. Overly protective, Eric thought sometimes, though he wasn't certain why. Maybe because they'd had no sisters, because their mother had died so young, and he was unaccustomed to the daily presence of a woman.

Eric suspected it was deeper than that. Maddalyn had come to them with all the force of an unexpected blizzard, and had become a part of their lives. She'd done her best to take care of all three of them. Cooking, mending, cajoling. Laughing at Conrad's lame jokes. Taking an interest in their future. Why else would she be so set on seeing Karl married?

Eric stepped over the bedroll that he'd tossed across the floor for himself, and opened the door

Thrill to the most sensual, adventure-filled Romances on the market today...

FROM  ✦ LOVE SPELL BOOKS

As a home subscriber to the Love Spell Romance Book Club, you'll enjoy the best in today's BRAND-NEW Time Travel, Futuristic, Legendary Lovers, Perfect Heroes and other genre romance fiction. For five years, Love Spell has brought you the award-winning, high-quality authors you know and love to read. Each Love Spell romance will sweep you away to a world of high adventure...and intimate romance. Discover for yourself all the passion and excitement millions of readers thrill to each and every month.

Save $5.00 Each Time You Buy!

Every other month, the Love Spell Romance Book Club brings you four brand-new titles from Love Spell Books. EACH PACKAGE WILL SAVE YOU AT LEAST $5.00 FROM THE BOOK-STORE PRICE! And you'll never miss a new title with our convenient home delivery service.

Here's how we do it: Each package will carry a FREE 10-DAY EXAMINATION privilege. At the end of that time, if you decide to keep your books, simply pay the low invoice price of $17.96, no shipping or handling charges added. HOME DELIVERY IS ALWAYS FREE. With today's top romance novels selling for $5.99 and higher, our price SAVES YOU AT LEAST $5.00 with each shipment.

AND YOUR FIRST TWO-BOOK SHIP-MENT IS TOTALLY FREE!

IT'S A BARGAIN YOU CAN'T BEAT! A SUPER $11.48 Value!

Love Spell ✦ A Division of Dorchester Publishing Co., Inc.

GET YOUR 2 FREE BOOKS
NOW–AN $11.48 VALUE!

*Mail the Free Book
Certificate Today!*

Free Books Certificate

YES! I want to subscribe to the Love Spell Romance Book Club. Please send me my 2 FREE BOOKS. Then every other month I'll receive the four newest Love Spell selections to Preview FREE for 10 days. If I decide to keep them, I will pay the Special Member's Only discounted price of just $4.49 each, a total of $17.96. This is a SAVINGS of at least $5.00 off the bookstore price. There are no shipping, handling, or other charges. There is no minimum number of books I must buy and I may cancel the program at any time. In any case, the 2 FREE BOOKS are mine to keep—A BIG $11.48 Value!

Offer valid only in the U.S.A.

Name_____

Address_____

City_____

State _____ Zip _____

Telephone_____

Signature_____

If under 18, Parent or Guardian must sign. Terms, prices and conditions subject to change. Subscription subject to acceptance. Leisure Books reserves the right to reject any order or cancel any subscription.

A
$11.48
VALUE

Get Two Books Totally
FREE —
An $11.48 Value!

▼ Tear Here and Mail Your FREE Book Card Today! ▼

PLEASE RUSH
MY TWO FREE
BOOKS TO ME
RIGHT AWAY!

Love Spell Romance Book Club
P.O. Box 6613
Edison, NJ 08818-6613

slowly. At least it didn't creak. He couldn't take it anymore, being this close to Maddalyn and not touching her. Knowing that she would welcome him into her bed. After the way she'd responded to him by the lake, he knew all it would take was a kiss.

There was a light burning down the hall, and it illuminated the figure who sat on the floor, his back to the wall, his hat down over his eyes. It was Conrad, and he had placed himself beside Maddalyn's door.

As Eric closed the door, Conrad lifted his face and grinned. "Good evening, little brother," he whispered.

"I thought you were at the saloon, or at Annie's," Eric whispered in a gruff voice.

"Nope. I'm on watch. In a couple of hours Karl takes over here and I get the bed." Conrad patted the carpeted floor he sat upon. "Can't sleep?"

"I didn't know we were standing guard," Eric said, lowering himself to his brother's side. "If you're tired, or if you want to go to Annie's for a while . . ."

Conrad snorted softly. "And leave the fox guarding the henhouse?"

"I suppose this was Karl's idea," Eric grumbled.

"Actually, it was mine," Conrad revealed, his voice filled with humor. "Karl was too preoccupied to notice what was going on at the supper table tonight, but I wasn't." The sideways glance Conrad shot his way held no humor at all. "If she's got you in such a knot, maybe you're the one who should go to Annie's."

It made perfect sense, but Eric knew a visit to Annie's wouldn't cure him, and he had no desire, at the moment, to lose himself in any calico cat's bed. Only Maddalyn would do. "Since when have the two of you decided to take up personal security again?" He couldn't disguise the bite in his voice.

"She deserves better," Conrad whispered.

"Then what was that stunt by the lake all about? Are you trying to kill me?"

"Just trying to bring you to your senses, little brother."

"It didn't work," Eric grumbled.

"I know."

Eric didn't have any desire to return to the room where Karl snored, at the moment. Sleep wasn't going to come quickly tonight, if it came at all, so he stretched out his legs and made himself comfortable there on the floor at Conrad's side.

"She is beautiful, isn't she?" Eric asked after several moments of companionable silence.

Conrad agreed with a low hum.

"She's different." It was inadequate, as a description, but accurate.

Conrad hummed again.

The silence stretched between them before Conrad spoke. "You could marry her," he suggested seriously.

"No, I can't," Eric informed his brother without revealing the bitterness that rose within him. "She can fix Karl up with Daisy, and find you a redhead, but I'm not getting married."

"She could make us gingerbread, even if I was wed to a redhead," Conrad said with a smile.

"Don't mention gingerbread to me now."

"Why not? I love Maddalyn's gingerbread."

"Shut up, Conrad," Eric growled.

"Well, if you're not going to marry her you're going to have to keep your distance," Conrad insisted softly.

"I know."

"She's too good for someone who only wants to screw her."

Eric's head snapped up at the crude, harshly spoken words. "I know that, too."

He should've returned to the room he shared with his brothers, but instead he remained where he was, sitting on the floor with his back to the wall and a surprisingly quiet Conrad at his side.

Five years ago he'd vowed never to marry again. How deeply was he bound by a pledge made when he was only twenty-four years old? A vow made when he was consumed with anger and confusion?

"She wouldn't stay," he whispered.

"Maddalyn?" Conrad asked.

"There's not enough for her there. It's isolated, lonely at times. It's cold in the wintertime, and the living is simple all year round."

"She doesn't seem to mind," Conrad whispered.

"She was only there for a few weeks. Can't you see it in her? She needs people. Nice things.

Linda Jones

Clothes and jewelry and parties and music. Didn't you see how excited she was about the dance?"

"You're selling her short, little brother. I didn't see any of that. You're still confusing her with Jane, and that's a very big mistake."

"They're both ladies."

"You said yourself that Maddalyn is different."

Eric shook his head. It was too much to ask for. He'd be satisfied to have her in his bed just once.

Maddalyn smiled down at the sleeping man on the floor. Poor Karl, all scrunched up like that, his head on his chest. She knew he'd been guarding her door, though she couldn't imagine what for . . . unless he was protecting her from his own brother.

The door just down the hall from hers opened quietly, and Eric took a quiet step into the hallway. He smiled at her, glanced down at Karl, and motioned for her to join him. Maddalyn stepped over Karl's stretched-out legs, lifting her red calico skirt so that it didn't drag across those long legs.

Eric held a finger to his lips, and then he led her silently down the hallway and down the stairs.

"Where are you headed?" he asked as they stepped from the hotel lobby onto the boardwalk. The morning sun slanted under the overhang. Maddalyn stood in the shade, but Eric was flooded with sunlight. It lit the golden highlights in his hair, and all but blinded her when she tried to keep her eyes on him.

"I should see the sheriff, don't you think? And

228

report what happened to the stage I was on? I assume it's been found by now." She tried to think not of the bodies, but instead of the abandoned stagecoach. It was impossible to see one without the other.

"You're right," Eric said. He walked close beside her, between her and the street. It was early, but there were lots of people out and about. "Sheriff Langston is . . . well, not much of a sheriff, but Olympia really isn't a very exciting town. Not enough money changing hands to attract many outlaws. Langston will probably just make a report to the stage line office and let them handle it."

"Well, I'll feel better when it's done."

Eric slanted his head to look at her, as if he were studying her as intently as he had her first day in the cabin, when he'd watched her from the photograph. "Are you worried about talking to the sheriff?"

"Just a little," she confided. "I've never had to . . . handle such business before."

He pointed out the building at the end of the street, a separate structure that he said contained the jail and the sheriff's office.

They were almost there before he spoke again. "What do you think of Olympia?" It was a casually asked question, the kind you might ask a newcomer you barely knew.

"It's very nice," Maddalyn answered, watching him closely. "And the people here seem friendly enough."

"For the most part," he agreed.

"You sound like you have reservations," Maddalyn said lightly.

"Well, it's all right. It's just different."

Maddalyn laughed. He was so transparent. "You're missing your mountain already, aren't you?"

He shrugged his shoulders, but there was a small smile on his face. "I guess that's hard for you to understand."

"No. I understand quite well. Up there everything's bright and green and beautiful. And quiet. I noticed that right away, you know."

"Did you?"

"As I was climbing the mountain, I stopped for a moment and held my breath, and listened to absolutely nothing. It should have been frightening, I suppose, because it only confirmed my belief that I was all alone in the middle of nowhere. But it was strangely peaceful. I'm afraid you're spoiling me. Why, last night it took me forever to get to sleep. People upstairs, people downstairs, people on the street. I swear, Eric, I think there were people in the hallway whispering into the wee hours of the morning."

His smile had faded, and in fact a small frown crossed his face. His brow was furrowed, and there were deep lines around his mouth.

"Is this it?" she asked when they came upon the building Eric had pointed out to her moments earlier.

"Yes," he said, oddly distracted. He opened the door for her and she stepped inside.

There was a man sitting at a weathered desk, his feet up, a tin cup and a pot of coffee sitting in front of him. He appeared to be half asleep.

The sheriff's eyes opened wide, though, as Eric closed the door, and he watched them with intense dark eyes.

"Where's Sheriff Langston?" Eric asked sharply.

"Retired." The new sheriff rose slowly from his seat. "You must be one of the Barretts."

"Eric."

"Kelvin MacIver." The sheriff offered his hand over the desk and Eric took it. "What can I do for you?"

"This is Maddalyn Kelly. She ran into some trouble a few weeks back. . . ."

"Maddalyn Kelly," Sheriff MacIver repeated, for the first time turning his sharp eyes to her. "Stagecoach robbery, right?"

"Yes," she said softly. "I was able to escape, but then I was trapped on the mountain by the snow."

He didn't give her much of a chance to talk, but only to answer the questions he fired at her. Had she seen the men? Could she describe them? Would she know them if she saw them again? Distinguishing marks? Accents? She told him about the limp, and that one of the bandits had been rather fat. That they both had gray hair, and that she was certain they were not young men.

It was dreadful. She saw the outlaws as she described them, relived quietly the fear and horror she'd felt as they'd killed the driver and Mr. Harrison.

The sheriff did, at last, offer her a chair, and she sank down gratefully. It was horrid, reliving every moment, seeing those men in her mind again.

Fortunately Eric stayed right beside her, and she was so grateful he had met her coming out of her room. She couldn't have faced the sheriff alone. He pressed her, harder and harder, until Eric insisted that he stop.

"Sheriff MacIver, might I ask you a question?" Maddalyn asked.

He smiled widely, wrinkling a somewhat handsome face, and she almost forgave him his vigilance. "Of course, Miss Kelly."

"Is there any chance of recovering what was lost? I'm not concerned about the clothes, or even about the small amount of money I had in my trunk. But my pearls. I would so much like to have them back."

"Pearls?" Eric asked softly.

"Yes," she said. "Just a small strand."

The sheriff shook his head. "I have to tell you, there's not much chance, especially after all this time. They've most likely been sold off."

"I see." Maddalyn sighed, unable to hide her disappointment.

"Pearls," Eric repeated again.

The door burst open, and a whirlwind dressed in britches and a wide-brimmed hat charged into the room. She was definitely female, no taller than Maddalyn but a bit fuller in the chest.

"You're going to have to talk to Ma," she blurted before she noticed that the sheriff was not alone. "Sorry," she said quickly. "I didn't know you were doing business, Pop. I'll come back."

"We're finished here," Maddalyn said, spying a single red curl that escaped from the too-large hat. "I'm Maddalyn Kelly, and this is Eric Barrett."

"Take off that hat, Kathleen," Sheriff MacIver ordered in a low, fatherly tone of voice. The girl did as she was told, and a mass of dark red waves fell from the confines of the hat.

Kathleen's eyes were glued to Eric, not that Maddalyn could blame her. "Where are the other two?" she asked. "There are three of you, aren't there?"

Eric lifted his eyebrows, and Maddalyn smiled. He had no idea what a picture the three brothers made, how extraordinary they were. She didn't doubt that every girl in town knew of the Barrett brothers, even if they did only make it to Olympia a few times a year. Goodness, if they knew that at least two of the Barretts were considering marriage there wouldn't be a moment's peace for anyone.

"Karl and Conrad," Maddalyn said brightly. "You must meet them, as well. Are you planning to attend the dance tomorrow evening?"

A wide grin split Kathleen's face. "Wouldn't miss it."

"Wonderful."

"Maddalyn." There was a warning in Eric's low voice, and she felt a chill run down her spine.

She ignored Eric and the chill.

"I know you have something to discuss with your father," Maddalyn said, stepping away from Eric and to Kathleen's side. The sheriff's daughter had dark brown laughing eyes, freckles across the bridge of her nose, full lips. "But I'm new to town, and there's so much about Olympia that I don't know. Would you be so kind as to acquaint me with the town and its inhabitants? Perhaps this afternoon? It's rude of me to ask, I know. . . ."

"And she's not normally so bold," Eric added lowly.

Maddalyn gave him a brief and cutting glance. Heavens! He looked like thunder!

"We could have lunch at the cafe," Kathleen suggested. "I've just been here a few months, but I can tell you everything you want to know about Olympia."

There was a bright light in Kathleen's eyes, and Maddalyn prepared herself for an equal number of questions about the Barrett brothers.

They made plans to meet, while Eric stewed. It wasn't her fault that Kathleen MacIver had fallen into her lap.

Pearls! Eric fumed as he led Maddalyn back to the hotel. He was such a fool. He'd almost convinced himself that she was better than that. Better

234

than Jane. That she might be satisfied with what he had. Pearls!

And he could hear her sweet Southern voice speaking to Sheriff MacIver. *Trapped* on the mountain. Trapped! If that was how she felt, he'd be damned before he'd ask her to return.

Conrad and Karl were pacing in the lobby, and their heads snapped to the doorway when Eric entered with Maddalyn. They looked as angry as he felt.

"Where the hell have you been?" Conrad snapped.

Maddalyn jumped in quickly. "I've been to the sheriff's office to report the robbery. He already knew, of course, and I suspect he thought I was dead, though he was too much of a gentleman to say so. Are they serving breakfast? I'm starving."

She turned toward the dining room, and the three brothers followed.

There was not a happy face among them, even as they were seated at a small table. Karl and Conrad were furious at being duped. Their charge had gotten away from them for a short time. Eric was feeling anger, disappointment, betrayal.

He had no reason to feel betrayed. None at all. Maddalyn wasn't his. She owed no loyalty to him, his mountain, his lust for her.

She had no idea what she'd done to him. She was meditative, no doubt planning a trap for Conrad.

Poor sap. Conrad didn't have any more of a chance of survival than Karl did. They were both doomed.

And all at the hand of an innocent-looking little girl with blond curls and stars in her eyes.

Chapter Sixteen

The place did have a wonderfully festive air, for a saloon, Maddalyn thought as she stepped through the bat-wing doors. The large room was well lit, and had been decorated with colorful banners and oddly attractive haphazard arrangements of spring flowers in containers of every sort: coffeepots, small bowls, even an occasional vase. There was punch in a huge bowl, and finger sandwiches on mismatched platters that were placed on the bar.

The music had already begun, provided by a trio of musicians who performed on a small stage, and several couples danced enthusiastically across the cleared floor.

Heads turned as she entered the room with Karl and Conrad directly behind her, but no one stared overlong. There were just furtive glances cast toward her and the two Barrett brothers who accompanied her.

She had no idea where the third and most stubborn of the brothers was. Eric had been curiously absent for the past couple of days, and when she had caught sight of him he'd worn a surly frown that was not—she was certain—like him at all. Perhaps staying in town was harder for him than she had imagined. Surely he would not attend the dance. If he didn't like crowds, he certainly wouldn't enjoy a social such as this one.

But he had asked her to dance—every dance. Obviously he had changed his mind, for he hadn't appeared with his brothers to escort her to the social.

Maddalyn glanced down briefly and smoothed the skirt of her dress—a simple gown borrowed from Kathleen. The material was a soft cotton, and the color was magnificent. It was a wonderfully bright blue, something Aunt Ethel would have heartily disapproved of.

Maddalyn adored it.

A rather short man dressed in clothing that was ragged but clean approached her, and Maddalyn smiled. For tonight, she would dance and smile and laugh, and she wouldn't even think about Eric Barrett. Of course, she would make certain that Karl and Daisy danced as often as possible, and it was time for Conrad to meet Kathleen.

The short man's smile died quickly as he lifted his eyes to look over Maddalyn's shoulder. Without a word, he did a quick about-face and disappeared back into the festive crowd.

"What on earth did you do?" she asked, glancing over her shoulder and up at a scowling Karl. If he scowled at every man like that, she'd likely pass the entire evening without a single dance.

"Nothing," he growled. "You don't want to dance with Lumpy. He's a no-good drifter."

Maddalyn sighed, trying to console herself with the thought that Karl only had her best interest at heart. But it would be a frustrating evening if he insisted on approving of each of her dance partners.

Another man approached, and Maddalyn smiled once again. This was a well-dressed young man, certainly not a no-good drifter like Lumpy. The gentleman returned her smile, and Maddalyn was literally swept off her feet as Conrad took her arm and all but dragged her past the young man as he led her to the dance floor.

Conrad was a good dancer, and he smiled down at her as he moved effortlessly across the floor. "Would you care to dance?" he asked belatedly.

"And if I say no?"

His grin widened. "Too late."

"Tell me." Maddalyn lifted her chin and stared into his face. "Is this how it will be all evening? Am I to be watched over like a helpless child?"

"That's a lovely dress," Conrad countered, ignoring her question. "Where did you get it?"

"I borrowed it from Kathleen," she said patiently. "You didn't answer my question."

Linda Jones

"Kathleen MacIver, the sheriff's daughter I've been hearing so much about?" Conrad's avoidance of one subject led the conversation exactly where Maddalyn wanted it to go.

Her smile widened. "Yes. I was hoping to introduce you to her tonight."

Conrad leaned in, placing his lips close to her ear. "Is she a redhead?"

Maddalyn laughed. "You are impossible. What difference could it possibly make? She's lovely, and quick-witted, and I've found her to be quite pleasant company."

"She's ugly, isn't she?" Conrad sighed.

When he saw Kathleen, she was going to knock him silly. Maddalyn chose not to tell him, at the moment, that the sheriff's daughter was very pretty, and had red hair to boot. "She most certainly is not ugly. True beauty comes from inside."

"Really ugly," Conrad muttered.

"Promise me you'll dance with her at least once," Maddalyn begged. "I told her that if she'd come to the dance, one of the Barrett brothers would dance with her. She'll be so disappointed. . . . Karl will be occupied with Daisy all evening, I suspect, and I have no idea where Eric is, so that leaves you."

Conrad looked down at her with an exaggerated grimace, as he effortlessly led her across the dance floor. "So I get stuck with her?"

"Just one single dance," Maddalyn said sweetly. "Will it really be such a chore?"

Conrad sighed dramatically, and Maddalyn

laughed. "Look," she whispered as she tilted her head and glanced past Conrad. "By the door."

Conrad spun her around, and when he saw what she had seen he smiled. A real, genuine smile that softened his sharp features.

Karl and Daisy made such a beautiful couple. Daisy was a tall girl, and did appear to be quite strong. But as Karl took her in his arms for a dance, she looked as delicate and fragile as any lady in the room. Karl towered over her, dwarfed her. Daisy had to tilt her head back to look into his face. She would've had to look down to dance with most of the men in the room.

Karl's dance lessons had paid off beautifully. He did not have Eric's or Conrad's grace, but he was confident, and moved almost easily.

"Aren't they a lovely couple?" she whispered.

"Yes, but—" Conrad began.

"Did you know that Daisy has been in love with Karl for years? She fell in love with him the first time she saw him riding into town. He walked into her father's store and ordered beans and coffee and that red calico. He looked at her just once—you know how shy Karl can be—but it was enough for Daisy." Maddalyn sighed.

"That doesn't mean they're compatible," Conrad argued. "You can't just . . ." He faltered, and Maddalyn knew he didn't want to offend her by voicing his obvious reservations.

"You don't believe in love at first sight?" Maddalyn asked.

Linda Jones

Conrad shook his head. "How can anyone? You can't tell what a person is like by their appearance. I've met some very beautiful girls who were less than beautiful inside."

"Then you shouldn't complain about dancing with Kathleen."

The grin he flashed at her was magnificent, joyful, and she wondered if Conrad had a care in the world. It didn't appear so at the moment.

"I walked right into that one, didn't I?"

"You most certainly did."

Maddalyn saw her then at the door. Bless her, Kathleen had taken Maddalyn's advice and left the boots and britches at home. Her gown was a lovely shade of green, and there was a matching ribbon in red hair that curled softly over her shoulders and down her back.

Conrad's back was to the door. "She's here," Maddalyn said softly. "Spin me around and have a look, as soon as you give me your most solemn word that you won't back out of your promise."

"I promised?"

"You did."

Conrad made a brief comical face, and then he spun her around.

She had never seen Conrad look completely amazed, but he did at the moment. There was no wicked smile, no wisecrack. Just a look of wonder in his eyes. The hand that held hers began to sweat.

"That's Kathleen MacIver?" he whispered, never taking his eyes from the door.

"Yes. You'll dance with her at least once?"

Conrad nodded, and spun around so he was no longer facing the door. He glanced down at Maddalyn with narrowed and suspicious eyes. "What I said a few minutes ago, about love at first sight being hogwash?"

"Well, that's not exactly what you said, but I do remember."

"I might have been wrong." His eyes sparkled as he lost his stunned expression and gave her a smile.

Eric leaned against a post, hidden in the shadows on the boardwalk on the opposite side of the street from the rustic building where the social was going on. Inside the saloon, people danced and laughed and waved at newcomers. The women were dressed in bright colors, and the men wore their Sunday best, starched and bathed.

He'd watched from the shadows as Karl and Conrad had escorted Maddalyn from the hotel, had seen Lumpy approach, look up into Karl's face, and do an abrupt turnaround. He'd watched without moving so much as a muscle as Conrad had spun Maddalyn onto the dance floor.

The swinging doors were open top and bottom, and so he could see a large portion of the room. Occasionally Conrad would spin Maddalyn out of his range of vision for a few moments, but they always returned to the center of the room. This happened twice before Eric realized that he held his breath when he couldn't see Maddalyn.

The realization only made him angry. She should have no power over him—none at all. She was just a pretty girl. As he tried to convince himself of that truth, Conrad dipped his head and spoke intimately into Maddalyn's ear. She smiled, and Eric's heart fell.

He wanted her too much. His fascination with her was no longer rational. Years ago he'd sworn that no woman would ever have power over his heart again. Giving up that power made a man do stupid things—make irrational decisions. It would never work. Maddalyn wanted socials and pearls—Eric wanted solitude and the necessities of life. No more.

The redhead was standing in front of the door, blocking his view, before Eric noticed her. She hesitated there, her full skirt held in her hands and off of the boardwalk. Eric saw the straightening of her back, as if she were preparing for battle, and then she passed through the swinging doors and became a part of the festivities.

Karl and his Daisy danced past, near the door. Hell, they were looking at each other like a pair of lovestruck calves. They didn't have eyes for anyone else in the room, and so the floor cleared before them, wherever their dance took them.

When the music stopped briefly, Maddalyn led Conrad to the sheriff's daughter. The music began again, and the three of them put their heads close together for only a moment before Conrad led

Kathleen MacIver onto the dance floor.

Maddalyn stood near the wide door and watched. Eric wished he could see her face. Would it be smug? Happy? She turned her head to watch Karl and Daisy dance by, and then turned her head to watch Conrad and the sheriff's redheaded daughter. Maddalyn tilted her head to one side, and the curls down her back danced slightly.

The man appeared out of nowhere, from just beyond Eric's line of view. It was a man Eric didn't know, too young and dressed like a dandy, a silly smile plastered to his face as he offered his hand to Maddalyn.

She took it.

Eric's booted feet hit the dirt of the street that separated him from the festivities. His steps were slow but long. This was a mistake. He should go back to the hotel room and let Maddalyn have her fun.

They were dancing. Maddalyn left a decent-size space between herself and the man, but she smiled up at him, and he was obviously entranced. Who wouldn't be? The woman had a smile that could take the bark off a tree, melt a frozen lake. Make a man do the most incredibly stupid things.

Eric stepped into the room, never taking his eyes from Maddalyn and the man she danced with.

Maybe it was true that he couldn't keep her, that she didn't belong on an isolated mountain. Maybe it was true that she was a spoiled lady who thought she could come into their lives and change everything with her matchmaking and her smiles and her kisses.

The only truth he knew at the moment was that he couldn't and wouldn't stand there and allow another man to dance with her all night.

She'd promised all her dances to him.

Maddalyn smiled up into John Terry's face, in spite of the fact that he had horrible breath. He continued to tell his boring story, laughing all the while in places Maddalyn supposed she, too, was expected to laugh. It would have been very impolite to excuse herself in the middle of their dance, and even more impolite to suggest her reasons for wanting to do so.

She glanced over his shoulder as slyly as she could manage. Conrad was dancing with Kathleen again, as clearly entranced as Karl was. They both laughed, and Maddalyn contained a sigh. At least Conrad's stories were funny.

Karl and Daisy danced past, and John Terry stepped aside, as did the other dancers. For a moment, Maddalyn's smile was genuine. One of them would have found the courage to approach the other eventually, she was certain. All she'd done was speed the process up a bit. If ever there were two people made for one another . . .

"I'm cuttin' in," Eric said just as the song came to a close.

Maddalyn snapped her head around as John Terry released her and stepped aside. Eric practically scowled at the smaller man, and then he turned that less than happy face to her.

"What happened to your smile?" he asked softly. "You looked so content just a moment ago."

Obviously her contentment irritated him. "Sorry. Just because staying in town ruins your disposition doesn't mean that everyone else—"

"Shut up and dance," he said. The music began, Eric took her in his arms, and Maddalyn forgot how maddeningly infuriating he could be.

It felt so good to be close to him, to move across the floor in perfect synchronization without effort. Were they meant for each other, as Karl and Daisy were? At times like this, it seemed that was true. But she remembered his angry words. She was a *lady*. When Karl and Conrad had suggested marriage after catching them in a kiss, Eric had exploded. Why should he have to marry her?

If there was one thing Maddalyn was determined to have, it was a husband who wanted her, who loved her completely. She was willing to make compromises. Life was a series of compromises. But on that decision she was firm.

Eric liked his solitude. Needed it, the way other men needed air and food. He didn't need other people, and he certainly didn't need her.

"Who was that man you were dancing with?" Eric asked softly, and there was an oddly sullen note in his voice.

"John Terry," she answered absently.

"I've never met him."

"I'm not surprised." Maddalyn managed to give Eric a bright smile. "He's the barber."

The music ended, and they stepped apart. There was an awkwardness between them, a hesitation. What next? Out of the corner of one eye, Maddalyn saw John Terry making his way toward them, a determined look on his face. If she knew Eric at all, and she was pretty sure she did, she knew that if he walked away from this dance and out the door, he wouldn't be back. Not tonight.

Maddalyn stepped into his arms, and twisted so that his body was between hers and John Terry. "Do you think that perhaps just for tonight you could forget that I'm a thief and a lady and a matchmaker, and we could just dance?"

His features relaxed, and she could almost swear she saw a twinkle in his blue-gray eyes. Perhaps for once she'd said the right thing.

The music began again, and Eric swung her away before the barber could reach them. The sounds of a lone guitar filled the room, strumming and picking a familiar melody Maddalyn couldn't name. She finally identified it as a classical piece Doreen had tried to pound out on the pianoforte on occasion. When Doreen attempted this music it had been forced, harsh, quite unpleasant, but the strains of the guitar were hauntingly splendid.

Eric spun her easily, and they passed Karl and Daisy so closely the brothers brushed arms. A moment later Conrad and Kathleen twirled by, and Conrad gave Maddalyn a quick and very bright grin over the top of Kathleen's head.

This was euphoria. Maddalyn was certain she had never been so supremely happy. She was holding Eric, even if it were simply for a dance. Karl and Conrad were so obviously well suited for the ladies they danced with, and Maddalyn knew she'd had a hand in that. For a moment, as the three brothers and their partners danced in close quarters, Maddalyn felt as if, for the first time in her life, she had a real family.

Real family didn't have anything to do with blood. And for tonight, while Eric forgot that she was a thief and a lady and a matchmaker, Maddalyn was going to forget that the Barretts weren't really her family.

Chapter Seventeen

"I'm simply exhausted," Maddalyn said with a grin. Eric took her hand and held it as she stepped onto the boardwalk, folding his long fingers over her hand.

If this was exhaustion, it agreed with Maddalyn Kelly. Her cheeks were pink, her eyes bright, her hair just slightly awry. It reminded him of the first time he'd seen her, curled on his bed and fast asleep. Of that first night he'd held her, keeping her safe from the cold.

"Did you see Karl and Daisy leaving together?" There was real excitement in her voice, true happiness.

Eric gave her a noncommittal grunt that implied a positive answer.

"And Conrad and Kathleen?" She lowered her

voice, even though they were all alone on the boardwalk. "Aren't they a perfect couple?"

"Well, she is a redhead."

Maddalyn laughed softly, and swung out at him for a playful swat on his arm. "It's more than that," she insisted. "Surely you could see that."

"I only know that both my brothers must be besotted to allow me to walk you back to the hotel alone."

She didn't have an answer for that statement.

"I haven't been able to get within ten feet of you without an escort since we camped by the lake."

That wasn't exactly true. There had been that morning in the sheriff's office, but as far as Eric was concerned it didn't count. They hadn't been alone.

Pale moonlight lit Maddalyn's figure beside him, and she raised a hand playfully in the air before her. "We must forgive them for neglecting their duties when they are both so obviously in love."

He hadn't meant to snort. It should have been a lighthearted scoff at her fanciful notions, but it came out as a snort.

"You don't agree?"

"Conrad just met Kathleen tonight, and as for Karl and Daisy . . ."

"You needn't explain." She made a valiant attempt at keeping her voice light, but her earlier playfulness was absent.

"It's just that . . . things will change. They always do."

"Change how?"

Her question was so open, so innocent. Could she really believe that life was so simple? "Let's say Karl and Daisy get married. It's true he's been mooning after her for years, and maybe she's even fancied herself in love with him. Tonight they dance, and maybe they even kiss. She's wearing her best dress, Karl's just had a bath and a shave. They see only what they want to see, and they reveal only what they want to reveal."

Eric took Maddalyn's hand and drew her to the flat bench that sat in front of the dark general store. Here they were in shadows, with only a hint of moonlight to illuminate Maddalyn's puzzled face. She sat slowly, and Eric lowered himself to sit beside her.

"Six months, a year from now, the dance will be a memory. Karl snores. He eats like a one-man army, and he works long hours. Daisy will get tired of living on the mountain, so far from her family and friends in Olympia. When she and Karl actually have to speak to one another, do you really think they'll stay besotted?"

He expected a hot defense, but instead got a soft sigh. "You have such jaded notions about life. How can you live in such a wonderfully beautiful place and have so little hope for the future?"

"It's just a matter of being realistic."

"For heaven's sake, Eric." Maddalyn leaned toward him and laid her hand against his arm. He didn't move, didn't reveal in any way how that simple touch jolted him. But it did. "Perhaps I am too optimistic, but I think Karl and Daisy have a wonderful future ahead of them. Conrad and Kathleen, too."

"You can't be serious," Eric growled, but there was no bite in his argument. Maddalyn had somehow wormed her way against his side, and his arm found its way around her. "Conrad and the sheriff's daughter just met."

"But they're such a perfect match." She tilted her head back so that her face was lifted toward his.

She was warm and soft, and just looking down at her made him grow hard. He'd never wanted a woman like this, had never wanted anyone or anything with such intensity. It would be best if they continued to argue.

"They're too much alike," he said lifelessly. "They'd fight all the time."

Maddalyn squirmed slightly, and managed impossibly to place herself closer to him. Eric closed his eyes. Even after she was gone, he would be able to close his eyes and feel her like this. Her body against his, her scent in his nostrils, something intangible so deep inside it scared him senseless.

"I imagine they'll argue some, but I think they'll laugh more."

She was no fun to argue with. There was no venom in her words, no animosity at all. "Well, Conrad . . ." Eric searched for another point to debate, but his mind went blank.

"Do we have to talk about Karl and Conrad?"

Maddalyn asked wistfully. "We'll never agree. Let's talk about something else. You're a wonderful dancer. I never did thank you properly for rescuing me from that barber."

"I didn't even know you needed rescuing," Eric growled.

"Of course you did," Maddalyn whispered. "You always know. It's quite amazing."

Eric surrendered. How could he win when Maddalyn fought dirty? "Maybe you could thank me with a kiss," he suggested.

In the dim light he saw her smile slightly as she raised her lips toward his. "I thought you'd never ask."

Eric bent forward to meet her, wrapping his arms around her as she came to him. He wanted to be gentle, but he felt like a man having his first taste of fresh water after a month in the desert, as if it were the end of a long winter, and Maddalyn was the spring sunshine. As if he were starving, and only Maddalyn could save him.

He parted her lips with his tongue and tasted her deeply. After a brief hesitation she answered him, and he was lost.

He could feel the brush of her fingers against his jaw and his neck, a light, tentative touch that was like lightning through his blood. The world closed in on him, and there was only this.

She sighed, a little catch in her throat that made Eric's heart skip a beat.

The hand at his jaw fell slowly, trailing languidly

over his throat and his chest, until Maddalyn gripped the front of his shirt.

Hold on. He wanted to say the words aloud, but he wasn't ready to pull his mouth away from hers. Not yet. He moved one hand to her side and held her there, sliding that hand upward until his thumb brushed against her breast.

She quivered, and—damn it all—so did he. He felt it to his core, so deep and so hard he knew it would always be with him, that on cold winter nights he would sit by the fire and remember this kiss.

It was insane to follow his instincts and touch her, to take her in his arms again and again when he knew there was nothing for them but disaster. Did he think it would be easier to let her go if he allowed his body to override his brain for a time?

When he pulled his lips away from hers and trailed them down the column of her throat, she threaded her fingers through his hair. She clutched his shirt and grasped the back of his head, holding on for dear life.

Maddalyn sighed when he laid his mouth against the quick pulse at her throat.

"Oh, Eric," she whispered.

"Oh, Eric."

Oh, no. He would've recognized that sardonic voice anywhere. The pleasant fog that had surrounded him disappeared, and he pulled his lips away from Maddalyn. Her hands fell slowly, and they both turned toward Conrad's voice, only to find two hulking figures in the shadows. Karl was, as usual, silent, arms crossed over his chest, what was no doubt a furious face lost in darkness.

"We've been looking for you, Maddalyn," Conrad said lightly. Eric wondered if she could hear the thread of anger in his voice.

"Eric was walking me back to the hotel," she said breathlessly. Like a woman who had just been too well kissed. "And I was thanking him for saving me from the barber who had foul breath and told incredibly boring stories, and it's really all my fault, so you won't hit him, will you, Karl?" Her plea was fast and breathy and soft.

Karl didn't answer immediately.

"Maddalyn, don't. . . ." Eric began.

"Please?" She added anyway.

"All right," Karl grumbled. "Let's go. We'll walk you back to the hotel."

Maddalyn stood slowly, perfectly composed. How could that be, when Eric felt as if his world were falling apart, spinning out of control?

She turned her back on Conrad and Karl and smiled down at him. Sweet, shy, brilliant. She leaned forward just enough, and whispered just for him: "That was the best one yet."

Eric had no answer for her. Did she have any idea where kisses like that one could lead? Did she know that he hurt with wanting her?

"Come on, little brother," Conrad said as Karl took Maddalyn's arm and led her away.

"No," Eric growled, watching Maddalyn walk

257

away. She cast a quick glance over her shoulder and smiled shyly. "I'm going to sit out here for a while."

Conrad laughed harshly. "Yeah, I think maybe that's a good idea." He slapped Eric heartily on the knee and sat down in Maddalyn's place. A poor trade.

"I don't need any company," Eric insisted with a glower that was no doubt lost in the dark.

Conrad ignored him. "Did you see Kathleen MacIver? She's gorgeous, and she's funny, and she has the most wonderful laugh."

"And she's a redhead," Eric added.

"Yes." Conrad ignored Eric's sarcasm. "And she has the most beautiful freckles across her nose, and dark brown eyes." Conrad sighed, a disgusting, lovesick sigh. "Maddalyn's a genius."

"You don't mean that you're seriously entertaining thoughts of marriage to a woman you just met."

"Well." Conrad shuffled his feet. "It is a bit soon. I'm having dinner with her family tomorrow night, and there's a picnic after church on Sunday."

"You haven't been to church in over twenty years."

"Well, I'll be there Sunday. Afterwards there's one of those, you know, fund-raisers, where men bid on picnic lunches the women make? Kathleen tells me she makes great . . . something. I don't remember exactly what it was, but I'm sure whatever it is will be delicious."

His passion was suitably cooled, and Eric was once again jerked into reality. "The hotel serves a perfectly decent meal."

"You have no sense of adventure, Eric," Conrad said as he rose, slapping Eric on the knee once again. "None at all. You can have a decent dinner at the hotel, and someone else can bid on Maddalyn's picnic."

"She can't very well cook at the hotel."

"I know. That's why she's spending the day tomorrow at Kathleen's house." Conrad walked away, obviously distracted.

Eric rose to follow his brother. Maddalyn Kelly was turning out to be an awful lot of trouble.

But if he closed his eyes he could still feel her all around, and—at least for that moment—he knew it would always be that way.

She tried to sleep, but it just wouldn't come. She could close her eyes and feel as if Eric were still spinning her across the dance floor. She could still feel his lips on hers.

Maddalyn entwined her fingers and placed them over her heart. She was so excited, so happily agitated, that she doubted she would sleep at all.

She'd given up on Eric much too easily. Surely he cared for her, or else he wouldn't have danced with her all night, and he certainly wouldn't have kissed her that way. Something had happened to him, something that had made him wary of ladies and marriage. Someone, that Jane, had broken his heart.

She sat up.

"I can mend it," she whispered. Doubts nagged at her, deep worries that stole a portion of her happiness. What if she was wrong? What if he couldn't love her the way she needed to be loved?

Maddalyn slipped from under the covers and stepped to the window. The street below was quiet, still, with only an occasional lone man passing quietly.

Olympia had a charm all its own, but she missed the cabin on Eric's mountain. How odd, that she had become so connected to the place in such a short time. She didn't miss Georgia at all, not Aunt Ethel's proper parlor or her own cozy bedroom. She'd always been a visitor in that house, even as a child. Afraid to touch Aunt Ethel's pretty things, lest they break. Afraid to run and shatter the stillness of the house. Afraid, even more, that one day they would send her away, and that the unknown would be even bleaker than the life she knew.

But from the moment she'd stolen into the Barrett cabin she'd felt at home. An odd concept, that feeling of coming home.

She recognized the figure that passed stiffly on the street beneath her. There was not a man in town who could pass for one of the Barrett brothers, even from a distance, and this particular one was hers. At least for the moment.

He ran both hands through his hair, raking the

strands away from his face, as he took long strides down the middle of the quiet street. Why wasn't he in his room next door, sound asleep? Where was he going? He passed out of her range of view, and she lifted the window slowly and soundlessly and leaned forward until she could see him again. He had stopped in the center of the road and faced the only business that was thriving at this time of night.

Annie's. Maddalyn's heart dropped. The overheard mention of Bucktooth Annie's hurdy-girls had been brief, but enlightening.

Eric took several long strides forward before he stopped again, and Maddalyn had to bite her tongue to keep from calling out. That would be scandalous, but perhaps worth the scandal if it kept Eric out of that place.

But he just stood there, watching the door, and he raked his hands through his hair again before he turned away and walked—more slowly this time—back toward the hotel.

Maddalyn leaned against the windowsill and smiled, as content as she'd ever been.

Eric walked past the hotel, turned around, and stalked in front of her window again. Good heavens, the man was pacing—eyes to the ground—like a man possessed.

When he did finally lift his head and see her there, he didn't even look surprised to find that he was being spied upon.

"What are you doing?" he hissed.

"Watching you."

"Go to sleep."

"I can't," she whispered. "I'm too excited."

She thought he might have laughed, but the sound he made was too soft for her to be certain.

"I didn't tell you how much fun I had tonight," she said, tilting forward so that she was leaning out of the window from the waist up. "It was marvelous."

"Yes, it was." It seemed he was reluctant to agree, but he did, thrusting his hands in his pockets and looking up at her. There was such strength in that face, in the eyes she couldn't see nearly well enough in the moonlight. How could someone so strong be hurt so badly that he'd given up on love?

"So you did have a good time?" she asked.

He didn't answer her immediately, but stared up at her without moving. What else could she say? *Thank you for not going into Bucktooth Annie's?*

"You should get inside and close the window," he whispered gruffly. "You . . . might catch cold."

Maddalyn laughed softly. "If I didn't catch cold when I was sleeping in that cave on your mountain, I very much doubt I will on a balmy night like tonight."

"Good night, Maddalyn," he said softly, defeat in his voice.

"Good night, Eric," she whispered, but neither of them moved.

She would be content to stand there and watch him all night, his hair almost silver in the moonlight, the memory of his touch so clear she could still savor it.

"If you don't get inside and close that window, I might just climb this wall." A promise? A threat? A capitulation? It had the flavor of all three, and Maddalyn didn't know how to answer.

"If you climb the wall, I'll have to shoot you." Karl's voice was deep, sleepy, unmistakable. "I'm too tired to knock you down."

Maddalyn twisted to the side. Karl's window was open just a few inches.

"It's rude to eavesdrop, you know," she hissed.

"Good night, Maddalyn," Karl said, and the window slid shut. She knew he was still watching, waiting for Eric to move on.

But Eric didn't move on, and Maddalyn didn't turn away from the window. There might not ever be another moment in her life like this one. Perfectly romantic, the man she loved pacing beneath her window, looking up at her with the moonlight on his face. She wished, in that perfect instant, that he would climb the walls.

Even though she'd sworn it couldn't happen, that she couldn't give herself to a man who didn't love her.

But Eric didn't look, at the moment, like a man who didn't, who couldn't, love her.

"I really did have a good time tonight," she said to Eric, placing her hands on the windowsill and leaning forward as far as she dared. Her hair fell over her face, and in an instinctive motion Eric lifted his hands.

To catch her if she fell.

To hold her when it was cold.

To light a fire deep inside where she'd known only darkness.

"That's good." His hands fell slowly.

"Will I see you tomorrow?" she asked tentatively.

"Sure." He turned away from her, and then Maddalyn closed the window.

And she knew she wouldn't sleep a wink.

Chapter Eighteen

It felt too good, too perfect, like a dream that wouldn't last. The sun was shining, warm but not hot. The quilt they sat on—borrowed from either Kathleen or Daisy, he was certain—was soft. There was a gentle breeze that touched his face and on occasion lifted Maddalyn's curls just slightly.

"I can't believe you actually paid twenty dollars for my fried chicken."

Eric lifted his eyes to her face. He couldn't believe it either. He hadn't intended to bid at all. It was a stupid game, filled with false excitement. "I love fried chicken," he said nonchalantly.

He hadn't intended even to watch. As he'd told Conrad on Friday, the hotel served a perfectly acceptable dinner.

But his damned imagination got the best of him.

Linda Jones

He hadn't seen Maddalyn since Friday night, since she'd leaned out of the hotel window and all but dared him to climb the walls.

He hadn't been able to sleep after that, and had ended up dozing off near dawn. He'd missed breakfast, and Maddalyn had spent Saturday dividing her time between Kathleen and Daisy. It would have been foolish and much too telling to seek her out.

And so he found himself wondering what she'd pack in a picnic lunch. He wondered what she'd wear, if she'd pull her hair back or wear it down, if anyone would bid on her picnic. After all, she didn't know that many people in Olympia.

On that count he shouldn't have worried. John Terry, the barber she had danced with just once, was determined to win this one. He wasn't alone. At least four other men bid on Maddalyn's packed lunch and the privilege of sharing it with her, including Kathleen MacIver's brother, Gavin. He wasn't much taller than Maddalyn, and had a mop of red hair, freckles, and a gun strapped to his hip. Eric didn't approve of him. Of course, he couldn't say that he approved of a single one of the men who bid on Maddalyn's boxed lunch.

So he ended up paying twenty bucks for the lunch she laid between them, doubling John Terry's last offer with a resigned shout, and silencing the other bidders. The meal was arranged before them almost artistically, her fried chicken, potato salad, soft rolls, and, of course, gingerbread.

266

She was wearing another borrowed dress. It was white, blindingly bright in the sunlight, and there was lace at the collar and at the hem of the full skirt that covered her folded legs.

"You're awfully quiet," she said, handing him a full plate.

"You usually manage to talk enough for both of us," he said.

He worried for a moment that he might have offended her, but she just laughed lightly. "I do, don't I? Aunt Ethel believed that a child should be seen and not heard, and I tried—I really tried—to hold my tongue. Poor Mary Lynette got the worst of it. After endless hours of being silent or speaking just when necessary and in hushed whispers, I'd run into the kitchen and explode. Sometimes I'd start talking and I couldn't stop. She allowed me to ramble on, and when I was done she'd let me help her with the cooking. A bit of energetic kneading was good, she always said, for whatever ails a woman."

"And that's why you're such a good cook," Eric said. "You hid in the kitchen."

"I never thought of it that way," she confessed, "but I suppose it's true."

She picked at her lunch, eating a little of everything but not much of anything, while Eric devoured what she placed before him.

"Look," she whispered, even though no one was close enough to hear. The picnickers were spread across the church grounds, families and couples in the sun and in the shade. Maddalyn nodded her head to the side, and Eric glanced in that direction.

Karl and Daisy faced one another over a huge spread, appearing disturbingly domesticated. There was something very different about the shy Daisy. Eric had never thought of her as beautiful, though she was certainly attractive. But now—she was radiant and graceful, and lit from within, and in the moments he'd been watching she hadn't taken her eyes off of Karl.

Several yards past them, Conrad and Kathleen shared a quilt. They ate and talked at the same time, both of them gesturing with fingers that clutched bits of food, laughing frequently while the sheriff watched from a few vigilant feet away. Conrad either didn't know or didn't care that he was under surveillance.

"Aren't they lovely?" Maddalyn asked softly.

Eric grumbled, but without any conviction.

"No argument?" she prodded.

Eric pulled his eyes away from his brothers and fastened them on Maddalyn. It was the white dress, he supposed, that made her look so glowingly seductive. The color in her cheeks, the bright blue of her eyes, the deep red of her full lips—nothing real could be so perfect.

"Not today," he conceded.

The smile she gave him was brilliant.

When she looked at him like that it made him think—for one ridiculous moment—that marrying her wouldn't be such a bad idea after all.

He pulled his eyes away from her face and

glanced over her shoulder to the mountains that filled the horizon.

"You're ready to go home, aren't you?" Her voice was soft, like the breeze that brushed his face.

"Yes. I haven't been away this long for four years. That's when I brought Karl and Conrad in with me. They were both ready to leave Pinkerton's, and I had a big contract coming up."

"Like the railroad ties?"

He glanced at her inquisitive face.

"Daisy told me," she explained. "I hope you don't mind. Is it a secret? I haven't mentioned it to anyone else."

Eric gave her a small smile, a halfhearted grin. "It's no secret. Conrad knows."

She turned her head away from him and toward the mountain range. "Will you show me?" she asked, almost as if she expected him to refuse. "I tried to pick it out, but from a distance they all look alike."

Eric rose to his knees and pointed. His forearm rested on her shoulder, and she tilted her head to the side to better follow the line his arm created.

"I think I see," she said. "It's the best one, isn't it?"

He laughed. She always managed to take him by surprise. "Naturally."

"When are you going back?" The question was delivered in a falsely light voice.

"Soon," he conceded. "There's lots of work to do."

"I suppose I should telegraph Mrs. Hudson and explain that I've been delayed." Maddalyn moved her head away from him, and Eric dropped his arm. "I should have done that when we first arrived, but . . . but I got so busy with Daisy and Kathleen I just forgot all about it."

"Tomorrow will be soon enough," Eric said lamely. "The stage that runs to Buffalo and then to Sheridan runs twice a month, on Thursday, I believe. You don't have much longer to wait."

She agreed with a murmur and a nod of her head.

And the dream was over. In a couple of days he'd return home, and Maddalyn would go on to Sheridan. He wouldn't worry about her. She'd proven, over the past several weeks, that she was able to adapt, that she was tougher than he'd suspected when he first found her.

He would miss her. It had taken him days, weeks to admit that, even to himself.

Her shoulders rose as she took a deep breath. "I'm looking forward to continuing on to Sheridan. Not that the delay hasn't been pleasant," she added quickly. "Except, of course, for the robbery. You and Karl and Conrad have been wonderful to me, but it's time to move on."

Was she really strong enough? Was it enough that he wanted her more than he'd ever wanted anything? What did he really have to lose by asking her to stay?

He would survive if she said no. He'd gotten

along just fine before she came along, and he could live the rest of his life without her. If he had to. It would be worse if she said yes, and then in a few months or a few years changed her mind. He knew what that was like, but this time it would be harder. Much harder.

Eric wished silently that Maddalyn would turn around, but she continued to stare away from him, toward the mountain, presenting to him a stiff and strong back and a mass of golden curls.

"Miss Kelly," a bright young voice called, interrupting the reverie that had lasted too long. "Would you care to go for a walk?"

Gavin MacIver stood there, too young and too bold, blushing beneath his neatly combed red hair. He was dressed in his Sunday best, a boiled shirt and clean pants, and he clutched his hat in his hands. Eric waited for Maddalyn to refuse.

"I'd love to walk," she said. "It seems we're finished here."

She didn't turn to face him, hadn't looked at him since they'd begun to discuss her trip to Sheridan.

The young MacIver offered her his hand, and Maddalyn laid her white fingers in his palm. Eric watched freckled fingers close over hers as Gavin MacIver assisted Maddalyn to her feet. Only once did the young man dare to look at Eric, a fretful and fleeting glance.

Maddalyn must have seen the questioning glance.

"Don't worry about Eric," she assured him. "He

doesn't mind, not in the least."

She didn't even glance at him, didn't look over her shoulder or turn. She just walked away without giving him another thought apparently. And to think he'd been about to make a complete fool of himself—again. Over a woman who would never be satisfied with what he had to offer.

"Are you all right, Miss Kelly?" Gavin leaned in and asked his question with what seemed to be real concern. "You're awfully pale. Maybe we should stop and sit for a while."

"I'd rather walk, and please call me Maddalyn," she insisted, not for the first time. Several times over the past couple of days, Gavin had made a brief and frenetic appearance in the MacIver household while Maddalyn was present.

She would have preferred to sit, but she had to get away from Eric before she said something she was going to regret. He was so calm, and seemed to have no qualms at all when it came to sending her away! How could she make him love her when he didn't even seem to care if she stayed or went?

"Actually, I am feeling rather ill. Would you mind walking me back to the hotel?"

"How about I take you to the house? Ma can look after you."

"I'm not that ill." Besides, Bonnie MacIver was still enjoying her own picnic lunch not far from Kathleen and Conrad. "I just need to lie down."

They walked slowly down the boardwalk, and

Someone's Been Sleeping in My Bed

Maddalyn allowed Gavin to ramble. In a couple of days Eric would go back to his cabin and she'd be on her way to Sheridan. What else could she do? She couldn't very well propose marriage to him. Good heavens, she'd done everything but. It had seemed, after the dance and the kiss, a real possibility that she could make him love her. Perhaps he was truly a lost cause. Just because she loved him didn't mean she could heal his broken heart.

It would have been nice to have had a chance to try.

If he'd cared for her at all, if she meant anything to him at all, he wouldn't have spoken of sending her to Sheridan so easily.

"What do you say?" Gavin asked as they stopped at the hotel entrance.

An answer of some sort was expected, but she hadn't heard a word he'd said.

"I'm sorry." She tried to smile, but it was a poor effort. "I felt a bit dizzy for a moment, and I didn't hear the question."

"Supper tomorrow night, if you're feeling better. Conrad will be there, so I thought it would be nice if I had a guest myself. What do you say?"

"That would be lovely," Maddalyn said. And preferable to supper in the hotel dining room with Karl and Eric. Or just Eric, if Karl and Daisy had made other plans. "I look forward to it."

He smiled, a bright and innocent smile. He had to be close to Eric's age, but he seemed such a child. It was that boyish face, those guileless eyes.

There was none of Eric's suspicion there.

"I can't wait, Maddalyn." He brought her hand to his mouth for what she was certain had been meant as a charming caress. It was quick and sloppy, and it took all her self-control not to wipe the back of her hand against her skirt.

The evening turned out to be not a chore at all. Dinner was delicious, Conrad and Kathleen were gloriously happy, and Maddalyn hadn't seen Eric since the church picnic. Gavin was very attentive, perhaps too attentive at times, and Maddalyn turned, on occasion, to another member of the MacIver family for a moment of respite.

The sheriff and his wife were lovely hosts, and as the evening wore on it became evident that Kathleen and Gavin got more than their coloring from their mother. Bonnie MacIver was as energetic as either of her children, and spoke with a lilting Scottish accent that was enchanting. Kelvin MacIver had lost most of his accent, and Maddalyn thought it was a shame. Now he talked like everyone else.

After dinner, Conrad and Kathleen disappeared quietly. Maddalyn wasn't disappointed or surprised. The sheriff and his wife made excellent company for the evening, and their conversation was almost interesting enough to take her mind off of Eric. Soon, though, Bonnie MacIver excused herself with kitchen duties as an excuse. Maddalyn insisted on helping, but was ordered back into her comfortable seat on the sofa. Moments later, Sheriff MacIver made his excuse: a fat cigar he rolled through his fingers as he carried it to the front porch.

And she was alone with Gavin.

Maddalyn clasped her hands and stood. "What a lovely evening this was, but I really should be getting back to the hotel."

"Not just yet," Gavin said, sitting on the sofa and taking her hand to draw her down beside him. "I asked Ma and Pop to leave us alone for a few minutes."

Maddalyn felt her heart drop to the floor. No good could come of this. None at all.

"Maddalyn." Her name was a squeak, and then Gavin cleared his throat. "Would you marry me?"

For the first time that she could remember, Maddalyn was speechless.

"I know this is sudden, but you'll be leaving in a few days."

"How did you—"

"Conrad said you were going on to Sheridan." He must have seen the refusal in her eyes, because he interrupted her quickly. "I love you. I fell in love with you the first time I saw you, at the dance on Friday. You were dancing with that Eric Barrett, and I didn't know . . . I'd been out of town for a few days, and I didn't know who you were or if you were married or promised. It didn't make any difference."

Maddalyn made herself look up into his earnest

face. Wasn't this what she had always wanted? A man who loved her completely? Love at first sight. The most romantic notion. But of course it would never work. She didn't love him, and she never would. By loving Eric, had she condemned herself to a life alone?

And, faced with his sudden proposal, she had trouble believing that it could be real. He didn't know her. How could he possibly love her?

"I wouldn't have asked so soon, but Conrad said you were unattached, and might not be averse to the idea of marriage, when I tried to question him discreetly."

She doubted that Gavin even knew what discreet was.

"He even said that he wouldn't mind having you for a sister-in-law," he revealed in a low voice. "I guess that means we can expect an announcement soon. We could make it a double wedding."

The refusal that was on Maddalyn's lips died. Falling in love with Eric had ruined her hopes of a perfect marriage. Was it possible that she could, at least, be a distant part of the family she had made for herself?

"This is so sudden," she said, unable to assure Gavin with a smile. "Can I have a couple of days to think about it?"

His smile was bright enough for both of them, and Maddalyn realized that he had been prepared for a negative response to his proposal.

She could live in Olympia. It was a nice place,

and the people were friendly. Conrad would be her brother-in-law, Kathleen the sister she'd always wanted. Even Karl and Daisy would be a distant part of her family.

And Eric. What would he be to her, exactly? Nothing. As he was nothing to her now. At least she would be able to see him once or twice a year, unless he took completely to the mountain. Was that better or worse than never seeing him again?

"I can see you're giving my proposal serious consideration," Gavin said earnestly. "And I appreciate that, I really do. I'd like to make just one more point in my argument, if you don't mind."

"Of course not."

Gavin took her hand and held it lightly. Tempting as it was, Maddalyn didn't draw her hand away. "I meant what I said when I told you I love you," he said softly. "I'll always love you. I'll care for you, just like the vows say, in good times and bad. I'm ready for a family, Maddalyn." Bless him, he blushed red as a beet. "Marry me, and I won't let you regret it."

It was the perfect proposal, everything she had waited all her life to hear. Love. A family. Forever.

But it came from the wrong man.

Chapter Nineteen

"A double wedding?" Eric repeated, sinking down to sit on the side of the bed. Conrad stood over him, grinning like a fool, and Karl stood in the open doorway of their shared hotel room with a formidably determined expression on his face.

"Maybe even a triple wedding, if Maddalyn will say yes." Conrad leaned forward, bending at the waist and lifting his eyebrows suggestively.

It was, for Eric, the last straw. "Dammit, how many times do I have to tell you? You can't make me marry her or anyone else."

"I didn't say that you would be the groom, little brother," Conrad said as he backed away.

Eric saw it then, a flash of red behind Karl. That swishing, swinging calico skirt. Maddalyn, hiding herself from him, pacing in the hallway. And then

Conrad's words hit home.

"What do you mean?" he grumbled.

"Kathleen's brother, Gavin," he clarified. "He's asked Maddalyn to marry him."

Eric felt sick. Physically ill at the idea of Maddalyn married to someone else. She wouldn't.

"What did she say?"

Karl turned around, and a moment later Maddalyn stood directly in front of the oldest brother. She wrung her hands, then dropped them to her sides.

"What did you say?" he repeated, standing slowly. "Are you actually going to marry that red-headed nit?"

"I don't want to talk about that right now," she said, looking at the floor. "I just came here to tell you that I think I've made a terrible mistake. What if Eric was right all along? Conrad, you just met Kathleen. You don't really know what she's like. And Karl, I know you think you know Daisy, but you really haven't had enough time together." Maddalyn glanced over her shoulder and up at Karl. "I pushed too hard. You should take it slow. Maybe get married next year, if you still have a notion to do so."

"I don't want to wait anymore," Karl said softly.

"Neither do I," Conrad complained more loudly.

Eric didn't care about her too late second thoughts. He wanted an answer to his question. "Maddalyn, are you going to marry Gavin MacIver?"

She lifted her eyes to him then and began to wring her hands again. "I don't know," she admitted. "I told him I would consider his proposal."

"Oh, you did," he said through gritted teeth. "What about Sheridan?"

"Plans can change," Maddalyn said quickly. "And besides, I haven't really decided. He just asked me last night after supper."

"Last night," he repeated. And he'd thought Maddalyn had been avoiding him for the same reason he'd been avoiding her. Hell, it was awkward, wanting something he knew he couldn't have, trying to look at her and speak to her without showing the world how he felt, and all this time she'd been considering another man's proposal of marriage.

"When's the happy day?" Eric asked bitterly.

"Three weeks," Conrad answered. "We figure in that time we can make some progress toward the new contract and start two cabins. We can at least get the walls up. And the girls wanted some time to make plans, sew wedding dresses, and plan a party and such."

"You'll be going back to the mountain soon," Maddalyn said in a low voice, almost as if she were talking to herself.

"You'll come with us, won't you?" Conrad stepped forward and took Maddalyn's abused, overwrung hands. "If you decide to marry Gavin, we can make it a helluva day."

"What if I decide . . . not to marry Gavin?" she whispered.

"Then you can be my best man," Conrad countered. "One way or another, you have to be there. If not for you, none of this would be happening."

For the first time in two days, Eric saw Maddalyn smile. "I can't be your best man," she protested.

"Why not? Has Karl already asked?"

Maddalyn shook her head. "It's just not done. Why, it wouldn't be at all proper."

Eric wanted nothing more than to leave the room, to escape this talk of weddings and new cabins, of Maddalyn being a bride or a best man. Nonsense. It was the most ridiculous notion he'd ever heard.

But Karl and Maddalyn blocked the door, and Eric didn't trust himself to pass that closely to her—not even to escape from this room.

"Call yourself whatever you want, but I want you to stand up with me," Conrad insisted.

Karl looked over Maddalyn's head and nodded to Eric. "You'll be my best man, right?"

Eric shrugged his shoulders, and that seemed to be enough for Karl.

Maddalyn, who had a moment ago been pale and fidgeting, now smiled as if she owned the world. "When are we going home? Back to the mountain, I mean?"

"Day after tomorrow," Karl answered. "We have to finish up a few things around town, pick up supplies at the general store." He laid a hand on Maddalyn's shoulder. "If I get some material, would you make curtains for the new cabin? I know Daisy can sew, but I'd like things to be really nice for her when she first sees the place."

"Red?" Maddalyn asked, glancing over her shoulder at Karl.

"Whatever you think is best."

Eric was suddenly, inexplicably jealous. Jealous of his own brothers, because their friendship with Maddalyn had always been so easy.

And, of course, there was Gavin MacIver to ponder. How could she even *consider* marriage to that boy? He'd never be anything more than deputy sheriff to his pa, unless he took over his old man's job one day.

Was it any worse than the future he could imagine for her in Sheridan? In one way it was.

Gavin MacIver wasn't a faceless old man, like the one he'd imagined Maddalyn finally marrying. If he could ever make himself come to Olympia again, he'd have to see Maddalyn with her devoted husband sitting together in church, dancing at the socials, chasing fat redheaded children down the street.

Maddalyn and Karl were lost in a deep discussion about curtains. She used her hands to demonstrate for him what she wanted to do, and Karl nodded solemnly. As though this were the most important decision he'd have to make all day.

Her back was to him, and so Eric stared openly. She'd tied her golden curls back with a red ribbon, and the tresses fell to her waist. Wild. Bright. When she raised her arms and spread them wide, her fingers danced, delicate and so very pale. She used her whole body when she talked, and he watched her hips sway slightly to one side.

He couldn't deny that she was beautiful, and tempting, and he recognized his own obsession for what it really was.

A fascination that would fade with time.

She was, after all, first and foremost a lady. A fickle one, too much like Jane for comfort.

He hadn't thought about Jane in days. Not really. He'd forgotten, until tonight, how treacherous a lady could be.

His brothers should know better; but then, they didn't know the whole story. Nobody knew the truth but him—and Jane, if she remembered him at all.

She'd been beautiful and charming and tempting. When it suited her purposes. It had taken him months to discover what the real Jane was like.

It wouldn't happen again.

A swift and not so hard swat to the side of his head forced him to return to the present, and he snapped his head around to glare at Conrad.

"You're a fool," Conrad whispered as Karl led Maddalyn from the room.

Wait six months, Eric thought bitterly, and then we'll see who's the fool.

It was like a reprieve. Back to the mountain, until the wedding! Maddalyn paced in front of the open window of her hotel room. It was so stuffy here, even when the wind blew and ruffled the curtains and pressed the nightshirt she wore to her skin.

At least another two weeks of magnificent vistas, crisp air, and that blessed silence she hadn't known she'd miss at all.

And, of course, at least another two weeks of dealing with Eric.

He'd seemed noticeably upset at the news of Gavin MacIver's proposal, but before that . . . moments before that . . . she'd heard him protest to his brothers that they couldn't *make* him marry her.

Marriage to Eric Barrett would be a disaster. He'd never even mentioned the institution without using the word *forced*, or some other word that implied obligation. Goodness knows, she'd had enough of that in her life.

But she'd also decided that she couldn't marry Gavin MacIver. She'd known it ten minutes after she'd told him she'd think about his offer, but it wasn't going to be easy to tell him. He was so sweet, and she didn't want to hurt his feelings—but she couldn't marry him.

She didn't love him. She still loved Eric, would always love Eric. Was this God's idea of a joke? Eric was most likely still in love with the woman who broke his heart. Here she was, hopelessly in love with Eric, while Gavin claimed to be in love with her. Why was love such a tangle? Why couldn't it be simple?

She'd always thought it would be. When she'd paced in her own room in Aunt Ethel's house and dreamed of escape, the love that came to her had always been so easy. She'd meet the right man, fall truly, deeply in love, and he would feel the same for her. Otherwise it didn't work. Not at all.

If she were a violent person, she would seriously consider searching Jane out and throttling the woman.

Maddalyn saw the movement below, a man passing on the street while the rest of the town was still, and she stopped pacing to stand at the window. A cool breeze washed over her, comforting and somehow liberating.

It was Eric, of course, pacing once again in the middle of the street. He was more settled than he had been after the dance, and not once did he rake his fingers through his hair or look as if he were headed for Annie's. He was calm. Staid, in fact. Tonight his pacing was not frantic, but instead seemed almost reflective.

She should have felt some guilt for watching him so shamelessly, but she didn't. Every moment she spent studying him, talking with him, perhaps even touching him, would make a memory that would have to last her a lifetime.

So she memorized the moonlight on his hair, the way he stood, so strong and tall, a figure she would recognize from miles away. The moonlight illuminated the lines of his face, the strong jaw, the harsh planes.

As she watched he lifted that face to her. Had he felt her eyes on him? Was that possible?

"You're not asleep." His voice was low, but it carried quite well to her ears. Maddalyn could imagine that his words were borne on the wind, delivered to her by a higher power.

"No," she whispered. *I miss my bed. Your bed. I miss my mountain. Your mountain.* "Too excited, I guess."

Eric crossed his arms over his chest and seemed to plant his feet in the middle of the road. Like a warrior preparing for battle. "About the wedding, I suppose."

She had never heard the word *wedding* spoken with such sarcasm, such obvious distaste. "Don't you think it's exciting?"

He didn't move. Just maintained that rather barbaric stance. "I'm sure you and Gavin MacIver will make a charming bride and groom."

Maddalyn leaned slightly out of the window. She hadn't been thinking about Gavin at all. "I meant Karl and Daisy, and Conrad and Kathleen."

"What about Maddalyn and Gavin?"

Maddalyn sighed deeply. "I haven't given him my answer yet."

"But you've made your decision, haven't you?"

He was so far away, and she couldn't see his face nearly well enough. If only he'd shake his hands in the air, or laugh, or give her any sign that he cared one way or another. It would be so much easier if she could hold his hand, look into his eyes, ask him to kiss her once more.

"Yes, I have," she admitted.

"And?" he prompted when she didn't say more.

She could almost think that he was angry, frustrated, perhaps even jealous. "I hardly think it would be proper for me to tell you before I give Gavin his answer."

"I don't give a good goddamn what's proper, Maddalyn," he snapped.

"Should I tell you what I want?" she asked in a voice so soft she wasn't certain he would hear her.

"Why not?" His voice was harsh, the set of his jaw and his stance hard. Immovable. Like his mountain.

And he was waiting for her to continue.

Her hair fell free, and the breeze that had been blowing all night lifted those curls that shone in the moonlight. What was he doing here? Why did he feel compelled to stalk beneath her window like a lovesick suitor?

"I want what I never had," she said softly. "Love, a family, a real home. Most of all, I want a love that lasts forever."

"What you want doesn't exist." How could she be so naive? He could see it on her face, her belief that fairy tales were real, that love like that was possible. He could even see, in her moonlit eyes, that she thought he could be more than he really was.

"I think it does exist," she insisted. His denial hadn't dampened her beliefs. "Maybe it's not easy to find. Maybe not everyone finds it. But I will."

With Gavin MacIver? How could she even consider marrying that boy after the way she'd kissed him? Hell, he'd climb the hotel walls for another of Maddalyn's kisses, risk being shot by Karl, take her in his arms and order her not to marry Gavin MacIver.

But the truth was he didn't have anything to offer her in return.

"It's just a dream."

"Dreams come true, Eric." She leaned forward, until he was certain she was going to come tumbling forward.

How could she believe that? After the life she'd led, after the years with Aunt Ethel, how could she still believe in dreams?

And then, without asking, he knew the answer. Because he knew Maddalyn as well as he'd ever known another woman. Her dreams had kept her going. Dreams had been all she had during those years.

He had no right to destroy them, to finish the job of crushing Maddalyn that Aunt Ethel had started. If he'd had something like that—something to hold on to after Jane had left him—maybe he would be able to feel happiness for his brothers. Maybe he'd want to try to give Maddalyn what she wanted.

He waited too long to answer her. She said good night, smiled at him—a wistful smile, not one of her brilliant grins—and then she was gone.

His reaction angered him. He missed her. He

Linda Jones

wanted her to come back to the window, to lean forward and smile and talk about impossible dreams.

What would it take to rid himself of this obsession? He knew. Dammit, he knew exactly what he needed from her.

Everything. He wanted her beneath him, around him, calling his name. Only then would he be rid of this fixation. Only then would he truly be convinced that she was just another woman—like all the rest.

It was a dangerous thought. What if she said yes to Gavin MacIver's proposal? Would he go so far as to sleep with another man's fiancee?

Maybe she'd refuse Gavin's offer of marriage.

Maybe it didn't matter.

One more day in Olympia, and then they would return home. He'd have a full two weeks, maybe a few days more, to make it happen. A full two weeks to work Maddalyn Lorraine Kelly out of his blood.

He would be honest. He'd never speak of marriage, he'd never say that he loved her, he'd never promise more than pleasure. That he could give her without hesitation. She'd melted in his arms more than once, and hadn't shied away there by the lake when he'd touched her bare skin.

Maddalyn had cast a spell over him, a spell that made his mind spin with impossible dreams of his own. There was only one way to break the spell.

Before Maddalyn left the mountain, he would have everything he wanted from her. Her body beneath his, her surrender, his proof that she was just like any other woman.

Karl would kill him.

It would be worth it.

"It's not that you're not a very sweet man, Gavin," Maddalyn said. "It's just that . . . well, I don't love you, and I can't marry a man I don't love."

He looked every bit as hurt as she'd expected, his dark eyes taking on a hangdog expression.

"We just need some more time," he insisted.

Maddalyn had asked Gavin to meet her in front of the general store, hoping that he wouldn't make a scene for the entire town to see, as he very well might if they met privately.

"I don't think—"

"It's that Eric Barrett fella, isn't it?" Gavin snapped, not even giving her a chance to explain. "You know, I think I've been very understanding about you living up there with those three fellas all this time without any supervision. Why, it looks just awful, but I didn't say a word."

Maddalyn was rarely truly indignant, but she felt the ire rising within her. "There's no reason for anyone to concern themselves—"

"I believe it is my concern," Gavin interrupted her again. "When the woman I love makes a spectacle of herself."

"A spectacle?" Maddalyn repeated. "I suppose you would have preferred that I froze to death, rather than accept the Barretts' hospitality. How dare you?"

The anger fled from his face, and Gavin was hangdog once again. "I'm sorry. I didn't mean it. I just . . . I really do love you, Maddalyn."

"You can't possibly love me," she insisted, still ill-tempered. "You don't know me, not at all. Why, I have all sorts of bad habits."

"Such as?"

Maddalyn took a deep breath. "I do tend to talk too much, even early in the morning. It can be quite irritating."

"I don't mind."

"And I have a terrible temper. You haven't seen the half of it."

"I'll never give you anything to be angry about," he promised eagerly.

"I'm much too bossy. Everything has to be done my way, or I'm cross for a week," she promised.

"We'll do everything your way."

Maddalyn sighed tiredly. He was so fervent, so insistent. "Gavin," she said softly, "I won't marry you. I can't. I'm sorry."

He looked like a sullen little boy, almost pouty, and Maddalyn laid a hand on his arm. "You'll find the right woman when the time is right."

"I've already found the right woman," he insisted.

Maddalyn shook her head slightly. "No. Not yet, but she's out there, you just haven't found her. She's a very lucky woman, whoever she is."

She meant her words to soothe him, but he left her standing there, storming off silently and leaving her alone on the boardwalk.

It had been a terrible mistake to tell him that she would consider his proposal. If she'd refused quickly, it would have been much easier.

But the thought of being a part of Eric's family, however distant, had been so tempting. It was almost irresistible. Almost.

"Lovers' spat?"

At the sound of the harshly spoken words, Maddalyn spun around and glared at Eric. How long had he been standing there?

"Don't worry yourself. It's none of your concern."

Eric pushed himself away from the wall he leaned against and stepped toward her. "I didn't say I was concerned or worried, Maddalyn. Just curious."

She couldn't breathe correctly when he was this close. "I just . . . gave Gavin his answer."

"He didn't look too happy. What was your answer, anyway?"

Maddalyn turned her back on him. Insensitive lout.

But he caught her arm and spun her around. "What was your answer, Maddalyn?" His humor was gone, and he delivered the question seriously, almost as if it mattered to him.

"I told him that I couldn't marry him, that I intend to continue on to Sheridan and fulfill my obligations there." His grip loosened, but he didn't release her.

"On to Sheridan," he repeated lightly. "You've been a long time getting there."

"Too long," she agreed. "Much too long."

"And now another delay." He released her arm, allowing his fingers to slide down her sleeve and over her hand. "Just so you can be Conrad's best man."

"I'm not really going to be Conrad's best man; that's ridiculous. I'm just going to be a witness for the ceremony." She lifted her chin, and Eric grinned down at her serious face.

And it was such a lovely grin. Bright and clear, and at the moment full of mischief.

"Back to the mountain tomorrow morning," he said lightly.

She should have known that the reason for his rare good humor was the prospect of returning to the mountain. Maddalyn couldn't deny that she felt some of the same anticipation.

"You can't wait to get out of Olympia, can you?" she asked, no longer able to be angry with him. He looked so oddly content.

His grin widened. "I can't wait."

Chapter Twenty

"Are you sure you wouldn't rather stay with us?" Kathleen asked once again as Maddalyn watched Karl affix the last of her belongings to the pack mule and then turn to a waiting Daisy.

"It's very sweet of you to ask, but I'm afraid it would be awkward."

Gavin had not taken her refusal very graciously. As a matter of fact, she had already spotted him three times this morning, skulking and furtively watching the party prepare to leave. He tried unsuccessfully to hide behind posts that were too narrow, or else he spied on them from behind a dark window. He actually seemed to be sulking, and Maddalyn realized that Eric had been correct. Gavin was just a child.

"You could stay with Daisy," Kathleen offered,

"if you're worried about Gavin. I know it must be a difficult trip for you."

"Not difficult at all," Maddalyn said with a smile. "Besides, I have so much to do. Curtains to make, those two dresses you gave me to mend and alter. And the boys have so much to do, they'll need someone to cook for them, to make certain they take care of themselves."

"Don't worry about Gavin," Kathleen whispered, leaning in close. "He'll be himself in no time. I swear, he falls in and out of love as often as the wind changes direction."

It was a relief to know that perhaps what Gavin had felt for her was not real love after all, but some sort of infatuation. Rather like Conrad's earlier fascination with any old redhead. She'd have to be careful not to mention that tidbit of information to Kathleen.

Maddalyn liked Kathleen, and Daisy, too. More than she could have imagined. Their personalities were dissimilar, but they were both sweet, fun to talk to, generous with their time and their laughter. They had become friends so quickly it was amazing. But Maddalyn was anxious to return to the cabin, to spend a few more evenings sitting before the fire with the Barrett brothers. She might never have family like this again.

"Time to go," Eric said. She had expected Karl or Conrad to assist her onto Winchester's back. Eric had been avoiding her so blatantly she'd begun to expect his apathy for her. Why, he hadn't said a word to her since she'd told him that she'd refused Gavin's offer of marriage.

But there he stood, taking her hand and placing an arm lightly around her waist as she very cautiously seated herself.

Even though Winchester's back was not so far from the ground—at least compared to the horses Eric and his brothers rode—Maddalyn clung to Eric's sleeve until she felt securely seated. Oddly enough, he didn't seem to mind.

Kathleen was off to say good-bye to Conrad. Karl and Daisy had been saying their farewells all morning, it seemed. There were no tears, since the Barretts would be gone less than three weeks, and when they returned it would be to the finest double wedding Olympia had ever seen.

Of course, it was also the only double wedding Olympia had ever seen.

"Happy?" Eric asked, just a touch of sarcasm in his voice. Maddalyn pulled her eyes away from the cheerful couples and stared into Eric's face. "You have such a satisfied smile on your face when you survey your handiwork, it's hard to ignore."

She wanted to look away, he stared at her so intently, but to do so would have been a defeat. Maddalyn didn't exactly understand why; she just knew that was true. So she met his gaze squarely, without so much as a flinch.

"They're four very nice people," she said, grasping the saddle horn and straightening her spine. "I think it's marvelous that everything worked out so well."

He placed his hand at the small of her back, and it felt unexpectedly wonderful. Warm and strong, and for goodness' sake she could feel it to her bones.

"Will Sheridan wait for you?" he asked in a near whisper.

"I telegraphed Mrs. Hudson, and she replied that my position will still be available in a month."

He leaned in close to her, much too close, checking the reins and the security of her saddle. Surely he could have done that before she'd gotten settled.

Maddalyn actually breathed a sigh of relief when Eric moved away, and the beating of her heart could return to a normal pace. For now, she wouldn't pine or wallow in self-pity because she couldn't have the man she loved. The brothers mounted their horses and prepared to leave Olympia. Hallelujah. She was going home.

If she'd thought it were possible, Maddalyn would have suggested that they ride through the night to reach the cabin. Of course, that wouldn't do. The animals needed their rest, and the shaded path that wound up the mountain would be completely black at night.

But she was so very anxious to reach the top of Eric's mountain. It was a gift she had not expected to receive, a reprieve. A return to the Barrett cabin. She tried to convince herself that when she reached Sheridan she would settle in as nicely as she had with the three brothers, but no matter how hard she tried she couldn't quite make it work. Something special had happened to her when she'd entered that cabin, when she'd seen Eric's photograph, when he'd rescued her from the blizzard. It might never happen again.

She rolled onto her back and tried to count the stars above her head, hoping the mindless chore might lull her to sleep, but there were too many sparkling lights in the sky. Countless stars against a velvet black night.

"Can't sleep?"

Maddalyn jumped, startled nearly out of her skin. The night had been so quiet, she'd been certain everyone else was asleep, and had been for some time. But Eric's voice was clear and soft, without a hint of sleepiness in it. She rolled to her side so she could see him stretched out on his own bedroll.

"No. I . . ." She hated to lie, but she couldn't tell him that going back to his cabin was like going home. He would only see it as another attempt to trap him into a marriage he didn't want. "I've been thinking about the wedding, and Karl's curtains."

She kept her voice low, so as not to disturb Karl and Conrad. They slept close by, no doubt dreaming of Daisy and Kathleen.

"Why aren't you asleep?" she breathed.

Goodness, he wasn't a full five feet away. She could ignore that fact when she kept her back to him, but not now. If she reached out her hand, and he reached out his, they would touch. Wouldn't it be wonderful, to fall asleep with his hand over hers? A simple touch. Innocent, almost.

"I have a lot of things on my mind," he whispered.

"The railroad contract," she answered. "Two new cabins. Two new sisters-in-law. Goodness, it's no wonder you can't sleep."

He murmured an answer, and Maddalyn scooted just slightly closer to him. She didn't want to wake Conrad and Karl, after all. She brought the bedroll with her and slithered across the hard ground like a snake. "Sometimes, when I can't sleep, I close my eyes and think of something pleasant. A rose, a perfect sunrise, a beautiful painting. Not food," she added quickly. "Once I tried to think of the smell of freshly baking bread, which is most certainly pleasant, but I just got hungry. So there I was, unable to sleep and hungry to boot."

"Did you sneak into the kitchen for a midnight snack?"

"Oh, no," she breathed. "That would have been breaking one of Aunt Ethel's most steadfast rules."

"Don't you ever break the rules, Maddalyn?" Eric's whisper was so soft, so intimate, it made her shiver.

"Not usually," she confessed. "Sometimes, when there's no other choice, I simply do what I must."

"Me, too," he answered.

She could hardly hear him, so she scooted just a

little bit closer. "I know you're angry because I played matchmaker with Karl and Conrad, but I hope you'll forgive me. I just hate to see anyone alone."

"I'm not angry with you." His voice was no louder than it had been before, but Conrad stirred, muttering in his sleep and tossing on his bedroll just a few feet away.

"We should get to sleep," Maddalyn said, barely breathing.

Eric made a noncommittal noise deep in his throat and raised himself up so that his head rested in one hand.

"Close your eyes and think of something pleasant," she suggested.

She'd moved too close to him, even though she was still a distance away from his bedroll. Her heart beat fast, and her mouth went dry. It was going to be so difficult to walk away from him and pretend it didn't matter.

"I don't have to close my eyes."

"Of course you do. Otherwise it won't work." She made an attempt to sound perfectly normal, as if she didn't have any idea what he was thinking. Of course, that was another lie.

It would be heavenly to scoot across the space that remained between them, to place herself in his arms for the night. It was a scandalous thought, of course, and one that she didn't dare share.

But she remembered too well what his touch did to her. He brought her to life somehow, as if she'd

Linda Jones

been sleepwalking through life until she'd found Eric. Waiting, simply waiting for him to find her.

"Would you tell me about Jane?" she asked softly.

The moonlight illuminated one side of his face, and she saw the muscles there tighten, saw a muscle in his jaw twitch.

"I thought you said we should think of something pleasant," he growled.

Maddalyn bit her lower lip and moved just a little closer. She didn't want Conrad or Karl to wake and hear their late-night conversation. "I want to understand why you're so certain these marriages will end unhappily. I want . . . I want to give this woman a face. Jane. Such an ordinary name. I can't picture her in my mind, and I want to."

"I don't."

His answer was so harsh, Maddalyn resigned herself to never knowing any more than she already did. "Sorry."

For several long minutes he was silent, but Maddalyn didn't lie on her back and close her eyes, didn't bother with trying to picture in her mind a perfect flower or sunset. She would watch Eric for as long as she could, forget about sleep for this one night.

"Even Conrad and Karl don't know everything," he said at last. His anger was gone, and there was a resignation in his voice that captured Maddalyn's heart. He was so big, so strong, and still he could be hurt. Eric Barrett was not invincible after all.

302

"She wasn't here for a few days, like they think. She lived in the cabin for four months."

"Oh." Maddalyn sighed. Somehow she had wanted to be the only woman who had ever run that household. To cook in that kitchen. To sweep the dirt the boys tracked in off the floor. The only woman to watch Eric by the light of the fire at the end of the day.

"I was just getting the logging business started, which meant there were weeks when I couldn't even get a letter to her. I went to Boston to visit, when I had the opportunity, to make our final plans. Karl and Conrad were working undercover at the time, so I couldn't reach them with the news of the wedding. Jane's mother was giving her a hard time about settling for me, and Jane decided she didn't want to wait. Neither did I. So we forgot the planned engagement and were married in St. Louis on our way home."

Maddalyn's heart sank, and she felt physically ill. Married.

"Jane Reese Barrett," he whispered. "That was her full name. You want a picture? She was beautiful. Black hair, green eyes, twenty years old, and sought after by every eligible bachelor in Boston. I worked security for her father for six months, and that was how we met."

His voice was cold, emotionless, but with every word Maddalyn felt more anxious.

"She hated it here from the first day. It got worse as the weeks passed and I had to spend most of the day cutting. In those days, before Karl and Conrad came in with me, I had a few hired hands that lived down the hill, and we had enough orders to keep us busy every day. It was a new business. I couldn't let the few contracts I had slide, but Jane never understood that. She'd never seen her father do any actual work; everything she wanted was just . . . there."

"I'm sorry I asked," Maddalyn whispered. "You don't have to—"

"She hated the mountain, she hated the cabin, and before too long she hated me. Jane gave me an ultimatum. I could have her or the mountain. I chose the mountain."

"Eric—"

"Jane returned to Boston," Eric continued as if he hadn't heard her. "And after a few weeks I began to feel guilty. I hadn't tried hard enough; I hadn't . . . loved her enough. So I went to Boston to bring her back. To convince her to give our marriage one more try."

Maddalyn could see that he stared over her head, past her. One hand rested on the ground, a hard fist, and she reached out to cover it with her own hand. She half expected that Eric would pull away, but he didn't.

"I gave her family quite a shock. Jane, too. There she was, all dressed in black, surrounded by caring men who were there to console her after the death of her husband. Dead," he said coldly. "She told everyone that I was dead, because it was more socially acceptable to be widowed than divorced."

"What did you do?" Maddalyn rocked her fingers over Eric's fist, and he didn't seem to mind. The tensed muscles beneath her hand relaxed just a little.

"I tried to do the right thing, especially after her father told me that she was going to have a child. He was the only one who thought it would be best for her to come back with me. Jane's mother was all for killing me off and continuing with the grieving widow routine."

A touch of sarcasm entered his voice, his own defense against the pain. Maddalyn was careful not to show how ill she felt. Did he have a wife and child out there somewhere?

"But Jane wasn't coming back, no matter what. She took this . . . medicine. Half a bottle. NOT FOR USE BY EXPECTANT MOTHERS, it read in big letters across the label. She lost the baby, of course. That was her intention, though I don't think she intended to nearly die in the process. I sat with her, because I felt it was my duty, and I listened as she told me again and again that she'd rather die than come back to me. When the doctor finally said that she'd live, I signed the divorce papers her mother shoved at me and I left. I suppose there are people in Boston who still think I'm dead."

He'd told the horrible story without emotion, but Maddalyn knew now why Eric was apprehensive about marriage. He'd loved Jane, and she'd betrayed him in the worst possible way. Perhaps he'd never be able to forget what she'd done to him.

"That's why you don't care for ladies," she whispered. His hand relaxed, and she threaded her fingers through his.

All she got was another noncommittal hum.

"I'm sorry," she whispered. "Most ladies aren't like that. As a matter of fact, she doesn't sound very ladylike at all." Maddalyn found that she couldn't speak the woman's name aloud. Jane Reese Barrett. "Now close your eyes and think of something pleasant."

Maddalyn continued to hold Eric's hand, their fingers intertwined lightly, their palms touching. He needed that, she decided, even if he refused to admit that he needed anything at all from her.

"The view from that rock just a few feet from the front porch," she suggested, closing her own eyes. "All green and blue and gray, and stretching ahead forever and forever." That wasn't what she saw, of course. Behind closed eyes she saw Eric, and she could remember so clearly how marvelous she felt when he kissed her.

Maybe, if Conrad and Karl didn't watch over her like a couple of mother hens, he would kiss her again before she left for Sheridan.

It was a dangerous thought. Maddalyn was innocent, but not completely stupid. Mary Lynette had acquainted her quite well with what she knew of the male mind.

Soon kissing wouldn't be enough. Mary Lynette had told Maddalyn, very sternly, that men had no patience at all where their libidos were concerned. That it was up to her to draw the line, to make it clear that she was not to be abused.

The problem was, Maddalyn wasn't sure where the line should be, and she didn't think Eric would ever abuse her.

As she fell asleep, she had the most wonderfully wanton thoughts.

Eric woke suddenly, with the sharp jab of a boot toe in his back. On another morning, he would have jumped to his feet, but not today.

Maddalyn was snuggled quite contentedly against his chest, her face lifted toward his, her arms around his waist. She had managed to drag most of her bedroll with her, but had left a good portion of it trailing behind.

She was sound asleep and showed no signs that his movements had disturbed her at all.

"You've got some explaining to do, little brother," Conrad grumbled from above.

"Hey, I didn't move." Eric gestured with the one hand he could work free. "She did."

It didn't seem a satisfactory explanation, at least not to Conrad and a scowling Karl.

"Maybe you'd better get up," Karl suggested sternly.

Eric ignored his brothers and looked down at the woman sleeping in his arms. Had he really relented and told her the story he'd sworn never to tell? Her innocent, heartfelt words came back to him. *Tell me about Jane.*

Think of something pleasant. He had. He'd thought of Maddalyn, of taking her in the bed he'd found her in, of losing himself in her for a time.

It had been as useless as her baking bread, and he hadn't been able to sleep until she'd finally succumbed herself, and she'd rolled instinctively into his arms.

"I hate to wake her," he whispered. "She had a hard time falling asleep last night."

Conrad snorted, and poked Eric in the spine with his boot once again.

"Maddalyn," Eric called, keeping his voice low. Conrad finally wandered away, and Eric brushed a wayward strand of golden hair off of Maddalyn's cheek. She pursed her lips and wrinkled her nose and pressed herself against him. From the foot she wrapped around his leg, to the cheek she laid against his chest, she touched him.

"Time to wake up," he whispered.

Her eyes fluttered and opened slowly, and she gave him a listless smile. "Good morning."

She seemed to realize all at once where she was, and she stiffened and tried to move away from him. It was a short-lived and gentle struggle. Eric held her tight and leaned down to whisper in her ear.

"Don't tell."

She relaxed and lifted her face to him. It was such an honest face, so full of trust and innocence.

"I won't," she whispered, and Eric believed her. He trusted her with the only secret he'd ever kept from his brothers.

He didn't want their sympathy. He didn't want Maddalyn's either, but it wasn't sympathy he saw in her sleepy eyes.

It was love he'd seen there all along, and it scared him now more than ever.

He didn't want Maddalyn to love him, because he didn't know how to love her back. He didn't want her to trust herself so damned easily into his hands, into his arms. He didn't want her to become a part of his life, because he knew it wouldn't last.

Loving and losing Jane had hurt.

Loving and losing Maddalyn would destroy him.

Chapter Twenty-one

Walking up the hill to the cabin, Maddalyn felt her excitement grow. Home. For a while longer, at least. When she crested the hill she couldn't stop the smile that spread across her face. Impossibly, it was more beautiful than before. Shining, splendid, waiting patiently for their return.

Karl was already complaining about his growling stomach, and even Conrad had claimed an unusually strong hunger. Tonight she'd prepare a supper they wouldn't forget. The table would groan under the weight of it.

Her own stomach was churning with excitement, and she knew she wouldn't be able to eat much, herself.

The air inside the cabin was a little stale, and Maddalyn opened every window in the house. The wind rushed in, fresh and cool, touching every corner. Bringing the cabin back to life.

"Home sweet home," Conrad called jovially as he carried in the first load of many that would have to be made from the bottom of the hill. He deposited the parcels from the general store on the kitchen table.

Eric and Karl were close behind him, and they were laden as well.

Maddalyn carried the bolt of white material to her room and deposited it on the foot of the bed, and then she spent a moment standing at the window. The land beyond was much more magnificent than any town would ever be. It was fresh and green and magical, and for a while longer it was hers.

And for a while longer Eric would be hers. Perhaps not in the way she wanted, but if it was all she could have, she'd take it gladly.

Perhaps they would, after all, finish what they'd started by the lake. Eric wanted that, she knew, even though he didn't love her. She could love enough for both of them, for a while.

"Where do you want these?"

Maddalyn turned away from the window. Eric stood in the doorway, filled it. He held her bundle of belongings, spare shirts and the dresses Kathleen had given her, the comb and brush and hand mirror Daisy had insisted she take. It wasn't much, but it was bundled neatly and wrapped in burlap.

"On the bed will be fine."

Someone's Been Sleeping in My Bed

He was different here, not as tense or as ornery. But he had changed, and it was more than the comfort of being home.

Maybe he had accepted that what was between them was not going to change. She had. It hadn't been easy, to acknowledge that she would never have Eric's love, that he had none to give. If he had been able to accept that there was something between them, even though she was a lady, then perhaps her remaining days on the mountain would be pleasant ones.

He dropped her bundle on the bed, but instead of leaving the room he joined her at the window.

"Look," he said, pointing over her shoulder, and Maddalyn turned.

A deer stood at the edge of the heavily wooded forest, alert, head up, magnificent and beautiful. Maddalyn held her breath and watched the animal that barely moved.

Eric placed a hand on her shoulder and stepped closer to her, pressing his body against her back. She could have moved forward half a step, but she didn't. It felt too good.

His other hand rested lightly at her waist, and then he kissed the top of her head. It was a brushing of his lips so brief, so easy, it came and went much too quickly. Then he lightly rested his chin there where he'd kissed her.

"It's a doe," he whispered.

"She's beautiful."

"This time of year they're everywhere. See that?"

313

He lifted his hand from her shoulder and pointed again.

Maddalyn saw movement in the trees, saw a small deer passing uncertainly through a clearing.

"That's probably her fawn."

His hand returned to her shoulder, and they stood there for several minutes without speaking.

"What's this?" Conrad called loudly from the doorway, and Maddalyn and Eric both turned toward the caustic voice. Conrad stepped into the room boldly, his eyebrows lifted high in obvious disapproval.

"Look," Maddalyn whispered, and Conrad stepped to the window, standing beside her and doing his best to displace Eric.

Conrad smiled brightly as he glanced out the window. "Supper!"

"Conrad Barrett," Maddalyn said sharply. "She is not supper. She's a mother."

He gave her a look that was properly contrite and still more than a little condescending.

"So we can only shoot deer that have no children? Should we stop to ask first? Pardon me, madam, but do you have any little ones?" His smile widened. "And what about fathers? Is it fair to spare a doe's life because she has reproduced, and not spare the buck as well?"

"I don't particularly care for venison, personally," Maddalyn informed him calmly.

"Come on, Eric," Conrad called, turning away from the window. "We've got a lot to do, and only a couple hours of light left."

The hand at her shoulder trailed away, the fingers trailing across her back in what Maddalyn could almost imagine was reluctance.

Those first few days passed much too quickly to suit Maddalyn, and she didn't see Eric nearly often enough. The pace of their lives had changed; there was so much to do with the railroad contract and the building of two more cabins on the mountain.

Conrad chose the site for his new home not far from Eric's cabin, in a clearing surrounded by imposing pines. Maddalyn had visited the spot Conrad had chosen only once. The cabin he and Kathleen would live in would be all but hidden in the forest.

Karl was building a new home down the hill a ways. The back of his cabin would be nestled against the side of the mountain, rather like a gambler with his back to the wall.

Maddalyn had sewn curtains for all three cabins, white and lightweight. She had made them as simple as possible. No lace, no frills at all. Nothing but a flat curtain and a tieback.

There was even a curtain hanging in Eric's bedroom, the bedroom she had taken over during her time on the mountain.

She had also been doing her best to mend their best suits, dark trousers and jackets, white linen shirts and silk neckties. There were popped seams to be repaired, stains to be cleaned, buttons to be sewn on.

Of course, Eric didn't have a proper dark suit. The trousers had been shortened for her own use, but then they had been placed in that trunk of discarded clothes, and she'd had no way of knowing that it was his best pair of pants. She did manage to round up a decent pair of trousers that Karl had outgrown, and along with Conrad's second-best jacket they made a fine suit.

One evening, on her second night back in the cabin, Maddalyn had tried to sneak into the main room after Conrad and Karl had retired, for a word with Eric. Just a word, that was all she wanted, a quiet moment alone with the man she loved. They were never unchaperoned. He left the cabin in the morning with his brothers, and they returned together in time for supper. She didn't even cook the brothers a noontime meal anymore. They took what Maddalyn considered a poor excuse for a proper dinner with them.

Conrad and Karl were maddeningly diligent in their efforts to keep Eric away from her.

She had not, of course, had a chance to speak with Eric on that evening or any other. The hinges on her door squealed horribly as she eased it open, and before she'd entered the hallway, Karl and Conrad were there.

And time was running out. Every day that passed brought her closer to the end of her time in this place.

Someone's Been Sleeping in My Bed

Today was laundry day. The sun was shining brightly, and there was a warm breeze blowing gently. She'd run a rope from the cabin to a sturdy tree and back again, and from that rope hung damp clothing that would, she hoped, dry before nightfall.

For a long moment Maddalyn stood very still and watched. The sun on drying clothes and bedding that whipped in the wind, the cabin surrounded by trees so tall and strong and old, the sky that was—on this afternoon—the most magnificent shade of blue.

It tugged at her heart much more strongly than it should have, and she hugged her arms to her body.

Why wasn't life more like her dreams? Why did Eric still love Jane? She knew that was true, that he mourned the desertion of his wife more than he dared to admit.

"It should have been me," she whispered to herself. "If he'd loved me I would have loved him back. If he loved me, I would never leave this place."

Talking to herself again. What would Aunt Ethel say?

Eric stood in the shadow of the trees and watched. The wind lifted her curls and made her red skirt dance, but she didn't move at all.

He was a fool for detouring from the path between the cabins Karl and Conrad were so intent on finishing, but he hadn't been able to help himself. She was there, alone, and he'd almost been able to convince himself that he'd be satisfied with a glance.

There was something about Maddalyn that called to him, an insistent tugging that stayed with him all day and all night, as he lay awake by the dying fire and even in his dreams. She was always in his dreams.

And now, with the sun on golden curls that fell unrestrained down her back, she was too tempting to ignore. She watched the laundry before her as if there were something there to see, something mesmerizing.

At the end of the line, a stark contrast to the workshirts and pants that were spread wide, to the white sheets that flapped in the breeze, there danced two flimsy-looking pieces of clothing: a chemise that was lined with lace and a pair of bloomers.

He knew damn good and well that there had been no replacements for those garments in the trunk of discarded clothing Maddalyn had scrounged in.

He didn't try to soften his step, but if she heard him coming up behind her she gave no indication.

Every word, every touch, every moment had been leading to this. He didn't believe in love anymore, but he knew that he needed her. Even that concession was more than he wanted to admit, more than he wanted to give.

She must have heard him coming, because when

he wrapped his arms around her she didn't flinch. Maddalyn showed no surprise at all, not even when he lowered his lips to her neck and pulled her back against his chest.

Maddalyn tilted her head to one side and Eric trailed his lips along the shoulder that revealed itself. He wanted to taste her, to touch every inch of her tender skin.

Did she know that he needed her? She lifted one hand to caress the back of his head, a gentle touch that spurred him on.

She was warm and soft, and he caressed the breasts beneath his old shirt with his fingers and the palms of his hands, quick and easy, feathery touches. Her nipples hardened in his palms, and he could feel the quickening of her pulse beneath his lips.

The buttons slipped through his fingers, and he slid his hands beneath the shirt to touch her skin. Silky, perfect skin. Rounded breasts he held gently, a flat stomach that quivered as he trailed his fingers across the taut muscles.

He buried his face against her neck, and her curls brushed his face and his throat. That gentle sensation, the brush of her hair against his skin, was crystal clear, intense.

Beneath the tender assault of his hands, Maddalyn trembled. The nipples beneath his palms were pebbled, and her heartbeat, the heartbeat he felt with his lips and his hands, raced.

He wouldn't let her go, not this time.

She turned in his arms and lifted her lips to his, offering him her mouth. He took it, harder than he had intended, and then he gentled the pressure.

There wasn't enough time—would never be enough time—to make love to her the way he wanted to. Not if they had the day, the week, a long winter. Maddalyn ran her hands slowly up his neck, through his hair, to hold him tight as she teased his tongue with hers.

It was a kiss like the others, deep and almost painful. Maddalyn pressed her body against his, crushed her breasts against him, and met his passion with a need, an urgency that matched his own.

She wouldn't be sorry. He wouldn't leave any room for regret.

When he lowered his lips to her breasts and took a nipple in his mouth, a cry caught in her throat. Surprise. Passion. Hunger.

She was so beautiful, with the sun on her pale skin, glistening on dampened nipples he kissed and kissed again.

Maddalyn breathed his name, a plea and a question that was more than he could stand.

He knew it was wrong, even as he took her in his arms and claimed her mouth with his own. It was also undeniably right, and holding Maddalyn was the only sane and reasonable response to an insane world.

They worked their way toward the cabin until they stood between two walls of drying wash, sheets that caught the sun and made their hideaway bright. Maddalyn managed to unfasten his shirt and spread it wide, and examined his chest as thoroughly as he'd examined hers.

He lifted the red calico in his hands, bunching up the material and raising her skirt until he could lay his hands against her thighs, against her bare hips, until he could grasp her buttocks and pull her against his arousal.

Eric dropped slowly to the ground and brought Maddalyn with him, so that she sat across his thighs. Sitting in his lap, she rained kisses on his mouth, his neck, she caressed his flat nipples with her tongue.

"I feel . . ." she breathed, lifting her eyes to his, "I feel like we've waited forever for this."

He answered her with a deep kiss, and he slipped his hand between her legs. Maddalyn moaned when he touched her, and spread her legs wider for him. She held nothing back, showed him no reluctance, no uncertainty. He had been prepared to coax, to seduce her if need be, but she came to him as if they'd been together a thousand times before.

His fingers touched her gently, and he felt her grow ready for him. Wet, hot, rocking easily against his hand. Giving herself completely over to instinct.

Eric watched her face, the growing wonder there, the mounting desire that filled her eyes. He didn't doubt her innocence. He knew no man had ever touched her but him, had ever brought that light to her eyes.

The tail end of a drying sheet whipped behind her, framing her passion-filled face for him in a picture he knew he'd never forget.

She locked her lips to his once again, and Eric slid a finger inside her tight sheath. Maddalyn deepened the kiss, held on to him fast, rocked against his hand. He felt the tremble that worked its way through her body, touched her harder, faster, until she cried out against his mouth and quaked in his arms.

The tremors died, and her kiss softened. "Oh, my," she whispered. "Was that . . . was that . . ."

"Yes, it was, darlin'."

She pulled her face slightly away from his and gave him the softest, most seductive smile. Maddalyn placed her hand in his lap, brushing her fingers over his arousal. Her eyes widened just slightly as she began to unfasten his trousers.

When his manhood sprang free he saw the first sign of doubt on her face.

"Are you . . . absolutely positive that this will work?" she asked breathlessly.

"Absolutely," he whispered.

Her doubt fled, and she took him in her hands. Her touch was hesitant at first, as she explored the feel of him, and then her touch grew firmer. Eric lifted her, set her above him. She straddled his hips and lowered herself slowly. Torturously slowly.

She was wet, and so tight it was all he could do

to wait. He wanted to plunge deep, to have all of her—now. But he didn't. He allowed her to take him slowly, until he met the barrier of her virginity.

Maddalyn took his face between her hands, laid her lips against his, and in one swift movement took all of him. She was still for a moment, and it was all Eric could do to remain motionless. When she began to move again it was with a certain rhythm, an instinctive cadence that matched the throbbing in his blood. A primal beat they found only together.

She whispered his name—*Eric*—a breath against his mouth, his throat. Even that sound, his own name against his lips and his skin, was a caress.

He heard the quickening of her breath, and Maddalyn began to move faster, more urgently against him, until he folded his arms around her and thrust so deeply into her she would never be able to deny that he possessed her.

Tremors rocked him, grabbed him and wouldn't let go. Maddalyn held on as if to let go would mean death. She cried out softly and convulsed in his arms once more, and Eric clutched her in his arms, afraid to let go, afraid for this to end.

Maddalyn collapsed against his chest, laying her head against his shoulder and breathing deeply. He was still inside her, still a part of her.

Had he really thought that this would cure him of his obsession?

"I cannot move," she whispered.

"That's all right." He lifted the hair away from her face so he could study her face. Her cheeks were pink, her lips swollen, her eyes bright. "Neither can I."

She smiled so easily, and then she planted a lazy kiss on the side of his neck. "I suppose I should be shy now, and cry and carry on, and declare that this never should have happened."

"Should you?"

"Yes, but I just don't have the energy to do so. Crying and carrying on take a lot of work, you know."

Eric smiled at her teasing words. She kissed his jaw with a maddening lethargy, touched him with gentle exploring fingers, his chest and shoulders, his rib cage and hips.

And he knew he would have to have Maddalyn again and again to rid himself of his appetite for her.

"Tell me everything," Maddalyn insisted with a smile as she sat herself at the table with three very tired-looking men. "I don't want to see the new cabins until they're finished, or at least almost finished, and I can hang the curtains."

"There won't be any glass in the windows until after the wedding," Karl reminded her.

Poor Karl, his eyes drooped. Conrad was silent, focusing all his attention on the food before him. Maddalyn felt bad for them: they were working so very hard, cutting in the morning, and working on the new cabins in the afternoon, exhausting themselves as they prepared homes for their brides.

She had tried, throughout the meal, not to stare at Eric. Whenever she did glance his way, he grinned at her—a wicked grin that certainly would have told anyone who saw it exactly what was on his mind. If Karl or Conrad had been paying a bit of attention, they certainly would have known what had happened that afternoon.

Maddalyn's face grew warm at the thought. She should be ashamed, she should be absolutely horrified at the way she'd behaved, but there was no shame or horror in her heart.

It had been more beautiful than she had imagined, and certainly more powerful. The earth had stopped spinning, for a time, while Eric had been a part of her.

From across the table he smiled at her, and a foot lightly brushed against her leg. She moved away, but his foot found her leg again, and this time she didn't bother to withdraw it.

Stop that. She mouthed the admonishment at him, but his grin only widened.

"I'm making the kitchen twice as big as this one," Karl said, never taking his eyes from his plate. "When the new stove I ordered comes in, and I get all the shelves built, and I run in the pump, it'll be the finest kitchen in Wyoming Territory."

"Leave it to Karl to concentrate all his energy in the kitchen," Conrad grumbled. "Wait till you see the porches on my cabin. Front and back, the length of the house, with sloping overhangs on both sides. I'm even building a small porch off the big bedroom, and putting a door there, with a window on either side."

"It sounds lovely," Maddalyn said, never taking her eyes from Eric. If he was willing to live dangerously, so was she. "I can't wait to see them both."

The meal continued that way, Karl and Conrad talking about the cabins they were building for their brides while Eric stared at her silently. He ate slowly, licking his lips while she watched. It made her heart beat faster, and so she returned the favor. She licked her lips and then her fingers, while Conrad talked about the fireplace he was building. Eric actually blushed.

Maddalyn knew Eric didn't love her, though she tried to push that certainty to the back of her mind. She loved him completely, the way she knew love was supposed to be. And he did feel something for her. Perhaps it was simply physical, the sort of passion that would eventually burn out, but it was strong.

Strong enough to make Eric come to her, even though he had an understandable aversion to ladies.

It was enough, even though she knew it wouldn't last. There were just a few days left, and then she'd leave the mountain and continue on to Sheridan.

In those few days, she intended to make enough memories to last a lifetime.

Chapter Twenty-two

Maddalyn gathered the edge of the quilt to her chin and stared at the closed door. She had tried to leave it open just wide enough for her to slip carefully through. Of course, that hadn't worked. Not at all. Karl had appeared at her door, bidden her a yawning good night, and shut the screaming door firmly.

There was no way she was getting out of this room without alerting the entire household.

How could she possibly sleep? This big bed was suddenly lonely, too broad and too empty for her alone. Like a single bean all alone in the center of a fancy platter. If she could only have Eric beside her, if she could hold on to him in the night and sleep in his arms, the bed would be just right.

Frustrated, she rolled away from the door and

faced the window—and there he was. Standing outside the window with his forearms on the windowsill and his chin resting on folded hands. She should have been startled, but it wasn't surprise that made her heart race.

"Eric." She sat up and allowed the quilt to fall to her waist. When she whispered his name he smiled at her, a welcoming smile in the moonlight.

He pushed the panes of glass high and boosted himself up and through the window, casting eerie shadows across the floor as he entered her room silently and crossed the floor on bare feet.

There was no question that she would welcome him into her bed, into her arms for the night. While this cabin was her home Eric belonged to her, and she would risk everything to keep him close.

Eric sat on the side of the bed and reached out to her, smoothing her hair away from her face, trailing his fingers over her cheek and down her throat. His welcoming smile faded.

"I couldn't stay away," he whispered.

"I know."

Their whispers were soft, breathy words that wouldn't carry beyond the room, beyond the bed, even.

He undressed her without the urgency of their afternoon encounter. Each button of her nightshirt—of his old shirt—was unfastened and then followed by a tender kiss. On her mouth, her throat, her shoulders. When he stripped the shirt from her, he touched her with exploring fingers that were roughened and yet tender. As though he'd never touched her before. As though he'd never seen the breasts he caressed, the bare arms he trailed his palms down.

He owned more than her heart; he owned her body. It responded to his touch, even to the questing of his hungry eyes, with an ever-increasing throbbing, an ever-growing urgency.

Maddalyn reached out and unfastened his shirt. Her hands trembled, but she moved as deliberately as he did. They had all night, and she wanted to make this a night to remember. She wanted to see all of him, to taste him, to feel him deep inside her body.

She peeled the shirt away and laid her palms against his chest. So strong, so hard, and yet she could feel his heart beating against her hand. It thudded in his chest, in a rhythm much like her own heart's. As though they were one even now, before they were joined, before he was physically a part of her.

He lay down beside her, taking her in his arms and placing his bare flesh against hers, and they kissed. Those wonderful kisses were deep and slow, fast and light. All was silent except for the rush of her blood and the pounding of her heart.

Eric's hands continued to explore her body, brushing over nipples that were surprisingly sensitive, traveling over her back and her thighs with a touch so leisurely she was certain he meant to torment her all night.

Linda Jones

It seemed he was determined to touch and kiss every exposed inch of her body, calmly and patiently caressing her neck and shoulders, kissing the crook of her elbow while he rocked a lazy thumb against the palm of her hand.

His hands were large, his fingers roughened by hard work, and still his touch was so very gentle. There had to be love in a caress so tender.

When he stroked her where she ached for him, Maddalyn nearly cried out. She'd never known what it was truly to need another person, to need a touch so badly she wanted to cry for it.

She unfastened his trousers and slid them over his hips, and he kicked them away. Eric positioned himself over her, pressing against her gently, waiting, prolonging this beautiful torture. Maddalyn wrapped her legs around his hips and thighs, reveling in it all. The feel of his skin against hers, the hot pressure of his arousal against her center.

She lifted her hips, and Eric pushed inside her slowly. Maddalyn closed her eyes. She would never again know anything as beautiful as this, as perfect, as heavenly.

Her hands explored his body as he had explored hers, sliding over his hard, muscled back, his tensed arms. Down his side to the hips that surged above her.

Eric moved within her, driving her to a point where all she knew was him. Where all she wanted was him. There was nothing but this meeting of

330

their bodies and the newly discovered rapture he took her to.

It grew, and finally shattered her. Eric fastened his mouth to hers, drove his tongue into her mouth as he drove his manhood into her body. The tremors shook him as well. She could feel them, could feel him shudder as his seed was released inside her. It was hot, insistent, and she embraced it as she embraced the feel of all of him. His tongue, his chest against hers, the strong thighs beneath her legs.

The warmth stayed with her, a tingle that filled her body and her heart. This was what it was like to be a part of something more than she had ever known. To love, to be needed. Not to be alone.

Eric's kisses were lazier now, without urgency. They were still joined, but he kept his weight off of her, leaning on forearms that rested by her head. They were such lovely forearms, so strong and well muscled. Like the rest of him they were completely male, powerful and splendid.

"I tried to leave the door open," she whispered against his lips.

"Did you?"

Maddalyn smiled and wrapped her arms around his neck. "I knew you would come."

"I wasn't sure that you would have me," he whispered.

What would he say if she told him that she loved him? Heart and soul, the way true love was supposed to be. If she had any hope that he would return her love, she wouldn't have hesitated.

He wanted her, and that was all she could expect from him. They had this, this wonderful physical harmony that would, if Mary Lynette were correct, fade with time. Of course, they didn't have much time.

"Did you really think I would send you away?" she whispered. "After this afternoon?"

He relaxed, kissed her again, smiled languidly. "No. And I wanted you in my bed, here where I found you."

Neither of them mentioned that they only had a few days. It would have broken the spell, stolen the magic. Eric rolled to the side, and Maddalyn rested her head against his shoulder. He held her nestled in his arms, and with his strong and warm body against hers, she slept.

Eric watched Maddalyn without caution, without caring if Conrad or Karl saw the gleam that had to be in his eyes. The firelight flickered on her face, on the green dress that lay across her lap.

She'd been sewing on the dress all evening, from the time she'd finished in the kitchen and joined them in the main room. She'd tried to keep her eyes on the alterations, but she did lift her eyes to him and smile on more than one occasion, a smile so bright and telling it made his heart skip a beat.

Karl and Conrad seemed not to notice. Were they blind? It seemed he knew everything Maddalyn was thinking, when she was dreaming of him, when she was remembering his touch.

But his brothers were half asleep by the fire, happily exhausted, counting the days until the wedding, and ignorant of Maddalyn's telling smile.

He was having impossible thoughts himself. Thoughts of keeping Maddalyn with him always, of asking her not to go to Sheridan, not to go back to Georgia—but to stay.

She'd made it clear on more than one occasion that living on an isolated mountain was not what she wanted, but maybe that had changed.

Maybe the power they created together was enough to change her mind, as it had changed his.

But there was still a nagging thought in the back of his mind, an insistence that this wonder wouldn't last. That Maddalyn would, in time, turn him away as Jane so often had. What they had seemed to be perfection, but Eric knew nothing was perfect.

He turned away from her to stare into the fire. She wasn't Jane. At times he was able to accept that, especially when he held her. Jane had never so openly accepted him into her bed, had never lost control beneath him. He had fooled himself into believing that it took time for inexperienced women to learn to enjoy being with a man, but Jane had never learned.

And Maddalyn had never hesitated to embrace him fervently. She'd made no demands, had taken with as much enthusiasm as she gave.

He didn't want to let her go.

* * *

Night after night he came to her, climbing through the window she had once used to escape from him. Maddalyn waited for the feeling to fade, for the urgency to show some sign of diminishing.

It didn't. Every night she wanted him more, and Eric showed no sign of tiring of her. They didn't mention the fact that soon she would be leaving, but Maddalyn felt it. It stole some of the joy in her heart, a little more every day.

Until the last night came. She was ready, her belongings gathered together, and they would be leaving in the morning. Karl and Conrad were so excited, so overworked, so distracted, that they hadn't even noticed the change that had come over her. Maybe it wasn't as obvious on the outside as it felt inside.

Eric hadn't smiled so widely when he'd come to her tonight. His lovemaking was not so tender, but was more insistent than ever. Harder.

But now he held her gently, her head against his shoulder, her leg entwined with his. They had never talked much during his nighttime visits, but tonight he had been completely silent, hadn't said a single word since he'd joined her in their bed.

He thrust his fingers through her hair, raked them lazily through the curls. Perhaps he hadn't mentioned the fact that this was their last night together, but she could feel the tension in his body, in the rigid muscles in his neck and arms. She rested her flat hand against his chest and wondered silently how she would survive being alone again.

It had always been hard, but now—now that she knew what it was like to be a part of something more—the lonely nights would be unbearable.

She laid her lips lightly against his skin.

"Marry me," he said gruffly, and Maddalyn's head came off his shoulder.

"What did you say?"

He turned his face to her, unsmiling, half in shadows. "I said marry me."

"Why?" Maddalyn whispered. She didn't ask too much. He didn't have to love her, even though that was what she wanted more than anything. If he'd just tell her that he needed her, that he wanted her, it would be enough. She would make it be enough.

"It makes perfect sense," he grumbled. "I'll be in this big place all by myself after Karl and Conrad move out. I'm a lousy cook, and you don't really know what's waiting in Sheridan."

"Perfect sense," she repeated.

"Yes. And anyway, I took your virginity. I should marry you."

"You should," she repeated flatly.

His voice was so cool, so matter-of-fact. "What if there's a child?" he reasoned. "What kind of a man would I be if I just turned you out?"

Maddalyn bit her tongue. She wouldn't have a man who wanted to marry her so he wouldn't have to cook. Because he felt it was the right thing to do.

"And if there's not a child?" she asked calmly.

Eric shrugged his shoulders. "Even if there's no baby, you were innocent when you came here. I can't just—"

"How very noble of you, Mr. Barrett."

She didn't know if it was her tone or the use of his formal name that got his attention, but Eric sat up and frowned down at her.

"What's wrong? I thought . . . that maybe you wouldn't be completely opposed to the idea."

"There are things that I want from marriage, Eric. I don't think you can give them to me."

She said the words very calmly, but it was evidently the wrong response.

Eric exploded from the bed. "Like pearls," he hissed. "Dances and damned picnics."

Maddalyn wondered for a moment if it would do any good to set him straight. It didn't matter. He didn't give her a chance.

"I should have known better than to ask," he muttered as he stepped into his trousers. "I won't change my life, not even for you," he insisted as he went to the window with his shirt in his hand.

He spun on her and shook that shirt in her direction. "You never should have come here, Maddalyn Kelly."

"I know," she whispered.

"Maybe you'll find what you want in Sheridan."

"Lower your voice. You'll wake Conrad and Karl," she warned.

"I don't care." Eric took a single step toward her

and stopped. "What are they gonna do? Beat me up? Damned if I care. Force me to marry you? Not likely."

He claimed not to care, but he had lowered his voice considerably. His words sent a chill down Maddalyn's spine. *Force me to marry you.* It was her worst nightmare, a lifetime in a house where she wasn't wanted. Where she wasn't loved.

She didn't know how to explain, and she had no chance in any case. Eric slipped out of the window and she was left alone.

Their passion hadn't died a slow death as she'd expected, but had exploded in her face.

Eric slipped his shirt on as he paced on the edge of the cliff. Why was he surprised? Why had he allowed her to surprise him with her refusal?

And she'd been so clear. *There are things I want, Eric. I don't think you can give them to me.* He should thank her for being honest with him, for not allowing him to make a fool of himself.

He should be angry with himself for being simpleton enough to think that a few nights would rid him of his passion for her. It was her fault. He hadn't expected her to return that passion so ardently, so openly. He had expected she would hold something of herself back.

She hadn't. And every night had been extraordinary. Unexpected. And he'd gone to her each night with his obsession stronger than before.

He didn't want to lose her. He didn't want to

come back to an empty cabin, and have to sleep alone in that damn bed.

But he would. By God, he wouldn't allow Maddalyn to ruin his life.

Eric sat on the edge of the rock and dangled his feet over the side. The drop was sheer, the surface below so far that in the night it was only darkness.

He could make his excuses, stay behind tomorrow. Karl and Conrad would protest, but in the end they'd still be just as married. It would be cleaner, easier, to send Maddalyn away with them and stay here where he belonged.

It wasn't an option he considered for very long. If he stayed behind Maddalyn would know that she meant more to him than he dared to reveal. Karl and Conrad—somehow they would know. He was amazed that they hadn't already figured it out. Until tonight he hadn't really cared.

No one would ever know what it cost him to let Maddalyn go. Especially not her. He would smile and laugh and celebrate his brothers' marriages. He would see Maddalyn off, wave good-bye, smile at the stage that carried her to Sheridan.

He wouldn't ask her again to stay. No matter how badly he wanted just that. No matter how badly he ached at the thought of coming back to this cabin without her.

Maddalyn would find what she searched for in Sheridan. Pearls and socials. Waltzes and civilization. A man who could give her all that and more.

Chapter Twenty-three

"Isn't it nice that they've given us the same rooms we had last time?" Maddalyn asked as she climbed the familiar stairs. She knew Eric was there, directly behind her and carrying her modest parcel of clothing. He'd been maddeningly civil to her since she'd refused his marriage proposal, and so of course the least she could do was be courteous in return.

"You'll be right at home," he said lightly.

Naturally, upon arriving in Olympia, Conrad and Karl had gone directly to their brides, leaving Maddalyn alone with the one Barrett brother she found it impossible to handle.

Eric escorted her to her room and deposited her bundle of clothing at the foot of the bed. And then he deposited himself at the edge, bouncing lightly and testing the mattress.

"What do you say?" he asked casually, giving her a roguish grin. "One for the road?"

One for the road. How thoroughly disgusting. Maddalyn reminded herself that she'd known all along how Eric viewed their relationship. There had never been any love involved, at least not on his part. It had been just a bit of fun for him. *She'd* been just a bit of fun for Eric Barrett.

"I don't think so." She kept her voice as apathetic as his, and turned her eyes out the window. "We wouldn't want your brothers to discover what we've been up to, now would we? Good heavens, they'd be scandalized."

She peeked at Eric from the corner of her eye. He made no move to leave her bed, but instead listed back and positioned his hands behind his head. "Well, we wouldn't want to scandalize Karl and Conrad, now would we?"

Eric caught her eye, and patted the mattress beside his hip. The grin he gave her was positively lecherous.

Maddalyn wanted to cry, though of course she would not. She'd known that Eric didn't love her, but she had thought for a few wonderful nights that she meant something to him. Something more than one of Annie's hurdy-girls.

"But hell, darlin'," he continued when she remained silent. "The wedding's tomorrow, and you're off to Sheridan the day after that. We won't have many more chances. Might be worth the risk of a little scandal."

Maddalyn turned to Eric. His feet were on the floor, and he reclined crossways on the bed while he stared at her boldly. She couldn't return his smile, couldn't pretend to be so nonchalant about her departure.

"That's a *no* face if ever I saw one," he drawled, sitting up and running his fingers through his hair. "Too bad," he said in a voice that revealed to Maddalyn just how little he cared.

The door was slightly ajar, and Maddalyn heard bright, laughing voices drawing near. Karl's heavy step on the stairs, Conrad's laugh. Kathleen and Daisy talking excitedly at the same time.

Eric heard it, too. "Talk about scandalous," he said as he went to the door. "The wedding's not until tomorrow." He raised his eyebrows in mock indignation. "And there's just the one other room. We may have to leave."

"Eric," she hissed.

He stepped into the hall as the others arrived, and with squealing greetings Kathleen and Daisy entered the room and closed the door behind them, leaving the three Barrett brothers in the hallway.

They continued their greeting with hearty hugs, and Kathleen handed Maddalyn a fat parcel wrapped in brown paper and tied with string.

"What's this?" she asked, sitting on the side of the bed. The mattress was still warm from Eric's body.

"It's for you to wear to the wedding," Daisy spoke up, while Kathleen watched and waited for Maddalyn to unwrap the package.

"I can't," Maddalyn began. "I altered the green dress you gave me, Kathleen. It will suit just fine."

"Open it," Kathleen ordered. "You must wear this dress. Daisy and I both worked on it especially for you. I hope it fits. There's not much time for alterations, but you and I are about the same size, so I think it will be just right."

"You shouldn't have," Maddalyn said as she untied the string. "With all you had to do . . ." Her voice cracked. No one had ever made an effort on her behalf like this. She'd never gone wanting, but she'd never had anything specially made just for her, either. She'd worn Doreen's castoffs, cut down and altered to fit. She'd done most of that work herself. On occasion Aunt Ethel had ordered a ready-made dress for her, but the funds had always come out of the trust Maddalyn's mother had provided, and Aunt Ethel always complained about the cost for weeks afterward.

She'd never owned a gown like the one that revealed itself as she unfolded the brown paper. It was made of heavy yellow silk, and there was lace trim at the neckline. Maddalyn lifted the gown and stood to hold it before her. The skirt was flared, and the sleeves were full. The color was a delicate yellow that reminded Maddalyn of the wildflowers that grew around Eric's cabin, of spring on the mountain.

"I don't know what to say," she whispered. "It's beautiful."

"I have a small bunch of silk flowers to attach at the waist," Daisy said. "But I didn't want to wrap them. I was afraid they'd be crushed."

"Y'all shouldn't have gone to so much trouble."

"If not for you, we wouldn't be getting married," Kathleen said simply. "And besides, when Eric sees you in this dress it might turn into a triple wedding. Have you ever heard of such a thing?"

Maddalyn placed the gown gingerly across the bed. It gave her an excuse to turn away from Kathleen. "That's certainly not going to happen."

"Conrad said—"

"Eric asked me to marry him and I said no," Maddalyn said quickly. She didn't really want to know what Conrad had told Kathleen about her relationship with Eric.

Behind her, Daisy sighed. "Why?" Kathleen asked sharply. "I thought you two were as good as married, after you turned down Gavin. Conrad said—"

"Eric doesn't love me." Maddalyn used her best no-nonsense voice, the one she planned to use on unruly students. "I don't ask for much, but when I marry I'll expect my husband to have some affection for me."

"But Conrad said—"

"Conrad is a very sweet man," Maddalyn said briskly. "But he doesn't know everything there is to know about me, or even about his own brother."

She smiled at a frowning Kathleen. "I'm excited about going on to Sheridan. It's time for me to go."

"But . . . I thought that you would stay. It won't be the same without you."

It took effort, but Maddalyn smiled brightly. "Perhaps when school is not in session I can come for a visit. Sheridan's not so very far." It was a lie, and she hated to lie to her friend. She wouldn't visit Eric. She couldn't stand it, to see him and have to leave again.

"Think about staying," Kathleen urged as she made her way to the door. "I have to run home. Promised Ma I'd help her with supper."

Like a whirlwind she was gone, and Maddalyn turned to Daisy. The tall woman had been silent, for the most part. Of course, with Kathleen in the room it was often hard for anyone to get a word in edgewise.

"I thought you would stay, too," Daisy said softly. "We'll miss you. I know Karl will miss you. If I had any sense I suppose I'd be jealous, but I'm not."

"Karl and Conrad have been wonderful to me," Maddalyn admitted. "They're like the brothers I never had. I'll miss them terribly."

"And Eric?" she asked.

Daisy saw too much. She silently observed what went on around her, and she saw through Maddalyn's facade.

"You love him, don't you?" Daisy prodded when Maddalyn didn't answer.

"Yes," Maddalyn admitted. It was so wonderful

to tell someone, anyone. "I've been in love with him all along, but he doesn't care for me at all."

"He asked you to marry him."

"You should have heard his reasoning," Maddalyn said angrily. "Love had nothing to do with his proposal."

"Are you sure?" Daisy's words were soft, thoughtful.

"Positive," Maddalyn assured her. And she was most positive. Eric couldn't love her while he was still in love with the wife who'd deserted him. She glanced down at the magnificent gown on the bed. "I can't thank you and Kathleen enough for this gift."

"You're changing the subject," Daisy accused softly.

"Do you mind terribly?" Maddalyn asked with a sigh. Talking about Eric wasn't going to change anything, and it only made her feel worse, more lost and alone than ever.

Daisy shook her head, and their conversation turned to wedding plans.

Eric stared down at the whiskey he didn't want. Hiding out in the saloon—what a chickenhearted act.

But he needed a break from smiling at Maddalyn, from pretending to be happy for his brothers. He wasn't a good liar. It was work for him. Damn hard work.

But of course he wouldn't have to keep it up for

long. He'd stand up at the wedding ceremony, drink a toast to the idiot brides and grooms, and then—the next day—he'd put Maddalyn on the stage.

"Drowning your sorrows?"

Eric lifted his eyes from the table to the deputy sheriff who leaned forward. Gavin MacIver wore a smug expression that made Eric want to ram his fist right into that freckled face.

"I know how you feel." Gavin took a chair, uninvited. "When Maddalyn turned me down I was downright depressed, myself." The deputy smiled, and Eric had to remind himself that Gavin MacIver was wearing a six-shooter, and he himself was unarmed.

"When Kathleen told me that Maddalyn had refused your proposal, too, I thought maybe I'd still have a chance." The boy lowered his voice. "I'm doing a little detective work. Maybe if I can impress her enough she'll stick around for a while, maybe even change her mind about marrying me."

He should have known that Maddalyn would confide in Kathleen and Daisy. Should have expected it, in fact. How much had she told? Simply that he'd proposed and she'd refused him? Or had she shared everything? The girls would, he supposed, relate what they knew to their soon-to-be husbands.

"Good luck," Eric muttered.

Gavin's grin widened. "Thanks. No hard feelings, huh? After tomorrow we'll be kin."

A less than comforting thought. "Yep."

"Well, I gotta get back to work."

"More detecting," Eric added in a low voice.

Gavin nodded solemnly as he rose from his chair.

So Conrad and Karl would know he'd proposed to Maddalyn and she'd turned him down. That he could live with. But he knew they wouldn't leave it alone. Conrad, for certain, would most likely talk his ear off, asking questions, doing his own detective work. Conrad was nothing if not tenacious.

Maybe when Maddalyn was gone he'd tell his brothers the truth. Head off their questions the only way he knew how, and tell them that in spite of their diligence he'd found his way into her bed. That he'd tried to do the honorable thing and marry her, but she wouldn't have him.

He couldn't give her enough. She'd been honest enough to tell him that to his face.

If the truth were known, Karl would likely beat Eric senseless, and at the moment that prospect was tolerable. More than tolerable. Because he wanted, at that very moment, to swing out at someone or something, and Karl made a nice, big target.

Karl and Conrad deserved to experience some of the pain of this disaster. From the first day they'd pushed him and Maddalyn together.

One of us could marry her.

You're the one she's sweet on.

You're a little sweet on her, aren't you? Just a little bit?

Why had he listened to them? Why had he fallen into the trap they'd set for him?

Eric grasped the glass of whiskey before him, but he didn't drink. He couldn't afford to lose even an ounce of control if he was to survive the next two days.

"It really wasn't necessary for you to walk me back to the hotel, Gavin," Maddalyn protested politely. She had been looking forward to taking the short walk alone. All the MacIvers, and Conrad as well, were excited about the wedding, and the supper conversation had been lively. Maddalyn usually enjoyed bright and energetic talk over the supper table, but tonight she had definitely not been in the mood.

She told herself and everyone else that she was tired, and that was true. But that wasn't the reason she'd been anxious to escape.

She wanted to be alone. She couldn't really remember a time when she'd sought solitude, but all she wanted to do right now was curl up under a nice soft quilt and stop pretending. Cry, if she felt like it. Scream into her pillow, if that would do more good.

But Gavin had insisted on escorting her to the hotel, even though the distance was short and it wasn't yet dark. And he talked, oh, how he talked, about some sort of secret investigation he was conducting, some sort of surprise he had for her.

Maddalyn listened with half an ear. Where was Eric? He'd declined the MacIvers' invitation to supper, and she'd heard him refuse Daisy as well. She shouldn't wonder where he was, worry if he was eating a proper meal or not. He didn't deserve her concern.

"I saw the dress Kathleen was sewing on," Gavin said as they reached the hotel entrance. "And I can't wait to see you in it."

"It was very sweet of her and Daisy to go to so much trouble," Maddalyn said, leaning back slightly to glance through the main entrance and into the dining room. She could see about half the tables from this position, but she didn't see Eric.

"Wait till you see the surprise I've got for you." Gavin leaned forward as if he actually intended to kiss her right there on the boardwalk in front of the hotel. But Maddalyn was fast. She muttered a quick good night and spun away and through the doorway before he had a chance to lay his lips on her.

She glanced over her shoulder and watched him walk jauntily away, apparently undeterred by her blatant avoidance of his kiss.

"Nice move."

She nearly jumped out of her skin as she spun to Eric. The scoundrel had been on the other side of the doorway the entire time. "What on earth are you doing, lurking behind the door and scaring me half to death?"

349

"Lurking?" he repeated.

"Yes, lurking." She took a deep breath and sighed. "Sorry. I'm not usually so jumpy."

His grin widened. "I don't usually lurk."

He was poking fun at her, turning her words around and using them to his own advantage. "You missed a lovely supper," she said politely, raising her chin. It would be easier to face him if he weren't so blasted tall. "Mrs. MacIver is a wonderful cook."

"But if I'd joined you, you might have missed out on Gavin walking you home. He's probably of a mind that three's a crowd."

He would know she was a coward if she turned and ran, and Maddalyn didn't want Eric to know how difficult it was for her to carry on even a simple conversation with him. She wouldn't cry, and she wouldn't run.

"He's planning some sort of surprise," she blurted.

"Maybe he's going to propose marriage again," Eric said calmly.

Maddalyn felt the blood drain from her face. That possibility had never occurred to her.

"You look a little peaked, darlin'," Eric said with mock concern. "Maddalyn MacIver," he said with an accent that mocked Kathleen's mother. "Has a nice ring to it, don't you think?"

"I'm very tired," Maddalyn whispered. "I think I'll go to my room now."

She spun away from him and climbed the stairs.

How could he be so distant? It only proved to her that he didn't care. She closed her eyes in distress when she realized that he was very close behind her, his footsteps matching hers on the steps.

"*I* have a surprise for you, Maddalyn," he whispered.

She turned toward her room and fumbled with the key she grasped in her hand.

"Well, not a surprise, exactly. The word *surprise* brings to mind a sneak attack. An ambush. Something unexpected, that maybe you don't even want. I would never give you anything you didn't want."

Maddalyn faced the door to her room, but she didn't unlock it. Eric was directly behind her. She could feel the heat pouring off of him, and when he placed his hand on her shoulder she turned to confront him.

She'd begun to believe, in their last days together, that she knew Eric, that she understood him. But she stared up into the face of a stranger, a man who could make light of the most beautiful time of her life.

There was nothing she could say to make him understand what she felt, how important he was to her. But as she studied him, his smile faded, and she saw a spark of the old Eric, of her Eric, in his eyes.

"Kiss me good-bye," he whispered. His casual attitude and wicked grin were gone. "We may not be alone again before you leave."

"We may not," Maddalyn agreed. She glanced down the long hallway and found it deserted. What could it hurt, one last kiss? A kiss good-bye.

He took that as a yes and lowered his mouth to hers hesitantly, as if it were the first time and he wasn't sure of her response.

The first time they'd kissed he'd told her to pretend his lips were honeysuckle.

Maddalyn closed her eyes. She never knew what to expect from Eric. She certainly hadn't expected a sweet yet deep kiss like this. He didn't lay his hands on her, but for the fingers that lightly touched her shoulder. And in the end he was the one who pulled away, leaving her with an empty ache deep in her heart.

"Good-bye, Maddalyn," he whispered.

Chapter Twenty-four

He had every intention of leaving Olympia long before the wedding. Last night, when he'd stood outside Maddalyn's hotel room and kissed her good-bye, it had been just that. Good-bye.

Eric didn't know or care what kind of surprise Gavin MacIver had cooked up for Maddalyn. He didn't even care anymore what Conrad and Karl thought. What they knew. He only knew that he couldn't face Maddalyn again, and he couldn't keep pretending that it meant nothing to him to watch her leave.

Karl and Conrad slept deeply, blissfully unaware of the dangers of the institution they were about to enter of their own free will.

Eric crept down the stairs like a thief, quiet, watchful. It made no difference if he stayed for the

Linda Jones

wedding or not. Come tomorrow Karl and Conrad would be married, and Maddalyn would be gone.

Nothing could make him stay in Olympia for another day.

The sun was just rising, and a few of the residents of Olympia were up and about. Daisy's father flung open the doors to his business and waved at Eric. Eric waved back as he crossed the street, but turned away from Karl's future father-in-law and toward the stables where his horse was housed.

When he was almost in front of the stables, Eric made the mistake of turning toward the hotel. Just for a quick glance. He knew it was a mistake when he saw Maddalyn leaning out of her window.

If she'd been watching him, if she'd waved as Daisy Colter's father had, he would have waved back and continued on. But she didn't even see him. Her gaze was fixed far above his head, over the rooftops. She didn't stare at him; she stared at the mountain.

Eric stepped into the shadows of the boardwalk, leaning against the solid wall of the barbershop. From here he could watch Maddalyn, and she'd never see him.

Her hair curled wildly, as if she'd just risen from the bed. If only he could see her face more clearly—if only she would smile, or laugh, to assure him that he was doing the right thing by leaving before he said something he was going to regret.

But she didn't smile, didn't appear to be at all

354

content. She just stared toward the mountain she'd climbed and claimed.

The sun crept higher in the sky, bathing the street in bright light and striking Maddalyn's face, and still she didn't move away from the window. He would have given his soul to know what she was thinking, what mesmerized her so completely.

At last she moved, but only to brush her fingers against her cheeks. Wiping away tears? If he stepped into the street and made his presence known, if he stood beneath her window and asked her again to stay . . . would she?

Approaching voices startled Eric, and he glanced down the boardwalk. Gavin MacIver was talking in hushed tones to Lumpy, handing the drunkard a full bottle of whiskey. Lumpy leaned close to MacIver when he replied, one hand clutching the neck of the bottle, one hand holding the breast of his tattered jacket as if it were a fine suit. Against his will, Eric smiled. Lumpy was a part of the boy's important investigation?

When he returned his gaze to the hotel, Maddalyn was gone. The window was shut, the drapes drawn, and he could almost imagine that his earlier view of her had been an illusion, that he'd seen only what he wanted to see. Hell, how could he leave now?

"There you are, little brother," Conrad called as he stepped from the hotel entrance and into the street. "Have you eaten yet?"

Eric shook his head.

Linda Jones

"Good. Have breakfast with me. I swear I'm starving, but I also feel like I'm going to puke."

"Hard to resist an invitation like that," Eric said as he stepped from the boardwalk to meet his brother halfway.

"Nerves, I guess," Conrad confided in a lower voice when Eric was near. "Kinda like getting shot at."

Eric smiled at the fitting comparison. "How's Karl taking it?"

Conrad laughed, a short guffaw. "I swear, he's in worse shape than I am. He rolled out of bed a few minutes ago and turned a shade of green I don't think I've ever seen on a person before."

"I tried to warn you," Eric said lightly. "This is what you get for ignoring your little brother's advice."

Had it really been such good advice? Eric was actually beginning to wonder.

"Daisy tells me that Eric asked you to marry him, and you turned him down. Is that true?"

Leave it to Karl to get straight to the point. Maddalyn reached up and straightened his collar. She couldn't allow him to go through the ceremony with one corner sticking straight up. "Yes, it's true," she admitted softly. "But I don't want to talk about that now. Less than an hour from now you'll be a married man. Very shortly this church will be filled with friends and family who are here to celebrate the happy occasion."

356

Someone's Been Sleeping in My Bed

"He said you wouldn't stay." Karl ignored her request to leave the subject alone. "Even in the beginning, when he first found you, he said a lady like you wouldn't be happy on the mountain. Do you think Daisy will want to leave one day? Do you think she'll get sick of living up there so far from town?"

Maddalyn sighed. She could hear the doubts in Karl's question. "I think you and Daisy will be very happy, no matter where you live."

"Why did you turn Eric down?" Karl's voice was soft, and Maddalyn could hear the concern in his voice. For her or for Eric?

Maddalyn straightened Karl's jacket, and tried to keep her voice light. "He only asked me because you and Conrad are both getting married, and he felt left out. He's afraid he'll have to do all his own cooking."

"But—" Karl began.

Conrad burst through the double doors at the front of the church, and then closed them solidly behind him. "There's my best man," he said brightly. He started toward the altar, but stopped halfway down the aisle. Conrad slapped a hand over his heart. "Who, by God, looks very little like a man at the moment."

Maddalyn smiled at Conrad's comically delivered compliment. She curtsied, holding yellow silk between her fingers. The dress was magnificent, she had to admit. Daisy had given her a small bouquet of white silk roses to attach to the waist, and

Kathleen had provided matching yellow ribbons and a white rose for her hair, which was piled high on her head. Only a few carefully arranged ringlets touched her shoulder.

The neckline of the yellow gown dipped just a little too low, and Maddalyn had tugged at it all morning, trying without success to force it higher.

Conrad joined them, and Maddalyn straightened his collar and jacket as she had Karl's, even though it wasn't necessary. "My, you two look so handsome. I never would have thought, when I first saw the three of you, that y'all would turn out to be such dapper gentlemen."

Eric joined them not long after Conrad, and Maddalyn had to clasp her hands and hold back the words that came to her lips.

He was every bit as finely dressed as his brothers, in Conrad's second-best jacket and Karl's hand-me-down trousers, and she resisted the urge to reach out and straighten his collar and his jacket. They needed the adjustment no more than Conrad's had.

She could almost convince herself that it had been a mistake to refuse his proposal. That, in time, she could make him love her. When he looked at her intently, as he did now, when he kissed her, when he touched her, she knew he had to harbor some affection for her.

"Can't convince either of you to change your minds, can I?" he asked in a teasing voice, tearing his eyes away from her and grinning widely at his obviously nervous brothers. "It's not too late."

His offer was halfhearted, without any real uncertainty, and Maddalyn could almost imagine that Eric felt a bit of joy for his brothers, that he held some hope for their future, even after marriage.

If only he could find some hope for his own future.

The ceremony was beautiful. The six of them stood at the altar, Eric on one side and Maddalyn on the other, while the preacher recited and prayed aloud and finally asked the all-important questions.

Maddalyn tried to keep her eyes on the beautiful brides and the fidgety grooms. They were so well suited, so happy, so contented.

But on occasion her eyes turned to Eric. Each and every time he was staring boldly at her. Without a smile, without a smirk, without a frown. Just watching, those eyes as intense as she'd imagined them to be when he'd gazed at her from his photograph that day she'd discovered it on the mantel.

And he didn't look away when she caught his eyes, didn't turn to the couples who stood between them or to the preacher who performed the ceremony. He continued to watch her, as if he had every right to do so.

Maddalyn began to wonder if she'd given up too soon. If it wasn't love that made Eric look at her that way, what was it?

* * *

Eric couldn't remember ever going to a party in a general store before. Evidently it was the only place in town that was big enough, but for the saloon, and the Barrett brides had vetoed that idea.

Shelves had been moved aside, goods had been stored elsewhere, and enough food to feed the town for a week had been laid out.

The room was still too small. It was a crush that Eric could have done without, would have done without if he hadn't been so determined to keep an eye on Maddalyn.

He'd watched her throughout the wedding. She was more beautiful than either of the brides. How could anyone keep their eyes on anyone else when Maddalyn was in the room?

John Terry had been dogging her heels, handing her lemonade and cake, talking into her face, following her when she tried to back away.

Gavin MacIver had spoken to her briefly early on and then he'd disappeared. More investigating, no doubt. Other men, men Eric didn't know, spoke to Maddalyn, smiled at her, and she smiled at them in return.

But it wasn't her brightest smile; it wasn't the real Maddalyn. She held something back.

He hadn't seen the real Maddalyn, smiling and openly delighted, since she'd watched his brothers say their marriage vows.

Did she save those unguarded moments for him? It was a wonderfully terrifying thought.

The afternoon threatened to last forever, but

eventually the crowd thinned. The younger children were taken home with promises of their waiting beds. A few of the older partygoers yawned and waved good-bye. All afternoon he'd watched Maddalyn from a distance, but now she made her way toward him, yellow silk in her hands as she lifted her skirt just off the floor. He had time to move away, to leave, but he didn't.

"Wasn't it just a wonderful day?" She stopped a couple of feet away from him.

"If you say so," he agreed without enthusiasm.

"You're such a cynic."

"About marriage? Yes."

Maddalyn sighed, and her chest rose and fell. He, and everyone else, could see entirely too much of that chest. When she took a deep breath he could see the globes of her breasts rising above white lace.

"If you're tired I'll walk you back to the hotel."

"Not yet," she said. "I want to stay until the newlyweds leave."

Eric nodded to the door, where Conrad and Kathleen tried to slip away unnoticed. They were unsuccessful, of course, and were practically mobbed by Kathleen's family and a gaggle of young females who all talked at once.

Maddalyn tapped his arm, and when he glanced down she pointed to the back of the room. Karl and Daisy were making a clean getaway through a rear exit.

"Are you satisfied now?" Eric asked softly.

Linda Jones

Maddalyn glanced up at him, waiting for clarification.

"Two of the Barrett brothers hitched well and good. Thanks to you, of course."

"They just needed a little push," Maddalyn confided in a small voice.

"What about me?"

She flushed, a pretty pink rising to her cheeks. "What about you?"

Eric waved a hand toward the flock of giggling young women who crowded around the door. "Aren't you going to pick one out for me?"

She turned absolutely red, blushed all the way down to the lace at her too low neckline.

"What about the black-haired one?" he asked in a low whisper. "The one in the pink dress."

Maddalyn glanced quickly toward the door and then returned her gaze to him. "She's too young for you," she hissed. "She doesn't look more than eighteen."

Eric smiled. "The brown-haired girl in the green dress?"

She didn't even look this time. "You wouldn't like her. Kathleen introduced her to me, and she talked constantly. She seemed rather bossy to me."

"For God's sake, don't saddle me with a bossy wife," Eric complained. "The blonde, the one over there in the . . . exactly what color is that?" He grimaced.

"Eric," Maddalyn interrupted sharply. "I'm

362

afraid you're going to have to find your own wife, if you decide to marry."

He knew Maddalyn wasn't completely indifferent, that she had some feelings for him. He'd seen it in her eyes, and in the brilliant smiles she seemed to save just for him. He'd tasted it on her lips. Affection, temptation, love, whatever it was, it wasn't enough. Maybe it was the prospect of spending her life on a cold, isolated mountain that made her refuse to marry him. If that were true, why had she looked toward it that morning as if she were saying good-bye to a beloved friend?

"Can I walk you back to the hotel now?" Eric offered. "You look tired."

"It's been a long day." She sighed. "But I don't need an escort."

"John Terry is coming this way," Eric whispered. "Maybe he can. . . ."

"Yes," Maddalyn said quickly. "Please walk me back to the hotel."

Eric offered his arm and Maddalyn took it.

"I didn't get a chance to tell you how nice you look today," Eric said when they were crossing the street. She kept her arm on his, but her touch was distant.

"Thank you," she said, more than a little distracted.

What was she thinking of? Who was she thinking of? "Did you learn what sort of surprise Gavin MacIver has planned for you?"

"No," she said listlessly. "Actually, I didn't see

much of Gavin today. I'll be leaving tomorrow, so I don't suppose I'll ever know."

She didn't seem to care about MacIver's surprise, and Eric couldn't say that he wasn't glad. "When does the stage leave?"

At the foot of the stairs Maddalyn disengaged her arm from his. She gave him her full attention before she answered; met his gaze and bit her lower lip. "Noon," she finally answered, turning away from him to climb the stairs. "The stage leaves at noon."

Maddalyn tossed on the bed, trying every trick she knew to get to sleep. She thought of the view from Eric's porch, of how content the newlyweds had appeared to be, but her thoughts always turned to Eric.

He was right next door, alone in the room he had shared with his brothers. Karl and Conrad had each taken rooms on the third floor, honeymoon suites, though Conrad had revealed to her that they were not much different from the rooms they'd occupied thus far. Just more expensive and one story higher.

Tomorrow morning she would be gone. On to Sheridan, where she should have been for weeks now. She'd have to think of her time on the mountain as a pleasant diversion, serendipity. A treasure she'd stumbled upon.

When she heard the doorknob rattle, she knew it was him. What was he doing, trying to open the locked door so he could creep into her bed and ask for *one for the road?* His nonchalant request had shocked her yesterday, but today . . . tonight she'd say yes. If it was all she could have, she'd take it.

After just a couple of minutes of scratching, the rattling stopped, and the door swung open. Maddalyn took a deep breath, steeled herself, and turned toward the figure in the doorway.

The figure that crouched there, a silhouette with the dim light from the hallway behind it, was not Eric. It was too short, too thin, and stooped over like an old man.

Maddalyn screamed. It didn't sound like a proper scream should, but thin and reedy. Much too weak. So she called Eric's name as loudly as she could.

The man in the doorway straightened slightly, then turned and disappeared.

Maddalyn stared at the empty doorway until Eric appeared there, holding the front of his trousers closed with one hand and gripping a gun she hadn't even known he possessed.

"What?" he growled sleepily.

Maddalyn sat up in the center of the bed. "Th-there was a-a-a man." She shook a finger at Eric. "He was right there, where you are. H-he, the door was locked, but, but, there was this scratching, and . . . he looked like a gnome."

Eric leaned against the doorjamb, and the hand that held the gun fell. "A gnome?"

He turned his head to glance down the hallway,

and he smiled genially. "Just a bad dream," he assured another hotel guest. "Sorry for the disturbance."

"It was not a dream," Maddalyn hissed.

Eric stepped into the room and closed the door. Without the light from the hallway, he was all but lost in darkness.

"Somebody just got the wrong room," he said. "Probably some drunk."

"Well, he scared me half to death," Maddalyn said. "I thought my heart was going to come through my chest."

"If you're okay," Eric said quietly, "I'll get out of here."

"I'm not okay," Maddalyn whispered.

It was an invitation, a plea for him to stay, but she wasn't certain that Eric would recognize it.

Eric was silent for a long moment. She couldn't even hear him breathing.

She could see him, a shadow in the dark room, as he laid the gun on her dresser. It sounded heavy, loud in the dark and silent room, the meeting of metal and wood.

He came to the bed and sat beside her and lifted his hands to her face. "You're all right. There's no reason to be scared."

"I know," she whispered.

"I can't stay with you. I can't comfort you the way you want to be comforted."

Maddalyn laid her hands over his. "Yes, you

can." She rose to her knees and slid her palms over his arms.

She kissed him, laid her mouth over his and parted his lips with her tongue.

For a moment he was still, and then she felt his surrender. He returned her kiss, he placed his arms around her and held her tight.

This they did right. Even when they couldn't agree on anything else, on love and marriage, on happiness that lasted beyond the twinkling of an eye, on hope—they had this.

It was more than physical, though Maddalyn wouldn't deny that the meeting of their bodies was beautiful. She needed Eric, and she loved him with all her heart. Heart and soul, body and spirit. Surely he felt that—surely.

He stripped the nightshirt she wore, an old shirt of his own, from her before he lowered her to her back. His hair fell across her skin as he lowered his mouth to her breast and took a nipple into his mouth. A jolt of lightning shot through her body, and Maddalyn forgot everything but the touch of Eric's hands and his mouth. Nothing else mattered, nothing but this wonder they created when they came together, the passion that consumed her.

And Eric. In spite of his protests, she knew he lost himself, gave something of himself over to her when they touched. He gave to her against his will.

Maddalyn couldn't stop her hands. They roamed over Eric's body, memorizing every muscle, the feel of his flat nipples beneath her fingers. Hardness and heat, that was Eric. He was a contradiction, a puzzle to her even now. What did he want? What did he need?

She slipped her hands inside the open front of his trousers, slid that single piece of clothing he wore away with a sweep of her hands.

He spoke her name against her lips, an unasked question in the whispered word. She answered Eric with a kiss that told all. That she loved him, wanted him, didn't want to leave him, ever.

The kiss went on, and Eric pushed her deeper into the mattress. He spread her legs with his knees, and Maddalyn lifted her hips. He brushed the tip of his arousal against her, there where her heartbeat was echoed with a torturous throbbing, and then with one thrust he filled her.

Maddalyn held him tight, clasped him to her with her arms and legs. He withdrew slowly, and then plunged deep again as she lifted her hips to take all of him. It was like a dance, but the music was the beat of their hearts and the rhythm of their pounding blood.

And so they danced in matchless harmony, in perfect synchronization. Time stood still, and there was only this, this joining that proved to her that love was more than she had ever imagined it could be.

The end came with an explosion, lightning coursing through her body, Eric shuddering in her arms. She whispered words of love, told him all that she'd held back.

They were still for several moments, with only the sounds of heavy breathing and beating hearts in the air. Eric tried to pull away from her, to withdraw from her, but Maddalyn held him in place with a gentle tug of the leg that was wrapped around his.

"Not yet," she whispered.

He lifted his head and looked down at her, his shadowed face looming above hers. "I should go." He breathed the words, as if he didn't believe his own hesitation.

"Stay with me," Maddalyn said. "Stay with me tonight."

He acquiesced with a kiss against her shoulder and a hand in her hair. "It doesn't last, you know," he whispered against her neck.

"What doesn't last?"

"Love."

So he'd heard her. She'd wondered if he had, if he'd acknowledge her love in any way. This was their last night together, and she didn't want to argue. She wanted to hold him all night long.

"It'll last for tonight," she whispered.

Eric fastened his mouth to hers, and moved just slightly within her. Maddalyn rocked against him, threaded her fingers through his hair.

He lifted his lips from hers just long enough to answer: "For tonight."

Chapter Twenty-five

Maddalyn stared out the window and nodded absently every few minutes. One of the other passengers, a Mrs. Tilton, had been going on about one subject or another since they'd pulled out of Olympia: Mrs. Tilton's grown daughter Holly and Holly's no-good husband; the neighbors she'd left behind in St. Louis; the weather, politics. As long as Maddalyn nodded her head on occasion, Mrs. Tilton was satisfied.

She was a coward. Maddalyn recognized that failing in herself, had known it was true as she'd sneaked out of the hotel while Eric slept. As she'd boarded the stage. As she nodded numbly at Mrs. Tilton.

If she weren't a coward she wouldn't have lied to the Barretts about her departure time. Kathleen and Daisy at the wedding party, Karl and Conrad as she'd straightened their jackets one last time, Eric standing at the foot of the hotel stairs. She just couldn't face all those tearful good-byes.

If she weren't a coward she would have wakened Eric with a kiss, and tried to convince him they could make love last for more than just one night.

If he'd even hinted that he felt as she did, she would have made an effort. But he hadn't, and she didn't want to live her life in a house without love.

It was the one sacrifice she wouldn't make.

"You're going to teach in Sheridan, you say?" Mrs. Tilton asked.

Maddalyn tried to concentrate on Mrs. Tilton's anxious face, the bright, small eyes, the upturned nose. "Yes." At another time, she might have told the entire story. That she was horribly late, delayed by a stage robbery that had left two men dead. That she'd climbed a mountain to escape, and been trapped there by the snow. She might have told of her plans for the Maddalyn Lorraine Kelly Academy for Young Ladies.

But today Mrs. Tilton was going to have to be satisfied with the simple answer she received, because Maddalyn didn't feel like talking.

The only other passenger, Mr. Johnston, slumped in a corner, eyes closed. His breathing was regular, but on occasion Maddalyn saw him barely open one eye. Of course, until the stage had arrived in Olympia, he had been the only one available to carry on a conversation with the talkative Mrs. Tilton.

"In my day," Mrs. Tilton continued, "it would have been scandalous for a young woman to travel unescorted. And into such wild country! Did you know that there's a notorious gang of outlaws that have a hideout somewhere near here? I hear they frequent Buffalo. Do you think we'll get a glimpse of them?"

Mrs. Tilton seemed more excited than afraid, Maddalyn decided. "I really have no desire to meet with outlaws, even those I have read about in the newspaper."

The older lady appeared to be insulted, but not enough to be silent. "I think it would be thrilling to meet such infamous figures. This is the wild West, you know."

Maddalyn turned away from the indignant woman and stared out the window. She didn't want thrilling; she didn't want wild. All she really wanted was a nice, quiet life on a beautiful, quiet mountain. All she really wanted was Eric.

Eric rolled over and reached for Maddalyn, but discovered he was alone. He lifted his head from the pillow and squinted when the bright sunlight hit his eyes. Where the hell was she? Her stage didn't leave until noon, and he knew he hadn't slept that late.

But a quick glance around the room chilled him. She'd left nothing behind. No hint that she'd ever been there. Her clothes, hair ribbons, the comb and brush Daisy had given her—all gone.

He fell against the pillow and took a deep breath. She'd done it to him again. Made him hope, and then left him feeling empty.

How many times last night had she whispered those damning words to him: *I love you, Eric.* Soft, trembling words he didn't dare to believe. But he wanted to believe that it was true.

He threw himself from the bed, propelled by his self-directed anger. Why couldn't he forget the past and take a chance? What if she did leave in six months, in a year? Hell, six months with Maddalyn was better than a lifetime of living alone. Maybe the love wouldn't last, but she loved him *now*, and even though he'd fought it hard, it was a losing battle.

He loved her.

He dressed quickly, pulling on his trousers. He was set to fetch a shirt from the other room until he saw the tail end of the shirt Maddalyn had worn to sleep in. It was lying on the floor where he'd tossed it last night, half under the bed. She'd mended the torn cuffs and replaced missing buttons. Eric lifted the sleeve to his nose. It smelled of her. Reminded him of how much he was going to miss her if she left.

The dining room was deserted, and the only employee in the lobby told Eric that he hadn't seen Miss Kelly that morning. Was she sitting in the office that did triple duty? Post office, telegraph office, stage depot. She had more than an hour before the stage was scheduled to leave, but where else would she go?

He made his way quickly down the boardwalk, tipping his hat to the ladies who said good morning, waving to the men who waved to him first. His greetings were halfhearted at best, as his mind was on the small building at the end of the boardwalk.

There was a lone clerk behind a tall desk, and he smiled at Eric broadly when the door opened. Except for the clerk, the room was deserted.

Where the hell was she? Eric started to close the door and search the rest of the town, but he had a thought and stuck his head back in the door. "The stage to Sheridan. Will it be on time?"

The diligent young man nodded abruptly. "I'm sure it will be. It pulled out of here right on schedule."

Eric stepped into the small room and faced the clerk. "Pulled out?"

The clerk nodded. "Yes, sir. On schedule."

"I thought it left here at noon." Eric felt as if he'd swallowed a boulder.

"No, sir. It's a ten-thirty stage, on the second and fourth Thursday of every month."

"Did a woman board here? Short," he held up his hand to indicate Maddalyn's height. "Blond, curly hair."

"Of course. Miss Kelly. We honored her ticket on to Sheridan, after that terrible incident several weeks back."

Eric shook his head. Gone. Sneaking away in the night like a thief.

"It seems everyone missed seeing her off," the clerk said cheerfully.

"Who else was by? The deputy? The barber? My brothers?"

Eric turned to leave. There was truly nothing to keep him in Olympia now.

"Two older men," the clerk answered the questions Eric had not expected a response to. "One had a nasty limp, and the other man was quite heavy. Would those be your brothers, sir?"

Eric turned in the doorway. "Two older men? Gray hair?"

The clerk nodded. "They just missed the stage, and they seemed very disappointed."

"When exactly did the stage leave?"

The clerk withdrew a pocket watch and checked the time. "Twenty-five minutes ago. Right on—"

Eric slammed the door on the clerk. The men who had robbed the stage and murdered two men were asking after Maddalyn. Did they think she could identify them?

It all came together. "Shit," he muttered as he ran down the street to the sheriff's office.

Kelvin MacIver was sitting at his desk, feet up, eyes half closed.

"Where's your boy?" Eric asked, slamming the door behind him.

"What's going—" Sheriff MacIver began.

Gavin MacIver walked through the door that led

to the holding cell, and before he could say a word Eric had pushed the deputy against the wall, grabbed him by the collar, and lifted him to face level.

"Tell me real quick about your investigation."

"I . . . I don't have to tell you nothin'." Gavin cut his eyes to his father, but Kelvin MacIver didn't rise.

"What investigation?" the sheriff asked lazily.

"I was just trying to get Maddalyn's pearls back for her. Nothin' came of it. I asked a few questions, that was all." His face was turning red, and his eyes bulged.

"All you did was spread the word that she could identify the men who took them, the men who murdered the only other witnesses, isn't that right?"

The sheriff muttered an oath behind him, but Eric didn't turn or relax his grip.

"If they hurt her, I'm going to come back here and kill you. Your pa might return the favor, but not till I'm finished with you." Eric dropped a gasping deputy to the floor and turned to the sheriff.

"I need a rifle." Eric looked at the stash of weapons behind MacIver's desk. "That Winchester will do just fine. Those Colts, too." He pointed to the pair that caught his eye.

MacIver quickly unlocked the case and handed Eric the weapons he requested, and then he followed Eric from the office.

"I can get together a posse," the sheriff offered.

"No time," Eric said.

Conrad and Karl, their brides on their arms, were walking down the boardwalk toward Eric and the sheriff.

"We wanted to see Maddalyn off," Kathleen called. "But we can't find her."

Eric reached the newlyweds and walked right through them, never slowing his step. They parted to let him pass, then turned and followed in his wake, and he explained what he knew.

He revealed the facts coldly. That Maddalyn was in danger, that the outlaws who had robbed the stage she'd been on weeks earlier were looking for her, were following the stage to Sheridan.

He didn't tell them that he felt as though his heart were going to come through his chest, that if she died, he'd just as soon one of them put a bullet in his head.

If he'd made her stay, she'd be safe. Always.

Karl whispered something to Daisy, and she ran toward her father's store. The others matched him step for step as he neared the stable.

Daisy appeared moments later with holsters and six-shooters for Karl and Conrad.

Eric watched his brothers strap on the weapons. "You don't have to come with me. I can handle it."

Conrad snorted, and Karl raised his eyebrows in disbelief.

"Give me twenty minutes," Sheriff MacIver offered. "I can put together a ten-man posse."

"No," Eric all but shouted. "There's no time."

Someone's Been Sleeping in My Bed

Kathleen helped the stable boy who led the three horses onto the street.

Karl mounted his horse first. "Besides," he said as Eric and Conrad jumped into their saddles, "we Barretts take care of our own."

"Why are we stopping?" Mrs. Tilton asked, leaning out of the window and getting a faceful of dust. Even Mr. Johnston, the silent passenger who had been pretending to sleep since they'd pulled out of Olympia, showed an interest in the situation.

Maddalyn's heart stopped. It was just like last time, when the stage had been robbed at the foot of Eric's mountain. The stage slowed but didn't stop, and a shot rang out as the driver fired his weapon.

Returning shots were fired, the driver cried out, and then the stage came to a complete stop.

The man who appeared at the door and threw it open was, no doubt, the man who had tried to enter her room last night. The limping man, small and gnarled, the man who had robbed a stage she was on before.

He smiled at her and waved his gun at the other two occupants of the coach. "Well, well," he said, his words muffled through the dusty mask he wore. "Howdy do, miss." He tipped his hat, lifting it just a tad from his greasy hair. "I hear you've been askin' about us."

"I-I, no, I most certainly have not," she said as calmly as she could.

Linda Jones

"Looking for them pearls, I hear." He patted his vest.

"My mother's pearls." Maddalyn sighed. "They're not really worth very much. Would you mind terribly giving them back?"

It was, evidently, the wrong thing to say. He reached into the coach, grabbed her wrist, and pulled her into the sunlight. Maddalyn looked up at the driver's seat, searching for assistance. None would be coming from the driver. He held a bleeding arm, and the other outlaw, the portly one, was just finishing a thorough job of tying the poor man up.

Mr. Johnston tried to exit the coach behind them, but the limping man waved his gun toward the stage and ordered the other passengers to stay put.

And then he turned the gun on her. Pulled her up against his chest and pointed the barrel at her temple.

"I want to know exactly what you told, and exactly who you told it to."

"I don't know what you mean. . . ." He pulled back the hammer. The clicking noise was loud, so close to her ear. Ominous.

"How did that deputy know what we looked like? Who else did you tell?"

Maddalyn was certain then that the outlaws intended to kill her, and the other passengers as well.

"He was the only one, and my description was very poor. I was frightened; I couldn't think

380

straight. Why, if you were to disappear right now, I wouldn't remember a single thing."

He laughed coarsely. "Smart girl, but you got smart just a little too late."

They lay prone at the top of the hill and watched the scene unfolding below. They'd been too late to stop the outlaws, and now one of them held a gun to Maddalyn's head.

Conrad and Karl had been talking strategy for what seemed like an hour, though they'd only been there a few minutes.

"All right?" Conrad whispered, patting Eric on the shoulder. "You're the best long-range shot. You'll have to do it. Give us to the count of one hundred."

"I can't do it. She's too close, and the bastard's got his finger on the trigger."

"You have no choice," Conrad said, and then he and Karl disappeared, Conrad scurrying silently to the right, Karl to the left.

No choice. Eric targeted the bandy outlaw, lining up the rear and the front sights. He'd never fired this rifle, didn't have any idea how accurate it was. Conrad had more confidence in his ability than Eric had in himself. It had been too long. Years.

He couldn't fire while that bastard had his pistol aimed at Maddalyn's head. He hadn't even begun to count, didn't have any idea where Conrad and Karl had gone.

She was wearing that blue dress Kathleen had given her, the one she'd worn to the dance. On that night she'd asked him to forget that she was a lady and a thief and a matchmaker, and he had. And they'd danced all night.

He couldn't fire while that pistol was pointed at Maddalyn's head. A jerk of a finger, and the weapon the outlaw held would discharge. He'd have to give the bastard something else to aim at.

Eric stood and sighted the target. The outlaw's attention was riveted on Maddalyn, and he didn't see the threat from the top of the hill.

"Hey!" Eric shouted. "You, down there! Heads up!"

The outlaw lifted his head, and in an instinctive move swung the pistol on the immediate threat. He didn't loose his grip on Maddalyn, though, and Eric wasn't sure he could make a clean hit. He took a step down the hill, and a shot rang out. It hit the ground in front of him somewhere, pinging off the rocks.

Eric was still too far away to be confident. He walked down the hill with the outlaw in his sights, and the pistol rang out again. The hefty partner, the one in the driver's seat, hid behind the wounded driver and fired. Eric heard a bullet whizzing by his head. That one had been close, but these outlaws were really not very good shots. The bullets hit, for the most part, wide and short, as Eric strode steadily down the slope.

The man in the driver's seat was fumbling with

bullets from his gun belt, trying to reload. But the man's hands shook, and bullets fell to the ground and to the floorboard at his feet.

The outlaw who held Maddalyn aimed and fired, but he too was out of ammunition.

When he came to the bottom of the hill, Eric stopped and planted his feet, aimed carefully. Close enough.

The outlaw was no fool. He dropped his weapon and ordered his partner to do the same. The man in the driver's seat obeyed the order, and shining bullets flew from his chubby fingers.

Eric didn't lower the rifle.

"Let the lady go," he ordered.

The outlaw shook his head and held Maddalyn tighter. "No. You'll shoot me if I let her move away."

"I can shoot you now," Eric promised. "It just so happens that I like that blue dress, and I'd hate to get blood and what little bit of brains you've got all over it."

The outlaw shoved Maddalyn away from him and threw his hands high into the air.

Conrad and Karl appeared on either side of the coach, their own weapons drawn, and only then did Eric let the rifle drop.

He hadn't fired a shot, and still he felt as if he'd been through a battle. It was seeing Maddalyn held like that, knowing that in a second she could be gone. Dead. That was what wore him out.

Karl held the two outlaws, one scruffy neck in

each hand, and Conrad comforted Maddalyn. Eric walked slowly toward the stage. Her back was to him, and Conrad had placed his hands on her shoulders. Eric listened for tears, for a wailing protest, but Maddalyn just looked up into Conrad's face and told him that she was just fine, thank you.

She must have heard him coming, because she spun on him. Instead of thanks, he got his ear bent.

"What were you thinking?" she asked, poking him in the chest. "Waltzing down that hill and allowing these men to shoot at you. Are you insane? What happened to your common sense? Why couldn't you have fired from behind that boulder at the top of the hill?"

"Sorry." Shoot, he was apologizing?

She relaxed the finger that jabbed at his chest, and grasped a handful of cotton. Her face relaxed, and she dropped her eyes.

"You could have been killed, Eric," she said softly, and then she loosened her grip and turned away.

"He's the man who has my pearls," she said, pointing to the outlaw who had held her. "Either in a pocket or sewn into the lining of his vest." She walked right at the scrawny outlaw Karl held tightly and patted his chest. "Right there."

Those damn pearls.

"Here," she said when her search was complete. She pulled a thread, the lining came loose from leather, and the strand of pearls fell into her hand.

She stared at the pearls in her hand for a long

time, and Eric stepped past Conrad to look at the stones she treasured. The stones that reminded him he couldn't give her everything she wanted.

The necklace lay on the palm of her hand, spilling over just slightly. It was a small strand, and the pearls were mismatched and irregular. They couldn't have been worth much, but a tear traveled down Maddalyn's cheek and into her palm, and she closed her fingers over the pearls and the tear that had joined them.

Maddalyn hadn't cried when she'd almost been killed, or when he'd almost been killed. That night he'd found her, lost, alone, frightened, she hadn't shed a single tear. But now he watched as she cried over a strand of pearls that could have been replaced easily. Cheaply.

"I didn't think I'd ever get these back," she whispered. Her voice cracked, and she wiped her cheeks with white fingers. "They're not even very pretty, I know, but they were my mother's. Uncle Henry gave them to me for my sixteenth birthday." She lifted eyes that were still too bright to Eric. "They're all I have of her."

Eric wanted nothing more than to hold Maddalyn as desperately as she held those pearls that were precious to her.

But he didn't make a move toward her, and a moment later she turned away from him, her eyes on her fist.

"Are one of you gentlemen going to drive the

stage on to Sheridan?" the woman passenger asked.

"No," Conrad said with a smile. "We're all going back to Olympia."

She and the other passenger groaned.

"We're supposed to be in Buffalo before dark," she whined.

"These men have to be turned over to the sheriff, and Olympia is the closest town."

Neither of the other two passengers cared for Conrad's explanation, but having no other choice they climbed back into the coach. Maddalyn joined them without protest, still clutching her pearls.

The outlaws were trussed up tight, and the trailing rope was attached to the saddle horns of their own mounts.

Conrad assisted the wounded driver into the coach, and Eric climbed into the driver's seat. Karl and Conrad mounted the outlaws' horses, and led the men at a brisk walk to the other side of the hill and the hobbled horses that waited there. Eric stayed on the road, and when Karl and Conrad and the bound and gagged outlaws met up with them, the party hit the trail for Olympia.

Eric leaned to the side and caught Maddalyn tilting through the window and watching him. When he caught her eye she slid back into her seat.

The pearls she'd mourned were nothing special, as far as jewelry went. They were a remembrance of her mother, nothing more. It made him wonder, for the first time, what Maddalyn had meant when she'd said he couldn't give her what she wanted.

And then he recognized the truth that he should have known all along. Hell, she'd told him, plain and simple, leaning from her hotel window and speaking of impossible dreams. Of family and home and forever love.

They had seemed to him, at the time, unrealistic. Harder to obtain than pearls and silk. The fanciful imaginings of a naive lady who saw the world as she wanted to see it.

It had never occurred to him, until now, that he could be the one to make her dreams come true.

Chapter Twenty-six

Maddalyn placed the pearls around her neck as they neared Olympia. Mrs. Tilton had been going on constantly, declaring that she was going to have a fainting spell, that this was simply more excitement than she could handle.

What would Mrs. Tilton do if her wish came true and she met the notorious outlaws she'd mentioned earlier?

Not receiving the attention she'd so obviously wanted, Mrs. Tilton had turned to another subject. The Barrett brothers. Since it was evident that Maddalyn knew them, all questions were directed to her. Even Mr. Johnston and the wounded driver seemed interested in her responses.

She told them very little. That the Barretts were friends, that they were retired from Pinkerton's, that they lived near Olympia.

Maddalyn didn't tell them about the mountain, and she certainly wasn't going to tell them that she was in love with Eric, the obviously daft man who'd walked right into a hail of bullets with that rifle in his hands.

But now, as she looked out the window, they left her alone. She'd heard whispers of "Poor girl, she must have been terrified," and once she heard Mrs. Tilton use the word "spell." Let them think she was in shock if they'd leave her alone.

Half the town seemed to be waiting for their return, lining the boardwalk on either side of the street, watching with solemn faces as the passengers left the coach. Conrad said something Maddalyn couldn't understand to his father-in-law, and in moments most of the crowd had dispersed.

The prisoners were handed over to Sheriff MacIver and Gavin. As Gavin took custody of the heavier bandit, he stared almost sheepishly at Eric. Eric, of course, merely scowled at the deputy. Something he did well.

Maddalyn had tried, herself, not to look at Eric too closely or too long. Except for the moment of his brief encounter with Gavin, there was an odd complacency to his facial expression and his posture. She'd expected anger from him, after her quiet departure that bordered on desertion. Perhaps he didn't care even that much.

Daisy and Kathleen came running down the boardwalk, and Kathleen all but knocked Maddalyn down with her greeting. When Maddalyn had righted herself and Kathleen released her, Daisy gave her a big hug, too.

"I'm going to shoot Gavin," Kathleen said seriously. "Pop told me, while Conrad and the others were going after you, what he did."

"What did he do?" Maddalyn asked.

Kathleen explained, talking quickly and in low tones. Daisy leaned in and listened, even though Maddalyn was certain she'd heard the story from Kathleen already. It was rather nice, the three of them with their heads together. It was like having sisters, Maddalyn expected, the way Eric had always had Conrad and Karl.

"You should have seen Eric," Daisy whispered. "He was livid."

"He threatened to kill Gavin, and I think he would have done it if those outlaws had hurt you," Kathleen added.

Maddalyn shook her head.

"Conrad was right all along," Kathleen continued. "He always said—"

"The three of them used to work for Pinkerton's," Maddalyn said sensibly. "This is probably the sort of thing they do all the time."

"I think Conrad was right," Kathleen said stubbornly. "I think—"

"Conrad doesn't know Eric nearly as well as he thinks he does," Maddalyn interrupted.

"They're brothers," Kathleen argued. "And I think Conrad was right when he said that Eric has loved you all along. From that first day."

Maddalyn shook her head. "No." Eric was a man who didn't even believe in love.

"Conrad said Eric was just too stubborn to realize what was going on, but that he'd come to his senses eventually."

Maddalyn continued to shake her head.

"Karl said the same thing, pretty much," Daisy added, and Maddalyn lifted her eyes to the tall woman.

If only she could make herself believe that it was true, that somewhere deep inside Eric did love her.

But he had told her himself that love didn't last. If he truly believed that, then whatever love he had inside couldn't possibly survive.

They were interrupted by an insistent tapping on Maddalyn's shoulder, and she turned to face Mrs. Tilton. "Are you going on to Sheridan, dear? It seems the stage representative has found another driver."

"So soon?" She'd thought to have a little more time with her friends, perhaps a chance to recover her senses, but if the stage was moving out, she'd be on it. "Of course. Yes, I'll be going on to Sheridan."

"One of those Barrett brothers," Mrs. Tilton informed her smugly, "has agreed to take the stage as far as Sheridan."

Maddalyn turned to face the stage. All three of the Barrett brothers were standing nearby, bickering as they'd been doing the first time she'd seen them. She stepped closer in order to hear their argument.

"You don't know what you're doing," Conrad said, pointing a finger in Eric's face. "Leave it to you to do everything backward. What about the contract? Karl and I can't finish it alone."

"Hire a crew," Eric said easily. "All the men you need."

"But I thought you didn't want—" Karl began.

"I changed my mind," Eric snapped. He looked over Conrad's shoulder and saw Maddalyn standing there, and he locked his eyes on hers while he spoke to his brothers. "Build a ranch, hire a crew, do whatever you want. I'm going to Sheridan to court the new schoolteacher."

"Now? You wait until she's leaving to decide to romance her? She's been under your nose for weeks. Where the hell have you been?" Conrad snapped.

Karl shoved Conrad lightly at the shoulder. "We were right. He's been crazy about Maddalyn since he found her sleeping in his bed."

"That's not true," Eric said decisively, and he didn't even have the decency to drop his eyes from hers.

Maddalyn turned away and started walking toward Kathleen and Daisy. Why was he going to Sheridan? To torture her further? Simply to find his way into her bed? A hand on her shoulder stopped her before she could take three steps, and she spun around. Eric placed his hands on her shoulders, and Maddalyn lifted her face to his, met his eyes even though it hurt.

"That's not true," he repeated. "When I first saw you sleeping in my bed, I was relieved you weren't a crazy old mountain man staking claim to the place."

"You don't have to—" Maddalyn began, but Eric silenced her by laying a finger over her lips. When she was silent he slid that finger away.

"You want romance, but I can only give you the truth. I could tell you that I loved you that first night, when I held you against the cold, but that's not true either. You were pretty and soft, and lost, and you needed me. It had been a long time since anybody had needed me for anything."

"Sheridan is so far from—"

"I could tell you that I fell in love with you the first time I saw you smile, but that's a lie. I knew then that you were the most beautiful woman I'd ever seen, that I ever would see. Damn near knocked me flat. The first time we kissed? I wanted you then, so much it scared me. That wanting gave you a power over me I didn't want to give. I've never wanted anything so hard in all my life."

Maddalyn looked for anger or frustration in his face, but Eric remained complacent.

He quickly searched the boardwalk, and Maddalyn did the same. Everyone had stepped away, and the newlyweds had their heads together over by the stage office.

"I suppose I should say that I knew I loved you

when we made love, but that's not entirely true." His voice was low, for her ears alone. "I knew then that I needed you. In my arms, in my life. I didn't want to need anybody, but I couldn't deny it.

"I watched you while Karl and Conrad were getting married. You were so happy for them, for their happiness, and I knew then that you were a special woman. A nice person. I suppose I've known that for as long as you've been with us."

He took a deep breath, steeled himself, and then he leaned closer, placing his face close to hers. "If I'm to be completely honest, I have to admit that I didn't realize that I loved you until last night, when I thought about going back to the cabin without you, and I realized that I couldn't do it."

"You said love doesn't last," Maddalyn protested softly. "And that's the only thing I ask for. A love that lasts forever."

"Prove me wrong," he whispered. "Let me give you everything you want."

Eric took Maddalyn's hand and led her to the middle of the street, past the stage and into the sun. "There it is." He pointed to the top of the mountain. "Home. You scaled that mountain, conquered it, made it your own. It was a quiet Southern Invasion, and it's yours now. Ours. I won't go back there without you. I'll follow you to Sheridan, get a job, court you, if that's what you want." He sighed deeply. "I swear, I'll hound you day and night until you agree to marry me and come back home."

Maddalyn took her eyes from the mountain and

searched his face for an answer. She'd always known it was an honest face, and there was nothing but sincerity there now.

"I want a lot from marriage," Maddalyn admitted, and she squeezed Eric's hand. "Love and companionship, passion and laughter, children. Lots of children. And I'll expect you to tell me every day that you love me, even when you've been working hard and you're tired and grouchy. And kissing," she added. "There should be lots of kissing."

Eric tugged at her hand and pulled her gently against his chest. "I love you, Maddalyn," he whispered, and then he kissed her. Slowly and sweetly, he molded his lips to hers. "Marry me," he demanded, his words a soft breath against her lips.

Maddalyn grasped the front of his shirt with her hands and realized exactly which shirt he was wearing. One she'd taken for herself, one Eric had removed impatiently last night. She smiled up at him. "Of course I'll marry you." She stood on her tiptoes and gave him a quick kiss. All of this was entirely improper behavior. They stood in the street, for goodness' sake, in full view of anyone who cared to watch.

It was very unladylike.

"I'm not quite as stubborn and indecisive as you are. I loved you that very first day, and it hit me like a thunderbolt."

Eric grinned. "You could have told me sooner."

"If I'd told you too soon you would have carried me down the mountain, snow or no snow, and been rid of me once and for all. Don't try to deny it."

He didn't. Eric took her arm and walked her back to the boardwalk. Conrad and Karl and their brides were lined up by the stage, expectant expressions on their faces. Mrs. Tilton and Mr. Johnston were seated in the stage, ready to go. They were in for a long wait.

"I think I'll wear the yellow gown Kathleen and Daisy made for the ceremony," Maddalyn said casually.

Kathleen jumped up and down. "I just knew it!"

Karl grinned and squeezed a smiling Daisy's hand, and Conrad laughed out loud.

"The preacher is available this afternoon," Daisy said softly. She blushed when Maddalyn looked at her. "Kathleen and I checked earlier, just in case."

"Good." Maddalyn sighed, and she glanced up at Eric. He nodded in approval.

"I'm not usually so impulsive," Maddalyn divulged, "but the sooner we get married, the sooner we can go home."

Eric held her hand as they walked down the boardwalk, and after they'd gone several steps he pulled her against his side. "You scared the hell out of me," he whispered.

"What about you? Walking down that hill waving that rifle in your hands while those bandits shot at you. Honestly, Eric. Do you really know how to use one of those things? You scared the . . . well, you know, out of me, too. You could have been

shot, wounded or even killed, for goodness' sake."
She held him tighter, frightened as much now by
the thought as she had been when she'd seen him
approaching the bandit who held her, unprotected.
"I really was quite frightened, you know." Eric
smiled down at her.

"First of all, I was not *waving* that rifle. Yes, I do
know how to use one, but I hadn't used that particular one so I wasn't certain that it would be accurate. And we won't have to worry about either of
us having the hell scared out of us again, because
when I get you on that mountain we're never coming down." Maddalyn sighed and wrapped her arm
around Eric's waist. That sounded marvelous.

Karl and Daisy and Conrad and Kathleen trailed
behind them, chattering constantly and all at the
same time. It was wonderful. A dream come true.

Eric loved her.

She was surrounded by the family she'd always
wanted.

And they were going home.

One Day, My Prince

LindaJones

Joe White is the most dangerous and best-looking gun-fighter in town, which makes him powerful enemies who bushwhack him and leave him for dead.

But Joe is saved. And though his woes dwarf those of his rescuers, the answer to their problems mirror the solution to his own. The seven newly orphaned Shorter sisters are in danger of being separated, and only a prissy schoolmarm named Sarah Prince can save them. And while the Shorters know that the bewitching Sarah is just what the wounded marshal is looking for, *he* doesn't know it yet. Miss Prince's kiss will open Joe's eyes to love—and one taste of forbidden fruit will keep them open forever.

___52388-4 $5.99 US/$6.99 CAN